A BLIND EYE

For Graham –

George Jony

A BLIND EYE

A JACK PARIS THRILLER

GEORGE FONG

coffeetownpress
Kenmore, WA

coffeetownpress

A Coffeetown Press book published by Epicenter Press

Epicenter Press
6524 NE 181st St.
Suite 2
Kenmore, WA 98028

For more information go to:
www.Camelpress.com
www.Coffeetownpress.com
www.Epicenterpress.com
www.GeorgeFong.com

Cover design by Scott Book
Interior design by Melissa Vail Coffman

A Blind Eye
Copyright © 2021 by George Fong

ISBN: 978-1-60381-795-0 (Trade Paper)
ISBN: 978-1-60381-796-7 (eBook)

Printed in the United States of America

To the men and women of the
Sacramento office of the FBI.

ACKNOWLEDGEMENTS

I WOULD LIKE TO THANK MY WIFE, Rebecca, and to my children Kyle and Rachel. The reality of the case this story is based on is what they lived through. While I spent six months living in the valley, they were the ones that took the brunt of life's daily burdens while I chased a ghost in the hills along side with the dozen of dedicated and hardworking men and women of law enforcement, fire authority, forestry, search and rescue, and every volunteer that came out to help find our missing tourists.

*"The difference between an assault and a murder
is that a murder has one less witness."*

— FBI Training Academy

CHAPTER 1

March 1997
Sacramento, California

Jack Paris

I FELT A SHIVER.

Some say it's the feeling you get when the ghost of the dead pass through you, but I knew what it really meant. It meant I had to face the truth.

I stood before a floor-length mirror and looked at myself. Black suit, the one I had bought for the occasion. Rain started to fall. Water droplets pooled on broad green leaves beyond the window, spitting onto the glass, giving a kaleidoscope view of the outside world.

My wife Emily was standing to my right. I could see her reflection over my shoulder. Genuine warmth, her smile, the kind that beamed with every good thought. She wore a silky white dress, the V of the front displaying her neckline. Her skirt fell just below her knees. It was a vision of grace and beauty.

She looked magnificent, elegant.

My son, Michael sat to my left, his fingers drumming against the arm of the high-back chair. He looked uncomfortable.

I posed. "Well, what do you think?" I asked.

He feigned a grin that couldn't have been more forced.

"Your Mom likes it."

His eyes sagged. Fingers stopped drumming. The rain started hammering at the window.

I pressed a hand on the front of my jacket, smoothed it down to the last button. "It was her choice," I added. I couldn't pick out a nice suit if it were labeled, *Nice Suit.*

Michael faked a smile but it quickly dissolved into a drawn tight lip and I saw his eyes glisten before they drifted toward the carpet.

I reached out and put my hand on his shoulder. His entire body buckled.

"It's okay," I said.

With a slight nod, Michael took in a deep breath, cleared his throat and gave me the grown-man look. "Time to go, pops."

I smiled. I liked it when he called me pops. Most of the time he called me *father*. It always sounded so formal, distant and overly proper, like I was the stranger in the room. Pops sounded like I belonged.

"Give me a minute," I replied. "I'll meet you in the hallway."

Michael paused uneasily, looked like he was considering whether to say something like, *'no, I'll wait,'* or *'do you want some company?'* But he didn't.

Hesitantly, he headed for the door.

I glanced over at Emily who was neatly folding a shirt I had tossed across a chair. Her green eyes met mine and I felt my throat tighten.

"You two are going to make a great team," Emily said.

I tugged on the double Winsor knot in my tie, acting as if it needed adjusting. I was buying time.

These past years had been difficult between me and Michael, maneuvering through a labyrinth of conflict and differences. Like walking barefoot through a field of broken glass. We didn't see eye-to-eye on most anything, and what we did agree upon felt akin to finding fault in one's soul. Me, being an FBI Agent, didn't help. I enforced the law while Michael ended up breaking them. Nothing serious, more like teenage angst. But it pushed us apart. We both knew how much we loved each other, never doubting the lengths we'd go to for one another. We just couldn't find a way to express it, get past the hurt. Under the circumstances we now faced, we were going to have to find a means to that end.

"We'll be fine," I heard myself say.

Emily nodded with a comforting assurance in her face that was undisputable.

I turned back toward the door, hearing Michael and the others just outside, talking, low, the words indiscernible but the tone, clear. They were voices of condolences. And there were tears. A soft patting of a hand on Michael's back, I could only imagine.

I looked back into the room and Emily was gone. The truth is, she was never there. Cancer took her. Left only to my imagination. Emily, the one that I could love no deeper, who fought to make life in a world of murderers and thieves a place of tranquil normalcy, was gone. The room suddenly felt cold and hollow.

I stood and smoothed my suit jacket, pressed my tie against my white shirt, and tried to gather my composure. I opened the door. Everyone stopped talking, all eyes now drawn toward me. Lips razor-tight, arms and hands fighting to find comfort. There were mummers of sympathies and empty consolation, reverberating in the small space louder than a marching band down a packed hall.

They came to Emily's funeral, to pay their respects. To see her off. I marshalled the energy to somehow convey the depth of my gratitude for coming but every word came through shuttered breaths. Once again, I placed a hand on my son's shoulder, and it was at that moment that I realized just how strong he really was. My daughter Justine following close behind, gently touched me and began to weep behind a cotton gloved hand.

We walked together into the next room, to see Emily for the last time and to do the one thing—at least for me—that would forever be a lie.

To say good-bye.

CHAPTER 2

Monday February 17, 1998 8:05 a.m.
Yosemite National Forest

SUNLIGHT REFLECTED OFF A SNOW-COVERED grassy mound, causing Mariposa County Sheriff's detective Hal Bellows to shade his eyes and squint.

Winter morning, the frozen air bristled as it thawed. I've never gotten use to the cold. Assigned to the FBI office in Sacramento, I'm more inclined to warmth. Hawaiian beach warmth. It was where Emily and I spent our honeymoon.

The National Park is in Mariposa County and Mariposa is part of my field office's territory; the Eastern District of California. If a crime occurs on federal land in the central valley, I got called.

Today, the sky was clear blue but deceiving. I had been standing in the shade for no more than fifteen minutes but still found myself pulling my jacket collar high around my neck to stave off a chill. Early this morning, Bellows called, said I should probably join him. That's how he always asked for me: *You should join me.* I knew by his tone, this wasn't a suggestion but a warning.

It took me a couple of hours to get into the national park with roads being closed due to the season's heavy snowfall and roads blocked from falling boulders. By the time I made it to the crime scene, Bellows had already started his investigation.

I didn't want to get in his way or interrupt his concentration, so I watched him as he stood before a small clearing that fell just outside several rows of tall evergreens at the edge of a dense section of forest.

The area was misted in cold damp air, giving the view as though peering through gauze. There was a dirt trail spotted with frozen pools of water, suspended pine needles, held in time. It snaked out from the tall snow-covered trees from the west, dropping out of sight toward the valley floor.

Bellows turned his head, studied the wall of dark green and white that surrounded the clearing. He dropped down slowly on one knee, formed his left hand in the shape of a curved blade and scraped at the snow down to blue ice, discovering patches of winter grass. Bursts of cold air flowed from the east, shaving snow off strained branches, detergent-size flakes drifting slowly to the ground. He lifted his chin, stared at the terrain and what lay above. I followed his gaze; eighteen hundred feet of gray stone climbing straight up into the air, sharp vertical striations, the result from thousands of years of harsh weather and shearing ice. The wind blew freezer cold against his exposed face and yet, I could tell it had no effect on him. There was almost a symbiotic relationship between him and the land. Hell, he was part of the elements.

I've known Bellows for a decade. We've investigated a number of death cases in the mountains and valleys within this massive track of land, the punishing climate always a constant and because murder never cares about jurisdictional territory. And one thing we have learned over the years together; if the cold didn't kill our victims, humans did.

The white-capped granite walls boxed us in on three sides, the fourth facing the valley, open to a sea of clear blue skies, brisk and clean. On another day, it would have been breathtaking. But today it was horribly stained. An unwanted and uninvited body of a young girl. Still, cold, and discarded like trash. It was the starkness of death, unfiltered, taken and left here most likely from the hands of one whose eyes were endlessly dark and merciless. I kept silent, staring at the expansiveness of this magnificent place, finding myself shiver—not from the cold—but from what had invaded it. It's the reason why guys like Hal and I come to this place. Our world, wondrous and dark, tranquil and isolated. Inviting and deadly.

Yosemite.

CHAPTER 3

I FINALLY HAD BELLOWS' ATTENTION.

He looked at me for about five seconds before turning back to the crime scene. That was my cue to head over.

I carefully stepped past the first layer of evidence markers, making sure I didn't disturb anything as I made my way to his side. Together, we studied the upper ridge, both pausing to observe the distraction above our heads. A dozen news reporters perched high on the ledge, cameras affixed on tripods with lenses that resembled cannons, like an artillery barrage pointed in our direction. Bellows shook his head in disgust. Amazed how fast reporters found their way to a crime scene, doubly so when a body is found. They were human blowflies.

Bellows peered over his right shoulder, eyes narrowing to slits. Two Park Rangers stood guard along a sagging stream of yellow evidence tape. He pointed at them with his chin like he was making me aware of their presence. Bellows never referred to them as Rangers, always called them *Federal boys*, like we were some special anomaly or from an alien planet. He was good with me, always being a reliable source of help in all our past investigations but I knew there was always a defined line between local agencies and us feds. It's something you just accepted, comes with the territory.

I continued to study the scene, stepping back to get a broader view. Gusts of wind rattled the long plastic barrier tape, like cards slapping against bicycle spokes. The area cordoned off to the small, contorted body of a young female, who lay in an exposed area of rubble and ice.

The number of cameramen and reporters grew along the ridge, distracting me. The pages in my notebook waved in the breeze, floating ice chips melted on the paper, blurring my words. Bellows ground his teeth, turned his head and spat. He muttered a string of obscenities, before flipping the bird at the gaggle of reporters. Bellows is a large man: six-six, two and a half, if not more with a thick graying Wyatt Earp-style mustache. Not a man the cameras would want to miss. I looked away, stifling a laugh.

Bellows jabbed a large hand at his crew standing along the edge of the crime scene and drew an imaginary line in the air. "Push out the boundary up along the road and keep the fucking press out." It was necessary to extend the crime scene perimeter, but it would also piss off the media. His idea of a two-for-one deal.

The winter had been unseasonably cold, the days threatening subzero temperatures as the thermometer plummeted at night, plunging deep into the negative digits. In the morning sun, the entire valley was blanketed in a thick crust of white that sparkled like sugar. I had been in and out of this valley for most of my life. I'd brought my family here on vacations, hiked the trails, and listened to the roaring power of spring melt. I always found the view nothing short of magnificent but right now I struggled to glimpse its beauty and questioned its safety.

The frozen ground crackled under heavy boots as I made my way up a hillside, stopping as we approached the victim's body. Bellows was to my right as we trampled a carpet of frozen pine needles and groundcover. I lowered my head and mentally calculated a checklist of what I needed to collect as evidence. Bellows broke the silence.

"Never get used to it, can you, Jack?"

"I'm not sure anyone should, Hal."

Dead bodies shouldn't be a part of anyone's daily activity. The irony was, up here, body dumps were as common as bear droppings. Base-jumping idiots to seedy-clients with bad debts. Bellows was often the first one to discover them stuffed in a crevice or a cold-water creek. Even with dozens of findings, the one thing we'd never understood: how anyone could dump a child.

He held still behind me, careful not to step into the crime scene, his thick torso casting an elongated shadow in the shape of an oversized arrow, pointing toward the victim's body, twenty feet beyond our position.

"I'm starting to doubt humanity," he huffed.

"Some people are just broken. They can't be fixed."

"Fixed?" Bellows crowed. "Christ-sakes, Jack. I say, put 'em down, like a rabid animal."

The Rangers gathered, started to set up a privacy screen; a large white tarp held up like a ship's sail by two aluminum poles. We made our way behind it and took a long pause. I knelt on one knee and rested my left forearm across my thigh while Bellows scanned the area like an animal looking for danger. The barrier gave me the ability to focus my attention on the victim without the distraction of the media. I held still, with a familiar sound finding its way into my head, the crispness of rustling branches disrupted by a constant buzzing noise. A droning tone, like the sound of a bow being drawn across the strings of a violin.

Blowflies.

They found the only patch of warm sunlight to nest. I stood, took a few steps forward, coming close enough to see every detail of the lifeless body. Bellows' head went on a swivel, studying the crime scene and pointing at everything out of natural order before pronouncing his assessment.

"She was killed here, in this clearing." He motioned to his left, swept an arm over an open area in front of a wall of tall evergreens. "Just outside that row of pines, not more than fifty yards away is the main path where the tourists walk." Bellows went quiet for a moment and I could hear his breathing becoming deep and heavy. "Everyone around with no one to see," he said. I knew what that meant, his anger boiling inside. Bellows took every death in the park personally.

I continued to scan the terrain, searching for clues the killer may have left behind. The area was blinding white. There had been a dusting of snow late last night. Evidence once visible could be hidden under a blanket of fine powder. Lips pursed, I glanced down, not at anything in particular. My mind filled with images of the killer, standing at this same spot not long ago.

"If you touched her," I thought, *"you left a part of you behind . . . somewhere.*

I was determined to find it.

Bellows called out as he turned his head toward his deputies who were milling around the scene. "Where are my photographers?"

I stood up and scanned for anyone with a camera who wasn't part of the media. I pointed downwind with my chin. "There."

From the corner of the road, three officers approached, cameras swinging like pendulums around their necks, black nylon bags slung over their shoulders. They marched in single file toward the crime scene. Bellows stood and fell in line behind them, guiding the officers through a narrow pathway in order to take pictures of the surrounding area.

"I want every inch of this landscape photographed from here to Sunday. If you find anything, I want to be the first to know."

Nodding in agreement, they moved as a team, photographing at every angle, entry and exit, broken branch, indentations. Cameras flashed, auto-advance mechanisms squealing a high pitch whine, reverberating off the thick wall of evergreens. Inch by inch, the land to be forever memorialized onto a dozen rolls of 35mm film.

A string of investigators crawled methodically toward the body. Bellows watched over the examiners while another cameraman followed, lockstep behind them.

More cameras flash, more whirl from the auto-winders.

Cigarette butts were retrieved for potential DNA, a glass bottle under a fallen branch for fingerprints. By the time they reached the dead girl's body, I had already formulated my planned examination. Bellows opened his pad and started taking notes.

I noticed there were more people on the hilltop. The tourist population had started to gather alongside the news crews.

Another contingency of Mariposa deputies walked a grid line along the north ridge, just below where the body lay.

I continued my focus on the lifeless figure, studying how she was left and the reason for her position, assessed her injuries. She had been struck at the base of the neck with a blunt object; that was obvious. Thin, rusty wire still wrapped around each ankle, cutting into her skin. That was telling. Frozen in place, on her knees, arms by her side, head pushed into the dirt. Her face was turned sideways, staring right at me. Eyes open and hazy, empty and distant. Blood splattered across her nose, eyes and mouth, matted in dirt and what appeared to be grease. The snow had melted then froze, leaving only patches of crimson in the ice around the girl's torso. Like an unwanted doll discarded and forgotten in the woods, lifeless. Left like discarded trash. There was a time the girl didn't have a care in the world, never had to worry about abductions and murderers. I couldn't help my eyes from welling up.

"How old do you think she is?" Bellows asked. "Fifteen, sixteen?"

"Seventeen," I said.

Bellows' brow creased with a row of deep lines, stare-sharpened into a question mark.

"I spoke to her mother." I pointed at the body. "Her name is Amanda Jenkins."

She was reported missing three weeks ago. Mother gave me her photo for distribution. I never forget a face. When Bellows called and said he had a possible child vic in the national forest, Mrs. Jenkins, resident of Mariposa County with a missing seventeen-year-old daughter, floated to the top of my mind. "Said she was a chronic runaway."

"Number three," Bellows barked. His words were sharp, accusatory as if to say, *I told you so.*

I reached into my jacket and removed a pair of latex gloves. Placing the opened end up to my mouth, I blew in a puff of air, all finger expanded as if waving. I slid it over my right hand, did the same for my left, and began a visual examination before touching the body. Cuts and scratches, possibly indicative of defensive wounds. May contain trace evidence. Gingerly, I placed my fingers on her head, guiding wet matted hair away from her face, making every effort not to move or disturb the body.

"You know it's under her, don't you?" Bellows said.

Staring only at Amanda, I forced back a response. "Wouldn't that be my luck."

I peered under my arm and back toward a cadre of deputies standing in the background, waiting to see what was to come.

"Get me a sheet to move her on." I instructed Bellows, surrendering to the inevitable. "Time to find out what's underneath her."

Bellows nodded and walked back to the crew to help find a large plastic sheet to transfer the body. Within a minute, he returned, carrying a large roll under his arm.

I took the roll and unsnapped the tie and, together, we laid the sheet beside her. We started to transfer her onto the tarp in order to capture any microscopic evidence stuck to her small frame, but in that moment of stillness and anxiousness, my attention broke, catching sight of falling winter leaves. They gently fell, bounced, and cartwheeled over her body. Some stayed while others were whisked away by a growing gust of wind. More leaves followed by pine needles. Bellows gritted his teeth. We both knew this was not a natural draft. This was man-made.

"Helicopters, Hal!" I screamed, trying to be heard above the *thump, thump, thump* of the rotor blades. "Here they come!"

Bellows looked up, grabbed tightly onto his Stetson, preventing it from being blown down to the valley floor.

With great speed, the air stirred to a frenzy, kicking up dirt and decayed leaves. Wet pine needles summersaulted in the air before falling like darts from the sky.

I yelled to a group of deputies stumbling in the whirlwind. "Get to a phone and tell those media assholes to get their choppers up higher before I shoot them down!"

The helicopter's blades continued to blow away evidence I fought to preserve as I shielded the body from the flying debris of dirt, ice, and pine needles. In that moment, something under Amanda Jenkins' left shoulder caught my attention. Flapping in the wind, a small piece of paper protruded out, threatening to fly away with the violent swirl. I quickly grabbed a corner, careful not to tear or damage it. As I fought to protect myself from the rotor blast, I bent down close to the body, peeling the sliver of paper from under her chest and placing it close to my face to read the words scratched in pencil. My anxiousness grew, knowing what I would see. Two words neatly written on the wet paper now glued to my gloved hand.

Catch Me.

TWO MINUTES LATER, THE HELICOPTERS HAD ascended and the turbulence started to subside. The air became quiet, the only sound coming from a passing winter's gust. Droplets of melting snow dripped from the trees. Soon the stillness was replaced by the sound of Bellows' boots trudging back toward me. I was still shielding Amanda's body as I caught sight of Bellows' shadow.

He leaned next to my right shoulder then glanced at the note. I could hear him breathe. "Same as the others?"

I straightened up and nodded. There were times I hated it when he was right.

"Same," I confessed.

Bellows pulled off his Stetson and dragged his sleeve across his forehead then said in a conceding fashion,

"Congratulations, Agent Paris. You got yourself a serial killer."

CHAPTER 4

Tuesday February 18th - 6:15 a.m.
Home, El Dorado Hills, California

THE ALARM WENT OFF EARLY BUT it didn't matter. There wasn't much time for sleep, having driven back from the valley late last night. Besides, I was restless, my head still in a fog, unable to shake the vision of Amanda Jenkins laying on that frozen grassland. Hate didn't come close in describing my feelings. Bellows and I had spent most of yesterday's daylight hours at the scene before the coroner arrived. We had canvassed the neighborhood, conducted interviews, checked and reviewed every ATM and liquor store camera. We still had more to do.

When night fell, I had to make a decision: go home and pack for a return to the valley or live in the clothes I was wearing for who knows how long? Although it was at least a two-hour drive on hair-pin roads back home, I opted for the clean clothes.

The sun hadn't risen yet, keeping the room gray and without shadows. Piled on a chair were neatly folded clothes I hadn't had time to put away. Not too long ago, Emily would have done it. She took care of everything. For my entire career, I lived life away from home, finding being in the heat of a case the addiction I craved, not appreciating the fact that I always had a place, a safe haven when the world turned a shade too dark. With Emily. Until it was too late.

After a quick shower, I pulled a white dress shirt, tie, and gray suit from the closet, sat on the corner of the bed and got dressed. I reached over to one of the stacks of clothes, searching for a pair of socks, preferably matching. It took me a second to realize I had been staring at the half-made bed for a long while, seeing the sheets on my side pushed, bent, and crumpled halfway down. Her side still neatly in place, crisp and unspoiled. The contradiction made my heart sink and constrict with pain. Seeing it made me question my decision, wondered if I should've stayed in Yosemite.

I walked over to her side of the bed, stood there for a moment and placed a hand on her pillow. The coldness of it felt like the emptiness of space. It was a miracle I was able to finish dressing.

Forty-five minutes later, I pulled into a long driveway, steering toward a large building buried in a mass of look-alike structures, a single story with a red brick facade. Smoked glass windows lined the outside like a ribbon around a box, a low wall bordering the circular concrete pad at the entrance. Isolated within a residential and college community, the facility was encased in thick, black steel bars with multiple array antennas, cameras and razor wire. An eyesore within a quiet, serene neighborhood.

I carefully maneuvered my bureau ride, a dark blue Crown Vic, through a series of concrete barriers, nosing the large sedan up to the overbuilt steel gate that surrounded the FBI Field office, jammed in the northwestern edge of Sacramento. The large sedan came to a crawl as I approached a small keypad that jutted out from a concrete slab. I waved my office ID card across the access panel and a set of numbers flashed up in random order. Typing in my private code, the panel beeped with each punch. The car idled for a minute before a green light blipped on and the large three-thousand-pound metal gate built to withstand an eighteen-wheeler at full speed slowly opened.

A voice crackled over the entrance intercom speaker. "Good morning, Agent Paris."

I waved at the surveillance camera perched high above my vehicle and took the first open parking slot before stepping out of the car. The air smelled damp, cut heavy with car exhaust coming from the vehicle maintenance bay.

A concrete walkway took me straight to a set of large reflective glass doors. I pulled on the thick handles. Warm air rushed out, hitting me like a slap in the face.

The lobby was dead quiet. Directly in front, a receptionist sat behind a wall of high-impact bullet-resistant glass, talking on the phone while another line chimed away. To my left, side-by-side portraits hung of the current US Attorney General and the Director of the FBI. The Top Ten board finished off the look, prominently displaying the most wanted, a true hold-over of Bureau tradition.

The doors leading to the workspace were locked with a guard standing at attention next to the metal detector. I'm an employee so I bypass the detector. I tapped my access badge against the card reader, punched in my passcode—again—and entered. My squad's bullpen was on the other side of the building. Getting there was through a long, narrow hallway that spanned the entire length of the building. Investigators at one end, the bosses at the other. Agents referred to the corridor between the two sections as the *Green Mile*.

Before I could make it to my desk, my Supervisor's secretary, Beatriz Gonzalez, stepped in my path and slowed. She pointed in the direction of Frank Porter's office before continuing on. "He wants to see you."

I entered the squad bay and continued past a maze of half-walls and cubicles. Telephones rang in the background, pictures of bank robbers, serial killers, and international terrorists pinned cock-eyed on corkboards along my path. Agents hunkered over their desks, talking in whispers. Most of them looked too young to be carrying guns.

I turned the corner to Porter's office and rapped twice, gently, against his doorframe. "Frank," I said. "I take it you want an update?"

Frank Porter looked up, peered over a pair of black plastic frame reading glasses with an affable look. He's an average sized guy, slightly stocky with a head of salt and pepper hair, more salt than pepper. He always had a smile, positive attitude, something he had not lost from years of dealing with assholes inside and outside of the field. Been in the Bureau of fifteen and change, doing time at headquarters and two other field offices before landing this gig as the violent crime supervisor. He stood up from his desk behind stacks of teletypes, electronic communications, and bureau publications. Reports from headquarters filled his in-box, unread, which were clear indications of how important he felt they were. The furniture in his office was not the typical government-grade. Rosewood table, credenza and stacked bookshelves were all neatly arranged. A man who knew what he liked. A television and an old video recorder were tucked in the corner with the world news running in the background. On the walls were awards and certificates of appreciations from agencies he worked with in the past. There was a photo of Porter shaking hands with the Director.

Porter reached out, his shirtsleeves rolled up above his wrists, taking my hand like he was glad to see you. And meant it. He was like that.

"Talk to me." Porter's face relaxed as he slid a notebook in front and grabbed a pen from his desk drawer.

I pulled my notes and went through yesterday's event chronologically, starting with Hal's initial phone call, finding the vic, confirming identity. Porter never looked up, the whole time taking notes as if he was preparing for an exam. I didn't get a chance to detail our findings before he interrupted me in an apologetic voice. "You get another one?" he asked.

I knew what he meant.

I nodded. "Yeah, we got another note."

His eyes went glassy and I could almost hear his jaw clench. I'd seen that look before. A boiler couldn't generate steam to billow any thicker.

"I have Chris coming out," I said. "His team will help examine what we collected."

Chris Hoskin oversaw our Evidence Response Team. His crew of agents and support staff are trained at the FBI Academy at Quantico in forensic examination. They travel wherever we need to collect evidence, whether it's a bank robbery or a terrorist attack. Hoskin's team was one of the first to mobilize and support body recovery efforts at the Oklahoma City bobming in '95. When they returned, they didn't speak much of what they saw, at least not to the outside world but I could tell, each one of them had been deeply affected.

"Bellows is turning over his evidence to us so we can send it to our lab. Hopefully, it'll generate some good leads." I flipped through my notebook one more time to make sure I covered everything. "Jenkins is in Mariposa and will be transported to the coroner's office in Stanislaus County later today. Autopsy's tomorrow."

Porter leaned back in his chair, creaked under his weight. "Mother been notified?"

"She's with her daughter at the funeral home."

There was a lull, neither of us saying much of anything. Porter has a daughter. She's fourteen, maybe fifteen. Has a picture on his desk with his wife, Jane squeezing each other somewhere on the beach or by a lake. Big smiles. I saw Porter giving the photo a glance before returning his attention back my way.

Porter asked. "You doing okay?"

He knew my situation, my two kids: Michael and Justine. They were grown. Michael, a chef in midtown at a top-notch restaurant, has his own apartment close to work because of his hours and Justine is in her sophomore year at college in Seattle. He knew how important they were in my life, especially now.

I nodded and gave Porter a short wave of a hand. "I'm fine, Frank."

Porter tapped the top of his phone. "I just got a call from the Special Agent in Charge at the U.S. Forest Service in the Yosemite National Park. Has himself two missing, a mother and daughter vacationing in the park."

The shift away from my case to this new report caught me off guard. One minute we were talking about the murder of Amanda Jenkins. The next, two missing tourists.

Is he suggesting they're related?

"They'd be treating it as routine," Porter said. "But there are some suspicious things about how they left their hotel room."

"What are they implying?" I put down my pen.

Porter placed both hands flat on his desk, took a moment before speaking. "They're concerned."

"Forest Service have reason to believe there's a connection to my case?" I felt my voice crack at the question.

He inhaled a deep controlled breath and panned a look of uncertainty before conceding, "I don't know what they're thinking. People come up missing in Yosemite all the time. Hell, the roads are as slick as a used car salesman. You can easily roll off the side of a cliff and no one would find you for months." He reached over and grabbed a separate notepad, turned to a page scribbled with bullet points. Lots of arrows and underlined words. "This is what I was told."

Porter started to rattle off detailed information about the case. I turned to a clean page, titled it *Case Two.*

"On February 13th," Porter started saying, "Maria Samuels, mother, age forty-one, and daughter Judy Samuels, age fourteen, checked into the Mountain View Lodge just outside the National Park's west entrance, near the town of El Portal. Hotel registry shows them planning a stay for a week. Two days later, the maid service advises management the guests in room 309 haven't been in their room since they checked in. Manager found all their luggage still in the room. The US Forest Service contacted Mariposa Sheriff's who dispatched a couple of detectives. They went out and photographed the scene."

"Bellows know about this?" I asked.

Porter shrugged, raising his reading glasses to the top of his head. "Don't know. It just came through from Park Service. Thought we should know."

Porter handed me a stack of reports that looked as if they came over a fax machine. I filtered through them, unsure of what I would find.

"How could this be related to my case?" I said. "Two vics, with one being an adult . . ."

Porter held steady, blank stare.

"My investigation involves only young girls." I shook my head. "Help me understand this."

"Whatever may be the case," Porter interjected, "they have two missing and you have three dead." He stood from his desk, walked in front of it and leaned on the edge, arms folded across his chest. This time, he wasn't smiling. I knew Porter didn't believe in coincidences but he didn't draw conclusions without all the facts either. "Right now, let's do a forensic examination of the hotel room and support the search efforts throughout the area. My guess is they're fine, maybe lost, somewhere. In the end, everyone comes home safe."

I heard his words but they didn't sound reassuring.

"Since you're already there," Porter said, "I need you to take lead on the search."

"I have a serial murder investigation, Frank."

"I'll get you help. Two, maybe three days, tops."

I nodded, understanding this wasn't a request. "Right."

I headed out of his office. The bullpen was empty, everyone was out covering leads. Beatriz shuffled between cubicles, tossing file folders and electronic communications on desks. Reports that need to be corrected, new cases being assigned, old ones being closed, or maybe just reminders to update their timecards.

I stepped up to my desk. Boxes of evidence, notes, and case files were stacked four high to my right. My area consisted of light blue walls, light blue book shelves and a light blue chair. Matching and modular. Stamped on the side of every piece of furniture were the words, *Made in Leavenworth, Kansas.* How appropriate. The modern-day work prison.

Slumping into my chair, all fingers intertwined, I sat in my cubby feeling uneasy. I rarely found myself here, opting to be out in the field where the real work existed. A thin layer of dust covered my desk with the exception of a spot where papers had once been stacked, looking like the chalk outline around a body. My eyes focused out the glass window that looked out onto the front gate thinking about Jenkins and now, another new case. Funny, I thought. It was a beautiful day.

Someone spoke, a woman's voice. Special Agent Heather Geonetta was leaning against my cubicle wall. She tossed a two-finger salute. "What's going on, gunslinger?"

She always had a way with words.

I tipped my head, threw her back a similar salute. "Same as always. Laundry, mowing, crossword puzzles . . . hunting serial killers."

Geonetta nodded matter-of-factly. "Yeah, me too."

I liked she had a sense of humor.

Special Agent Geonetta was fairly new, both to the bureau and the Sacramento Division. In her mid-twenties, five-five and a half (but always saying, five-six when asked), thick blonde hair brushed against the shoulders of a black sport jacket. She had an athletic build. Young, attractive, in great shape. Probably could run a mile in under six minutes. I hated her for that. Aggressive—but in a good way—Geonetta had helped me in past cases and I could tell that's why she was here now. The first time we worked together was in response to a bank robbery in downtown Sacramento. She was on the job less than a year and in need of validation from us old guys. She was the FNG (Fucking New Guy). And like all FNGs, it was a tradition; to gain respect, you got to earn it. Geonetta was no exception. She came screaming up in her Crown Vic, lights flashing, sirens blaring. Just like on TV. Terry Keenan was the PD detective on scene. I'd worked a lot of cases over the years with Keenan, a good guy, quick-witted and a real ball buster. He started chuckling under his breath, the feds again trying to corner the market on drama. Geonetta jumped out of her ride, held up her badge high and commanded, "FBI, we got this!" More laughs from the responding uniforms. A shit-eating grin from Keenan.

"Fuckin' feds," Keenan whispered loud enough for my ears only.

I pulled her aside, a little annoyed, a lot embarrassed. "You know the robbery's over," I said.

She held onto a lost expression for as long as she could before a tight-lipped grin overtook her face, one that said, *Gotcha!*

I looked over at Keenan, his shoulders rolling from laughter, barely able to breathe. The uniforms gathered around Geonetta and took her by the shoulders, like she was part of theirs, not one of mine. She crossed her arms, leaned against the group and held a smile.

"Dude," Keenan said. "Hook, line and sinker."

I had to admit; they got me good. And she did, too.

After we finished at the crime scene, I took her, Keenan, and a couple

of the straight-legged uniforms out after for drinks, my penance for
being a sucker. From that moment on, Geonetta proved herself worthy
and no longer the FNG.

"So, I hear you have another victim."

"Victims." I shrugged, holding up three fingers. "Plural."

"Related?"

I shrugged again.

"Bet you could use some help."

"Was that a question?"

Geonetta smiled, rolled a chair to my side of the cubicle and sat.
"Frank assigned me as your co-case agent on the missing tourists."

He could have told me when I was in his office.

"Media is already reporting on it, saying it looks suspicious," she added.

It was becoming apparent the case was taking on legs. This was more
than just an assist to the local authority. If this case was going to be
O&A'd, meaning opened and assigned, Porter was going to want more
than a forensic exam. He's going to want a significant amount of time
focused on it to see if there is a link between the two investigations. If
that were the case, I could use the help.

"Welcome aboard," I said.

"Let me deal with the missing tourists, give you time to focus on your
serial-murderer. If there's a connection, I'll find it."

Connection. I didn't want it to be true. But I couldn't discount it.

Geonetta reached around the cubicle wall and retrieved a file folder,
a couple of inches thick. She pulled a few notes from the top and started
reading.

"I already called Mariposa County Sheriff's," she said.

I craned back toward Porter's office and saw him watching the two of
us, seeing how I'd react to my new partner. Porter sharpened his stare,
which made it clear: *It's a done deal. Now get to work.*

"Spoke to the responding deputy," Geonetta continued, ignoring
my momentary distraction. "Said they interviewed the janitorial staff
at the Mountain View lodge and took photos of the room." Her fingers
sped down the page until she hit the bottom. "He did say their luggage was still there, including the daughter's medication, something
she needs daily."

*Strange. Why leave without your meds, especially if you're planning
on being gone for an extended period of time? Unless it was unplanned . . .*

"The weather is pretty bad up there," I suggested. "Accident, maybe?"

Geonetta pursed her lips. Instincts assumed differently. "They found blood in the bathroom."

That changed everything. I sat up in my chair, collected the paperwork from her hands and pored over the notes. "Where's Hoskin?"

"I called him," she replied. Said to meet us at the Mariposa Sheriff's." Geonetta took back the notes and returned them to her file. "I'm not saying this is related to your killings but don't you think it's a bit coincidental?"

"I don't believe in coincidences." I didn't want to admit it, even if I agreed.

"Neither do I," she said, "but I wouldn't bet against it, either." Geonetta stood. "I'm going home to pack. Should be in Yosemite by nightfall."

I said I'd meet her there. She shoved the folder under her arm before heading out. I fell back into my chair, thinking about Amanda Jenkins, the two before her, and how a newly reported missing persons case might have more in common than I wanted. The worst thing that can happen in a murder investigation is to have more victims. Today, things got worse. As I always did in the past, I picked up the phone to let Emily know I wouldn't be coming home.

But then I remembered: there wasn't anyone to call.

CHAPTER 5

Tuesday February 19th – 12:15 p.m.
Mariposa County Sheriff's Department –
Detective Bellows' Office

Hal Bellows

BELLOWS STOOD INSIDE A CRAMPED OFFICE, staring at a wall covered in glossy snapshots. Half were high school portraits, the other half a stark contrast of crime scene photos. Innocent eyes staring back before tragedy crossed their paths. It was the only reason why their faces hung on the murder board.

He had just returned from the Jenkins' crime scene, finishing up what he had left pending the day prior. Bellows opened a well-worn black leather satchel, pulled out a stack of papers and began to read. He jotted notes on a stack of *Post-it* stickers and slapped them onto his montage of related murders, his morbid mural of once-living faces. He stepped back, gaze held steady on the large corkboard with dozens of Polaroids, dog-eared and marked, pinned in sequential order, depicting a chronology of events that ended with a body recovery. It was frustrating to know that the photos, when placed together, completed a puzzle, revealing possible clues to a person who hungered for young girls. Just not enough to see the killer's face.

Bellows rubbed the weathered skin along his jaw line. The stubble on his face scuffed like sandpaper. He cleared his throat with a growl sounding like a Harley stuck in low gear. Trying to make sense of this mess, he turned away, tried clear his mind. His gaze caught sight of a new folder lying on his desk.

They arrive like uninvited guests.

It was placed on top of the stacks of other files left unaddressed because of the current crisis. His secretary had typed a label, which was neatly affixed to the edge of the folder. *SAMUELS, Maria—Missing Person 1.* He tilted his head a little more and caught sight of the other one: *SAMUELS, Judith (Juvenile)—Missing Person 2.* Bellows sharpened his focus before pushing his chair away and shutting his eyes.

They keep coming, don't they?

He took another deep breath, forced himself to return his attention to his most recent murder. Again, he reached into his satchel and removed a few pictures stuffed in a small white envelope and began sorting them in order of importance. He began pinning them on the murder board next to a 3 x 5 card with the name of his last victim, thick black lettering which read, "Amanda Jenkins—Victim 3."

Graphic shots of Amanda's body in every angle, laid out and posted like a clinical examination at med school. As they were hung, Bellows analyzed each one, hoping to discover some tiny detail that went undetected during the initial search. There was a thin folder that contained close-ups of two notes recovered from his victims. He tacked these too on the board, beneath each body where they were found. He knew better than to post the notes permanently. Too many people came and went from his office; he'd rather not share sensitive evidence like this with just anyone. Not even with other law enforcement officers. But he needed to see them with their victims. Removing the one found on Amanda's body, he compared it with the other two. Bellows aligned the words with each note, illustrating a near-perfect match. Every letter written in the same style, same size, same words. Nothing unusual about the paper, which appeared to be from a medium stock, recycled pulp, similar to high-volume notepads sold to commercial businesses or government offices. Maybe even a public school. Three sides of the note retrieved from Amanda's body had been folded and torn, leaving a straight but rough edge. One side cut clean, indicating it was from the bottom or edge of the sheet.

Bellows stepped back from the board, trying to absorb all the facts in front of him, never taking his eyes off the pictorial of bodies. One by one, he noted the similarities: all filthy, smudged with dirt and grease; loose hay embedded in their clothing. Malnourished. Killed by a blow to the head. Blunt force trauma. He sat down in his office chair and the spring squealed, the supports straining under Bellows' weight. He pushed off with one foot; the metal wheels slowly inched their way backward across the aged linoleum floor before coming to a stop, three feet from his original starting point. It allowed for an expanded view of the entire wall. Bellows rested his elbows on the arms of the chair, hands cupped in front of his mouth. He studied them in silence.

Then he read the names out loud, penned under each portrait. "Rene Walker—Victim 1, Anna Marie Taylor—Victim 2, Amanda Jenkins—Victim 3."

Bellows turned, looked at the missing persons folders again then back at the murder board, wondering if he was investigating one case or two. He felt the rush of a cold draft roll past his neck like cascading ice water. The window was closed. Bellows turned his attention back toward the murder board, squinted and whispered to the passing chill, "*All right. Tell me . . . who's next?*"

CHAPTER 6

Tuesday February 18th – 10:07 p.m.

B Y THE TIME I MADE IT to Mariposa, the sun had dipped behind the tree line. It didn't take long to locate the only motel chain in town: Best Western. Their bright sign shared a pole with the local Chevron gas station. The whole city center was about the size of a small strip mall.

I parked in the vacant lot and pushed through the front glass door. A bell chimed. The lobby was dimly lit, the manager watching a game show on TV. Five minutes and I was registered, handed a keycard to a room in the building around back. The manager returned to his game show and I left to call Geonetta, who told me she had already checked in and was on her way to the Mountain View lodge to meet Hoskin and the ERT crew. I told her I'd be there shortly.

"ROOM 233," I SAID TO MYSELF. Staring at the brass numbers pinned at eye level, I fumbled for the key card to unlock the door.

I stepped in, kicked on the lights and got my first glimpse of the accommodations. The room was decorated with a vintage '60s table lamp, what you'd expect to find in a small quaint town. Basically, a small box with a double bed and two wooden nightstands. The off-white walls, dark furniture, and muted yellow light bathed the space in a golden *Las Vegas* tint. There was a coffee maker and three packs of pre-measured pouches neatly arranged on the counter top, TV the size of a mini-fridge. No Ritz-Carlton but it was clean. Most likely, this going to be my home for the foreseeable future. I felt exhausted.

I tossed my suitcase on the bed and dug out a pair of boots and my winter jacket, took my Glock from my briefcase and holstered the sidearm before heading to the car. It had been raining hard most of the drive in. The rain had stopped and the air had started to freeze, feeling like crystalline needles prickling at my face. I slid the key into the ignition and the vehicle barked back to life. The wipers scraped slush off the windshield.

"Two missing tourists and three murdered kids." I needed to hear the words.

I drove out of the parking lot, turned up a path of glassy, white ice surrounded by black air. I was about twenty minutes from the Mountain View Lodge. I took in my surroundings and imagined the Samuels right here, at this spot, in the same weather conditions. Gloomy and unfamiliar. On a cold and dark winter night along a deserted road, anything could happen. A truck could veer across the dividing line for a head-on, a deer could jump out from a fog bank. A tree could fall in my path. Maybe Maria Samuels and her daughter would miraculously stumble out from a clearing. Wouldn't that be something?

Like I said, anything could happen.

CHAPTER 7

Tuesday February 18th - 10:59 p.m.
Mountain View Lodge

I T TOOK THIRTY MINUTES.

The lodge was sprawling. Rows of buildings stacked neatly along a tree-studded hillside. Lights twinkled in a neat row. The place possessed a rustic look that made it resemble a hunting lodge. Clusters of tall redwoods framed the entire complex and a mountain stream snaked parallel to the road. The air roared with the sound of rushing icy waters from high above to the valley floor. Snowmelt on a massive scale. Whitewater pounded against granite, and a cold hazy mist hung heavy in the night air. Most of the complex was dark but aluminum pole floodlights lit up an area around an opened door. I nosed the Crown Vic forward, heading toward the light. Out front, I could clearly see six FBI agents erecting equipment and draping tarps. The numbers "309" appeared prominently outside the room where the agents stood. Yellow tape separated the area from the rest of the lodge, a command to keep the general public far away. I pulled up to a stall about twenty-five yards away, where three black Suburban SUVs were already parked. It was obvious they were Bureau vehicles—lots of antennas, darkened windows and a large white number embossed on the back lift gate. I recognized Geonetta's car next to the SUVs. On the other side of the parking lot were two sheriff's vehicles. A deputy stood talking on a cell phone.

I stepped out of my car, threw an FBI plaque on the dash, and headed over to an agent by the name of Dave Minacci, who was guarding the perimeter. He was part of the Evidence Response Team. I didn't know him but knew about him. Dave was new to the team but not to devastation. Before joining the bureau, he was a Marine, did two tours in Afghanistan, another in Syria with the Kurds.

After exchanging pleasantries and a warm handshake, he took me over to Hoskin, standing on the other side of the parking lot. Next to him was Geonetta, knit cap and scarf with a hot cup of coffee in hand.

"I hear you're the lead on this abduction," Hoskin said.

My stare sharpened. "You've concluded it's an abduction?"

Hoskin made a motion like he wasn't committing, feigning ambivalence. He raised his hands, palms forward. "Not quite yet," he replied. "I just started the examination, maybe we'll get a better understanding of what happened."

"Were you able to get over to Hal's office? Collect the evidence of the Jenkins homicide?"

Hoskin shook his head. "Mariposa wants to address this first, ASAP. They want to know if there's a connection with the other murders." Then he added, "Whatever the case may be, we're working on the assumption these two missing are still alive."

"You think these two could be victims of whoever is killing the local youths?"

Hoskin flexed his shoulders, another sign of uncertainty. "Anything's possible." He hooked an arm and pointed to the other side of the building. "Let's take a walk. Bellows is inside the room now. He's got the ticket on both cases. He'll be able to update you on any commonalities."

We crossed the lot to a second row of building housing six guest rooms, Geonetta in tow. Green metal doors accented the natural brown paneling of the building. Bellows had just stepped out from the entrance to room 309, arms crossed in front of his large barrel chest. Agents out front were preparing to start their forensic examination.

He saw me and acknowledged my presence by jutting out his chin, upper lip invisible beneath his bushy mustache. "See what happens when you leave for a day?"

Geonetta handed me the cup of coffee and I took a sip. It had already gone cold. "Tell me if you think we have a cross-over with our serial murder case."

Bellows sucked air into his lungs and held it for several seconds before exhaling a moan filled with exasperation. "I'm hoping not, but the way my luck's been going, I can't discount the possibility." He pointed at the opened door. "I heard you found blood."

"What appears to be blood," Hoskin corrected. "But that doesn't mean foul play. Could have been simply a cut."

"Or could have been a murder," Geonetta chimed in.

"Let's not go there quite yet," I said. "I'm hoping they're just lost. It's a big park."

Bellows shook his head, unconvinced by my response. He glanced at his watch, tapped the crystal with a bent finger. "I've got to be getting back to the station. Besides dealing with our murder case, there's work piling up and I'm short-handed. Let's connect tomorrow. My office, around eight?"

We all agreed.

Bellows gave a quick nod, shook our hands, and trudged back to the parking lot toward a Chevy Tahoe. Squeezing into the driver's seat, he cranked the engine and the transmission rumbled as it was dropped into low gear. The vehicle nosed up to the exit, turned left, and disappeared down the unlit road.

Hoskin tapped Geonetta on the shoulder, pointed a finger at me and motioned toward the tourists' room door. "Follow me."

We walked up to the entrance, giving us our first look inside. Two queen-size beds with matching nightstands topped by brass lamps. A small white refrigerator was situated near the door, and on the side of a long dresser, four drawers, stacked two high. A large mirror was perched on top followed by a small 19-inch television. The examination had been on-going for about half an hour, agents methodically studying the walls for latent prints, tool-marks, out-of-place fibers. Anything microscopic.

Geonetta sounded anxious to get on with the case. "What have you got, so far?"

"Nothing remarkable." Hoskin puffed out his cheek. "But something's wrong. Place looks too clean."

I took a step forward, knowing the entry had already been processed and gave the interior a good look-over. The team was still working the scene.

Hoskin leveled a hand shoulder height and swept it left to right. "Most of the time I find blood, prints, and fiber everywhere," he said. "Even when there isn't a crime. Here, I got nothing." He looked around and back, eyes wide. "If this was the scene of a crime, somebody had time to clean up."

I looked at Geonetta. She looked at Bellows.

"I barely found any fingerprints. When does that ever happen?" Hoskin's voice picked up a staccato beat. "Imagine this: Guy stalks his target, learns the layout of the room, knows when there would be no witnesses . . ."

I nodded, knowing where he was going.

"Afterwards, he wipes everything. Knows he has time because he's been watching the movements of his victims, the staff, the other guests."

I stopped to let Hoskin's theory sink in.

Premeditated.

They were from out-of-town; no one knew them around here. What would have brought a premeditated crime to this small tourist town? And at the same time, the possibility of a serial killer? Like Frank Porter, I didn't believe in coincidence. But if there was a crime committed in room 309, the chances it was related to my serial killer couldn't be discounted.

Hoskin shrugged his shoulders. "Maybe we'll find our answers in what we collect here."

I pointed through the door. "I hope we find them out there."

Hoskin didn't respond, knowing he couldn't guarantee a safe conclusion. He turned back to the crew, who were now standing nearby, listening in on our conversation, nodding along. Most were covered in protective clothing, their bright white Tyvek jumpsuits, harshly contrasting with the natural colors of nature.

Hoskin shooed them away. "Okay, back to work."

The crew separated, returning to their duties. A female agent began photographing the outside of the lodge. Another took GPS coordinates on a set of footprints near the entrance porch. Plaster was poured from a plastic bucket onto tire tracks near the room. A handful of cigarette butts were located in a flowerbed. Everything photographed and collected, each marked, tagged and separated so that one could not contaminate the other for possible DNA and fingerprints. An agent in baggy tan colored cargo pants and a gray T-shirt under a dark blue Gortex jacket squatted by the doorframe, bending low, studying the wood through thick glasses. Black powder smudges covered his gloves as he methodically began dusting for prints. His horsehair brush twirled as the sparkle of magnetic powder floated in the harsh light coming from a portable flood lamp.

Four agents slowly entered the room. I followed them in. One of the agents finished dusting, put away his fingerprint powder kit, and retrieved the ALS, a shiny steel box resembling a small briefcase with a metal flex pipe, known as the wand, a color wheel at the end. He flipped a toggle switch and the cooling fan hummed as the agent clicked through various color filters, searching for the one that would trap the right wavelengths for his specific examination. Starting with bright white, he lowered the wand close to the ground, shining the beam at a slight angle, a technique known as *oblique lighting*. Oddly shaped elongated shadows danced across the floor.

He increased the angle toward the ground and more shadows appeared. As the light fell across the carpet, hundreds of tiny hairs and fibers sparkled, the shiny strands glistened as if sprouting from the floor. On their hands and knees, three agents crawled, retrieving samples with plastic tweezers, before dropping them into small, clear plastic baggies marked for evidence.

"Next," Hoskin said, walking over to the edge of the nearest bed. He squatted low, peered across the top of wrinkled bed sheets. A blue blanket was untucked at one corner, hanging low over the sides of the mattress. Hoskin closed one eye, aimed his view with the other. He was looking for body fluid residue. Hotels are cesspools for every bacterium known to man. Hoskin waved an agent over, the one carrying the ALS light. The agent dropped next to Hoskin, the heavy metal box steady in his right hand. He manipulated the wand with his left, shifting the color wavelength between 390 to 540 cycles per second. Anything blue or red glowed with the same effect a black light had on an Elvis painting.

Everyone donned amber colored goggles. Hoskin passed me a pair. "Put these on." I slid on the lenses and the room immediately transformed into a sea of yellow and orange. The lenses filtered specific color wavelengths causing blood or semen stains to appear black. The agent swept the room with the ALS wand, searching for any signs of trace evidence. Spatter marks materialized along the baseboards, a common reaction to chemical solution used by the cleaning staff. He brushed the wand up and down the walls like painting. Patterns that resembled versions of a Rorschach inkblot materialized in the light, disappearing as the beam moved on. He shifted away from the wall to the bedspread and sheets. They glowed with a distinctive pattern that could only be recognized as remnants from an active and robust guest.

Hoskin shook his head and whistled low. "No blood, just a lot of spooge."

That was Hoskin's attempt at technical terminology.

"Best we bag and tag. Let the lab boys play with it."

Without the ability to study each stain in detail on scene, Hoskin carefully folded up the bedding and sealed them in large paper bags, readied to be sent off to Quantico.

I watched the crew section off the room. A team member with the name *ROBINSON* scrawled in bold letters with a black marker on the back of his Tyvek entered the bathroom, taking samples of the water by snaking the toilet, tub, and sink drains. Wouldn't be the first time someone had used the bathtub to hack a body into pieces. If the tub *was* used, there was a possibility they could dredge up bone fragments, blood, or skin cells. I looked at the sink where the team reported a potential bloodstain. A small dark smear appeared on the cold-water handle. The item was photographed and swabbed for analysis.

Hoskin peered in the bathroom. "I can't say we'll find anything of importance here. The maid service had already come through, cleaned everything." He pointed at the handle. "Lucky we even found that."

It was unfortunate.

Hoskin glanced back at his crew and swirled an arm like he was spinning a lasso. "Start taking fiber samples."

The crew dug deep into their backpacks, coming up with their Gerber knives. Blades snapped opened. The agents took corners, started slashing and digging into anything fibrous. Paint chips from walls, wood slivers from the doorframe, chunks of weave from the carpet. It was legal vandalism.

"The management is going to be upset when they find out you're cutting holes in their carpet."

"That may be so," Hoskin said, "but I think they'll be more upset when they find out we're tearing out the carpet, wall-to-wall."

I turned and scanned the empty room. A coldness traveled up my spine, the kind you feel when imagining what went on in this room, the ghost of the missing acting out the part in your head. As much as I wanted to find nothing indicating a crime, Hoskin was right: it was all wrong, this scene, like a crooked square. I refocused on Hoskin. "I got a bad feeling about this."

Hoskin only nodded.

I took a closer second-look at the entryway door. No scratches, no dents. No one broke the frame, handle, or door. Clean. Like it was opened by someone with a key.

"Who has access to the room?" I asked.

Hoskin held up a hand, fingers popping one at a time. "Could be a host of employees. Maids, manager, maintenance workers."

"Have they all been interviewed?"

"Only by Mariposa County Sheriff's."

Geonetta returned with a fresh cup of coffee.

"Then I guess we better do it again," Geonetta said.

Hoskin gave a thumbs-up, then returned to his forensic examination.

He took a knee and started pulling up the corners of the carpet, preparing it for shipment to the laboratory division at Quantico, Virginia.

Tomorrow, the bureau would be buying Mountain View Lodge 500 square feet of new carpeting.

CHAPTER 8

Wednesday February 19th – 6:00 a.m.

THE ALARM WENT OFF BEFORE THE SUN BROKE. I awoke feeling groggy, a bit cheated, having gotten only four hours of restless sleep. The search at the Mountain View Lodge took longer than expected. I got out of bed and pulled back the curtains. Moisture clouded the corners of the window, coldness covering the glass like a blanket, frost cracking the pane. Outside, the ground was obscured in crystalline flakes, the air dark, gray, weighted. I couldn't shake the feeling of lead in my veins. I cranked up the heat, turned on the television, and listened to the local station while I showered and dressed. In the background, I heard the news already reporting on our missing tourists.

"A mother and daughter from Phoenix, Arizona, went missing while touring Yosemite National Park. Police are preparing to coordinate search teams to comb the hills in an attempt to find out just what may have happened to the two, who have been missing for almost three days. Snow falling on the upper ridge is going to hamper air support efforts."

I continued listening through the open bathroom door as the shower's hot water jackhammered against my back, try to find a reason not to get out. I didn't want to face the media waiting for an update at the Sheriff's station. More so, knowing they'd be asking if the disappearance of our tourists was some way linked to the serial murder investigation. And frankly, I wouldn't know how to answer that.

After getting dressed, I clicked off the television, stepped out of the room, and found a patch of sun to stand in, waiting for Geonetta to show.

Within a minute, she rounded the building. We went into the lobby together and each grabbed a cup of coffee before getting into my car. Up the hill, we turned right onto Tenth Street, just off Main. Small green signs marked "Sheriff's Office" were scattered along the way, the roads full of potholes. Slushy dirt and ice piled up on sidewalks. Small cottage-style bungalows lined both sides of the street. Cresting the hill, I caught sight of a High School in the foreground, tall evergreens and rocky cliffs for its backdrop. It appeared old and in need of a paint job. Students spilled out of three large yellow school buses parked in the turnaround while the drivers appeared lost in their routine. The innocence of what I saw caused my head to buzz, a collision of contradictions. It was a con-fluence of time and place out of sync. For me, it was foreign. Void of con-crete roads and tall glass buildings, the scene offered no large Hollywood billboard signs, no traffic jams. The air was too clean. It was certainly not the kind of town where you'd expect to pick up the morning newspaper to read about three homicides tucked between the funnies and classified ads. *Welcome to Mariposa; please set your clock back fifty years.*

The Sheriff's station was across the street. I pulled next to a cruiser and threw my car into park. The air had a sharp, cold bite to it as I stepped out.

"Feels like Christmas," Geonetta said.

Clouds of warm breaths trailed me all the way to the front door and into a small waiting room.

A woman's face peered out from a sliding glass window inside the entryway lobby.

"Good morning. We're here to see detective Bellows. Jack Paris and Heather Geonetta, FBI." I offered my credentials.

The receptionist's eyes narrowed under a bobbing head of silvery hair fashioned in the shape of a beehive. "Paris? Like the city . . . in France?"

"Yes, ma'am." I forced a smile.

"I'll see if he's in. Please take a seat." She picked up the phone, and a second later poked her head out of the small sliding glass window. "Detective Bellows is coming up to get you both."

A few minutes passed before a side door opened, Bellows crowding the frame. "Come on in." He strained a smile but couldn't hide the fatigue and dark rims circling his eyes.

I walked up and patted him on the shoulder. "You look like shit."

He considered the remark. "Thanks."

We followed him down a narrow hallway and rounded the cor-ner where we could see Hoskin and the crew already inside reviewing topographical maps and chart. Radios blared in the background with SAR teams calling in their coordinates.

Hoskin was handing out assignments to the agents. Search and Rescue was set to comb in concentric circles, starting at the El Portal entrance working their way north toward Tuolumne Grove. Another crew was starting up near the O'Shaughassey Dam, just south to Highway 120. Hoskin's team would join them in case something was found.

Bellows handed me a folder containing land maps of the valley, updated investigative reports, and a list of contact phone numbers. "Everyone here has one of these and we will be updating it every day. Cellular service is spotty up here. In these parts, analog phones rule. Your digital tech is worthless."

A large map blanketed the conference room table: Tuolumne, Mariposa, and Calaveras counties. Red hatch-marks, just beginning, were etched across large swaths of land, like the march of advancing armies.

"Since the news release, we've been getting hundreds of tips on the call-in line. Park Rangers are shagging down the leads but they're coming up dry." Bellows continued scanning the reams of reports. He shook his head in disgust. "They're all bullshit."

"Still don't think this is related to our serial killer case?"

Bellows looked at me. "Yesterday, I couldn't see how." He then shrugged his large shoulders. "Today? I just don't know."

Child killers don't often switch between children and adults. Generally, they get intimidated by adults and stay away when confronted. But these profiles are based on statistics. It's the exceptions that prove the rules.

Bellows scratched at his chin. "If our killer *was* involved with these missing tourists, I'd say it would have been unplanned, forcing him or her to kill. If that's the case, we should find a wealth of forensic evidence left behind . . . somewhere."

I turned to Hoskin, said, "What's your assessment?"

Hoskin removed a stack of notes from his briefcase, neatly tabbed and color-coded.

"There was something that caught my attention. Cigarette butts found just outside their door."

Our search found no indication either of the Samuels women were smokers.

"The maintenance crew said the area was cleaned the night prior. It appears somebody had been hanging around out there late in the evening."

There was a quiet pause.

"A stalker?" I asked.

"Strong possibility. I wouldn't rule it out."

Hoskin rolled a finger over the evidence list from the previous night. "The stuff we gathered is being sent back to the lab for DNA work up." He paused, tapped the palm of his hand with his Monte Blanc fountain pen. "Some other interesting things I observed out there." He walked to a table lined with photographs of Maria and Judy Samuels while on vacation. "We found a roll of film on the floor in the hotel room. Must have fallen from their carry-ons next to the suitcases. I had an agent run down to the local Walgreen's to have them developed. He stood there watching the employee process the film, ensuring no duplicate copies were made. We reviewed them last night and placed them in chronological order. The prints are date and time marked."

We studied the pictures, noting the camera's timestamps. The last photo showed a mark of 02 14 98 0746. That translated into 7:46 a.m. on the 14th, indicating the last verified time they were alive and in the room.

"The maid told the deputies she was in the room the following morning," Hoskin added. "She remembered seeing suitcases on the bed nearest to the window. When she returned the following morning, the room appeared the same."

"Doesn't look like they came back that night," Geonetta said.

"We then pulled the photos taken by the sheriff's detective during their investigation. Take a look."

We carefully compared the two sets, searching for any differences. I punched a finger in the center of one taken by the sheriff's. "Looks like a piece of luggage was moved."

Hoskin took his pen and pointed at the same one. "That's a jewelry bag." He tapped at the picture "It's empty."

"Maybe a robbery gone bad?" I said.

Hoskin hesitated. "Maybe, but if it was a robbery and things started going south, there'd be more damage, leaving me with a shit load of forensic evidence. Things just don't seem right." Hoskin bracketed the photos between his hands. "Look at the beds again. Nothing, no change." He waved a sharp pointing finger, alternating between the two sets of pictures. "Besides the luggage, they look exactly the same. Who rents a room for three days and never sleep in the bed?"

I could only draw the one logical conclusion. "They never returned to their room."

"Still doesn't tell us what happened to them."

"So," I said, "let's identify suspects with a motive."

For what we were looking at, our start was with sex offenders, known as two-ninety registrants. Yosemite had plenty. They come to hide, deep in the hills, to get away from the prying eyes of the law. A place to feed their addiction. Bellows and I had already interviewed dozens on our serial murder case. Now, we needed to go back and start again, to see if there was any connections to our tourists. "How many" Geonetta asked, "are in a mile radius of the lodge?"

Bellow's expression changed, eyes dipping toward the floor. "More than you can imagine."

He held his hands up in front of his chest. "I've already started preparing a list but I can't guarantee it's completely accurate."

I knew he was right. The valley is large and sparsely monitored. They squirrel away in trailers and rental cabins throughout the hillside on open and unmanaged land. Like a virus. Burrowed deep in the forest, they go undetected. The locals would prefer them gone, pack their bags and get the hell out of town. But they fill the menial jobs. Restaurant dishwashers, cooks, cleaners. And they work at the hotels and lodges. Like the one where the Samuels stayed.

Bellows and his deputies do their best to track every one of them to ensure they register as mandated by the State. Failure to do so is a felony but it doesn't seem to faze most of them.

Geonetta leaned between me and Bellows. "I'll start making contact."

Bellows nodded and then handed over the first draft of his suspect list.

I picked up a folder marked, *Interviews,* fanned through each report looking at the names. "Have all the lodge employees and guests been interviewed?"

"First thing we did after the two were reported missing." He pointed at the folder. "You should have them all there."

By 9 a.m. things were already being put into motion. I gave Geonetta a copy of the interviews for her to read, see who she thought may be worth revisiting, and identify employees or guests we missed.

Mariposa Sheriff stood up a command post inside a small conference room. It had already outgrown the space for the crowd of officers and investigators now assigned to this case. Bellows was put in charge to coordinate the logistics of nearly two hundred search team members from Mariposa, Tuolumne, the U.S. Forest Service, and the Bureau. Mariposa didn't have the resources to manage a serial murder and a missing persons case alone. They asked for help from the surrounding agencies and they got it. For now, the case belonged to Bellows. Even for a seasoned detective, the task was daunting. Four days had already passed since the Samuels were last seen. I sipped coffee while contemplating the odds they were still alive. In my mind, it wasn't good. If they were taken, without a ransom note, more than likely after this much time, they were dead. If they were lost or involved in an accident and exposed to a Mariposa winter night, they'd be dead. There was no activity on their credit or ATM cards. That's a bad sign. I didn't like the way this was heading. Whatever the case, I feared, we were looking at a recovery instead of a rescue.

Sitting at a corner table, I faced out toward a large window while sifting through newly delivered reports, pausing every so often to let the information soak in. Lots of possible leads, more likely, a hundred pages of red herrings. Nevertheless, I forced myself to give them a serious look, hoping something would stand out. Twenty pages in, my eyesight began to blur and I had to stop.

A bell rang. School just got out.

I looked out the window and watched the kids coming out of class, stand in front of the school, milling around, socializing. I looked past them, stared at the mountainous backdrop that stretched across my peripheral view, a hazy mist obscuring the tallest peak. Snow continued to fall. Like frosting on a cake. It was an enormous swath of land to search, I thought, even with the large number of volunteers we had.

"A needle in a goddamn frozen haystack," Bellows said walking up behind me. He had more reports in hand.

I sank into my chair and stared at the ridgeline as if it were a massive painting.

Panoramic.

"Two needles," I said. I pointed a finger at the large snowcapped mountain, the heavy mist growing ever thicker. "If they *are* out there, their time is about run out."

"That's if they're not already dead."

"You know, Hal, we still have a serial murder case needing our attention."

Bellow pulled the two Samuels folders from his stack of files and handed them to me. "Who says we stopped?"

At this point in time, I couldn't disagree. "Well," I said, "we better get some more help."

CHAPTER 9

Wednesday February 19th - 9:51 p.m.
Mariposa County Sheriff's Department

THERE WAS A BREAK IN THE CASE.

The phone on Bellows' desk rang just as I walked into his office. He swiped up the receiver and pointed to the chair next to his desk. Receiver pressed tightly between his ear and shoulder, he twisted toward the murder board. Bellows covered the mouthpiece, leaned his head back in my direction and informed me the call was from a Tuolumne County detective. I nodded and stayed quiet.

Bellow listened, saying little while jotting notes onto a legal pad. He tilted it my way so I can read it. Most of his writing was illegible, but I was able to decipher *burglary* and *custody*. I'd have to wait to get the full story.

"Okay . . . all right," he said before asking the detective, "Has he lawyered up?" Bellows listened for a response then kicked the wall with his large boot. "Well don't let him!" he shouted back. "We're coming over now."

He hung up, double-checked his notes, and scribbled more hieroglyphics. He glanced at the paper, then exhaled a long breath in a slow, low whistle. "Tuolumne County Sheriff's arrested a juvenile tonight on a car burg at the Captain's Lounge, a shit-hole just outside downtown Sonora. The bar owner heard a commotion in his parking lot and went out to investigate. Came across the suspect digging around in the trunk of a car. Kid started to freak out and according to the bar owner, attacked him. The owner was armed with a baseball bat. Gave him an attitude adjustment. A classic *wooden shampoo*. Then the deputies arrived."

"Is he okay?"

"He's fine," Bellows said, waving a dismissive hand. "When they searched the vehicle, the officers popped the trunk." Bellows was choosing his words carefully but I could see he had something of interest to say. "They found what looks like a kidnap chamber inside."

I had been taking notes. I stopped writing.

"Fully equipped with chains and handcuffs bolted to the trunk walls. Looks like the kid was searching for something to steal when he stumbled across a predator's car. Tuolumne Sheriff's is holding off searching the vehicle until they can get a warrant. They're aware of my three homicides and wanted to know if I was interested in coming out to see if it's related."

"Have they identified the owner of the vehicle?"

Bellows licked a thumb and flipped through pages of notes. "Yeah, a Robert Rae Olsen, Junior, 10851 East California Street, Tuolumne." Something he wrote caught his eye. "They ran his criminal history. A two-ninety registrant in Tuolumne County."

Sex offender. One we hadn't yet interviewed.

"You thinking what I'm thinking?"

Bellows picked up his keys. "Let's get a look at that car."

"Let's find Olsen," I added.

I grabbed up my briefcase and followed Bellows, who was already heading for the door. I turned and yelled over to Hoskin. "Wake your team," I shouted. "We have a vehicle that needs to be searched, bumper-to-bumper. I need to know who may have been held in that trunk."

CHAPTER 10

THE PAPERS TUMBLED OFF MY LAP and onto the floor of the SUV. Tires squealed along the icy pavement every time Bellows decided to make a hard turn. We pulled out of the sheriff's parking lot in a hurry, heading toward the Tuolumne sub-station. Bellows steered with one hand, holding up his cellphone with the other, hoping for cell service, as though black ice on the road was no big deal. He got through to the Tuolumne sergeant while I re-arranged the papers now jumbled and out-of-order. I quickly examined the Samuels case reports, searching for any references to a vehicle like the one seen at the Captain's Lounge. Maybe a mention of a Robert Olsen.

Bellows ended his conversation with the sergeant and slipped the phone into his jacket pocket. "They've canvassed the bar. No sign of Olsen. None of the patrons admitted knowing him either." Bellows rolled down the window and spat. "No surprise. Tuolumne is sending two deputies to his last known address."

Thirty minutes later, we pulled into a county lot in front of a large warehouse. Rows of gas pumps dotted the back of the large metal-framed structure. County trucks sat vacant and cold, sleeping dinosaurs on a black-tar oasis. Vapor lights hung over each of the six roll-up doors.

We entered the large building through a side door and into the open bay of the warehouse. A flatbed truck rested quietly in the middle, bathed in the florescent light buzzing from high above. The confiscated Impala was slowly being rolled off the back of the lift and onto the concrete tarmac. The driver unhooked the chains, dragged them back into a well-worn toolbox. We walked straight to the Impala, anxious to see what we would find inside.

Sergeant Kevin Malloy with Tuolumne County Sheriff's Department appeared from a small office. He walked over to Bellows and shook his hand. "Glad you could make it, Hal." Malloy glanced at the towed vehicle, an eyebrow raised. "May be the break in the case you're looking for."

Bellows stepped to the side, leaving me front and center. "Kevin, let me introduce you to Agent Paris with the FBI. We're working the murder cases as well as the missing tourists. We're wondering if there might be a connection. Thought he might be able to provide some assistance. He's got a whole forensic crew here. They may be of value."

Malloy hesitated, considered what it meant allowing the feds into the inner-circle. He eventually gave in. "Can always use the help."

I shook his hand. "What have you got so far?"

Malloy tugged at his Stetson.

"It all started with a call-out to the Captain's Lounge." Malloy cleared his throat as we walked toward the car. "Not one of our upstanding establishments," he added with a slight smirk. "Truth is, it's a repository for the town's assholes. A real shit-hole. Town council allows the dive to remain open, mostly to corral the local felons and troublemakers. Opposite end of town. We pop into the Captain's Lounge from time to time. Find most of our parolees at large there. Lots of drunks, drug dealers, and wife beaters. Makes our job easier having them all in one place."

"How did your subject stumble onto this car?"

"He said it was purely random. We spoke to him after being booked. Name is Robby Tyler. Got a record for B and E and some petty crimes, mostly juvenile. But I believe him. He didn't have any problem telling us what happened. Realized he'd rather be charged with auto burg than be a suspect in a kidnapping."

Smart decision.

"According to Tyler, it was around midnight when he picked out the car. Far edge of the lot where it was dark." Malloy hooked his thumbs on his tactical belt and looked at the car. "1967 pale blue Chevy Impala, two door. Clean, chrome trim, shiny wheel. Nice ride. Said he took a hammer and busted out the wing window. Got inside and started rummaging for valuables." Malloy hunched down and pointed a finger at the backseats. "That's when he found the chains and cuffs attached to the back wall of the trunk. It didn't take long for Tyler to know what he'd stumbled upon."

I looked through the back window and could see the seat already pulled back, the chains dangling out like a den of snakes. "A confinement chamber," I said.

Malloy tipped his head. "Exactly."

"You got a bead on where to find Olsen?"

"I got deputies running out to his residence now."

It wasn't more than a minute when a young deputy entered the warehouse and approached the sergeant with the news they came up dry at the Olsen residence. "Porch light off, no cars in the driveway."

Malloy didn't seem surprised. "Put out a BOLO for Olsen. He's a registered sex offender and most likely on probation. Find and wake up his P.O., get his residence searched. I want him found."

Bellows made a call to the on-duty Deputy District Attorney, brought him up to speed on what we had and to expect an affidavit for a search warrant on the Olsen residence.

I got Malloy to agree to allow our ERT crew to do the forensic search. It took about an hour for Hoskin and his crew to arrive. They stood in the warehouse already dressed in their Tyveks. With a final thumbs up from Malloy, they began searching the vehicle, starting with photographs and diagrams. Two agents started scraping dirt residue from under the tire wells. Insects were carefully tweezered from the radiator, help determine where the car may have traveled. The interior was dusted for prints. Another agent vacuumed the interior using a sterile filter, trapping the contents. The canister quickly filled with dirt, hairs and fibers, clues that could potentially tell us who was in the car, who may have been held against their will. Carpet samples were taken to be compared against fibers found at our crime scenes, including the Samuels' hotel room.

But it was the trunk I was most interested in.

Hoskin walked to the back of the car, the crew following closely.

The lock had already been picked open. I stood to the right of Hoskin, flanked by Bellows on my left. Hoskin nudged the latch and the trunk lid creaked open. The overhead florescent lights washed the interior in a blue tint, illuminating shiny metal chain-links zig-zagging, terminating onto large eyebolts welded to a metal plate attached to the side walls.

Bellows whistled. "Holy Mother-of-God."

"You got that right," I said.

Dirty industrial rags, gray from grease, scattered throughout the trunk—grease, like the kind we found on our victims. A stained brown comforter, more like a ball of fungus, was bunched up in the spare tire well. And a plastic gas can tilted sideways had been shoved in the corner along with some old navy blue worker's pants, pair of boots.

Hoskin waved a finger above the trunk and called out to agent John Gilliard. "Photograph everything."

Gilliard grabbed his camera and fired off a stream of flashes.

An agent started coiling the chains, placed a separate bag over the cuff at the end, then tagged and sealed them in a large evidence bag.

"I'm betting we'll get trace DNA," Hoskin said. "Hopefully confirm if your victims were here."

Another agent removed the comforter and placed it in a paper bag and sealed it with evidence tape.

"We got something," another agent hollered back.

I leaned over the agent's shoulder to see a large green duffle bag stowed in the spare tire well, hidden below the brown blanket. Hoskin stepped forward, removed the bag and positioned it on a large sheet of butcher paper. Slowly and methodically, he started pulling out the contents. More flashes from Gillard's camera.

I pushed my way forward to get a better look.

Hoskin stopped halfway through his examination and peered up at me. "Women's clothing."

I reached down and touched a torn blouse and a pair of dirty jeans, a hoody with what looked like a high school logo across the front. Something like my daughter Justine would wear. My throat tightened.

"I'd say, more like young girl's clothing."

CHAPTER 11

Thursday February 20th – 7:30 a.m.

THE SEARCH AND RESCUE TEAMS CONTINUED TO SCOUR the frozen hills. Horse-mounted deputies from Tuolumne County joined in, now with talk and rumors there may be a link between the two cases. The red hatch marks on the topo maps etched deeper into the mountainous range, albeit as a slow advance. The conference room, which had become a command post, was littered with half empty coffee cups and food bags from the local sandwich shop. Tired officers stumbled in and out, dragging the mud from the hillside onto the already worn linoleum floor. I had been in the CP for over an hour, briefing Quantico about the case and preparing them for what they were about to receive for analysis. With a dozen other high-priority cases demanding their attention, the analysts confessed they were hard pressed in getting to ours as quickly as I would like. I told them the more time they took, the greater the chance more people might die. I may have sounded overly dramatic but it was the truth. And frankly, I didn't care about other cases; I only cared about mine. After hanging up the phone, I had to step out of the command post to get some air.

The outside was as chaotic as the inside. Search teams swirled the parking lot, exchanging information about where to go next. SAR canines barked, anxious with all the commotion, handlers receiving orders where to send their dogs. Several sheriff's helicopters sliced through the sky overhead. I could feel the *clunk, clunk, clunk* from the lumbering sweep of their rotor blades reverberating off my chest. The weather was being kind for now and the sheriff's office was going to take advantage of it as long as they could. I walked to a clearing in the parking lot, looked for a favorable cell site and a quiet place to phone the office. The sun was out but the air was cold, making my fingers stiff and clumsy. I punched the numbers into my cell through gloved hands and waited for Porter to answer.

"It's me."

Frank Porter groused something unintelligible before saying, "Give me some good news."

"We may have something," I said. Porter listened as I told him about the discovery of Olsen's vehicle, the compartment and finding young women's clothing hidden in the back trunk. Olsen wasn't married, had no sisters, and was a registered sex offender. Our findings rolled off my tongue, like gas on a fire. Porter didn't say much but I could tell his assumptions were heading down the same path as mine.

"I have asked the lab to give the clothes priority," I said.

"What's your gut feeling?" Porter was asking if I was betting on DNA from my victims, the Samuels, or both.

"I won't know until I see the results. Until then, Mariposa and Tuolumne are continuing with a full-blown search of the area." I gazed over at the mountains, the snow that covered them, and followed a darkening layer of clouds, thick as concrete, slowly moving in my direction. "I am hoping if the Samuels are out there, they've found shelter, enough to stay warm."

"And alive," Frank added.

"Yeah," I replied. "Alive."

As I FINISHED MY CALL, BELLOWS WALKED UP with Geonetta at his side. He still looked tired but upbeat.

"Your partner located Olsen's mother under the name of Patricia Neumann," he said.

Geonetta handed me a folder containing property record searches and credit reports. There was an old driver's license photo of Neumann, long since expired.

"She's living in Copperopolis," Geonetta said. "Maybe with our boy, Olsen. I say we pay her a visit."

Bellows spoke in a tempered tone: "If we're lucky, we'll find Bobby Rae Olsen having cocktails with our tourists."

His levity didn't help settle my nerves. As much as I would have welcomed a break in this bleak moment, I had to face the fact that either the Samuels had fallen victims to bad weather or victims to bad people. Whichever the case, the weather was our enemy and the forecast wasn't showing signs of getting any better.

I retrieved my bag from the command post and we all met back in the lot. Bellows fired up the Tahoe. I pulled on the passenger door, threw my bag in the back, and pulled my safety belt across my chest. Bellows accelerated from the lot before I could hear the belt click. The joking had passed and the cabin went quiet. Geonetta sat up front. I saw her checking her left side to confirm she had extra magazines for her Glock. She wanted to be ready.

Thick storm clouds rolled closer like an angry mob and the mountaintop grew dark. Where we were, the sun still shone bright, rising high through a patch of crisp blue sky, the cold air taking control of the lowland. It was a slight break in the weather. I hoped the same would happen in this case.

The rear tires on Bellows' Tahoe chirped as it broke traction exiting the lot. Heading toward Copperopolis, I prayed our next contact would be with Bobby Rae Olsen.

CHAPTER 12

Thursday February 20th – 9:27 a.m.

I KNOCKED ON THE DOOR.

Bellows and Geonetta slipped around the back in case Bobby Rae was inside and decided to make a run for it.

The house was small, an unassuming wooden porch across the front. The whole place was in need of paint. I peered through a small window to the right of the entry door, rapping the glass with the back of my hand. "Patricia Neumann? FBI. I'd like to speak to you, please." I waited a few seconds and, hearing no response, I gently pushed on the front door to see if it was opened, all the time, resting my thumb on the safety strap of my holster. Door secured, I walked back to the window and again scanned the interior. The living room was quiet, everything in its place. Just then the front door cracked open and a slender old woman appeared. She shuffled into the opening and waved a frail hand, implying an invitation to enter.

"You must be looking for my son." Spoken as if knowing we were coming. She was no more than four foot seven, a wisp of a woman. I ventured to guess a soft breeze would carry her away like autumn leaves. Her hair was dominated by gray, with a hint of red, a shade reminiscent of her younger days, but neatly pulled back and tied, a proper appearance for a person of her generation. I noticed cloudy eyes, most likely impairing her ability to see clearly, but somehow I doubted it handicapped her.

"Is he here?" I asked.

"No, but come in," she said with the airiness of spun cotton. I wasn't sure if her tone was from politeness or the proficiency of years dealing with the problems of a troubled son. I followed her into the living room. "Please, sit. Can I get you something to drink . . . some tea?"

Bellows had returned to the front, and when he heard Neumann's voice, invited himself in. He ducked down a hallway and I heard him open a door.

I politely declined the offer of tea. "We'll only take a moment of your time."

She guided me toward the sofa. It almost seemed ritual. This wasn't her first rodeo. No subterfuge was going to work on a mother whose son treated the judicial system like a revolving door.

After rummaging around back, Bellows joined us in the living room. Geonetta still stood at the open door, watching the road and the open areas between the house and forest. Neumann sank into a rocker, cloth-covered Bible lay waiting by the seat. She picked it up and placed it carefully on her lap as if it were part of her dress.

"This book has helped me through some rough times," she confessed as a diminutive smile graced her lips. "Do you believe in Jesus, Agent Paris? To believe is to be righteous." There was a motherly confidence in her voice.

Bellows perused photos on the walls, discretely fanning through the mail stacked on the entryway table. I could see Mrs. Neumann was acutely aware of his activity but said nothing.

"Mrs. Neumann, where's Bobby Rae?" Bellows said.

Her cloudy stare drifted in the direction of his voice as though giving the question serious consideration.

"I don't know," she answered.

"Are you sure? It's important we speak with him."

Neumann's face tightened. "I know why you're here, detective."

I opted for a different tack. "Mrs. Neumann, Bobby Rae may have information to help us locate a person hurting children. He could help save a child's life."

She dipped her chin to her chest, eyelids fluttering. Had she ever heard these words before? Someone asking Bobby Rae for . . . *help*.

"I doubt Bobby Rae associates with anyone who would harm a child," she said. "He loves children."

"I wasn't suggesting otherwise."

The old woman smiled, lips thin and tight. I suspected she saw through my ruse.

"Mrs. Neumann, does Bobby Rae associate with any teenagers? Kids of, maybe, a girlfriend?"

Mrs. Neumann responded as though pricked by a needle, eyes squinting as she shook an arthritic, accusatory finger. "He's changed, Agent Paris. Bobby Rae is a kind, gentle soul. Whatever might have happened in the past is past. He's making amends with himself and the Lord." She patted the Bible on her lap and the speed of her rocking quickened. "He helps at the High School, volunteer work." Neumann straightened. "Detective Bellows, you should have known that."

Bellows stopped writing in his notebook. "What does he do at the school?"

"He cleans, maintenance, gets rid of the trash. After hours, he helps get the kids on the right school bus so they get home safe and sound."

Bellows flinched. Bobby Rae at the local High School, a wolf mingling with the sheep.

"He's reformed," Mrs. Neumann snapped.

"Is that where we will find him?" I asked.

She leaned forward in her rocking chair, "He's my son and I love him, even after all he has put me through. You're going to have to find him yourself." The old woman sat back and continued to rub the worn, cloth-covered Bible. The room went silent, Neumann's stare now far and distant.

I stood up knowing we weren't going to get any further with her. I thanked Mrs. Neumann for her time. "If you hear from Bobby Rae," I said, making the perfunctory offer. "Please have him call me." I dropped a business card on the coffee table covered by a crocheted doily, beside a glass jar sat holding wild winter flowers. "It would be in his best interest."

As I walked out the door, Patricia Neumann spoke, her tone still soft. "Mr. Paris, do you believe in karma?"

I looked back, focused on the woman.

"Because I do," she added. "Bobby Rae has done wrong and has been punished for his years of misfortune."

Misfortune?

"Now that he's doing well, it wouldn't be right to accuse him of a crime he did not commit. If someone falsely accuses another, they will be faced with their own karma."

"I'm not accusing Bobby Rae of anything," I said. "I'm trying to stop someone else from getting hurt. Your son may have the answers I seek."

A moment of brittle silence followed, Patricia Neumann pensive, as if wanting to say more. I looked at her hands. They were trembling. I sat quietly, giving her an opportunity to respond.

She didn't look up at me, just started talking into her lap. "Raising Bobby Rae wasn't easy. From my first marriage. A mistake. He was a child born with the devil in his soul, but over time he got him out. I can't say there aren't remnants." Her head lolled to one side, pupils starting to spread and darken.

"Has he ever been violent?"

"There were times," she confessed.

I pushed. "Hurt anyone?"

She didn't answer but I saw tears flooding her eyes and she turned away. She didn't want me to see the secret, a wound that never healed.

"I'm sorry for the things you've gone through, Mrs. Neumann. "But whatever Bobby Rae knows or has done is all his doing. Neither you nor I can change that. But he's got the chance to do something good here. He can do the right thing."

"Be careful of the direction you take, Mr. Paris. You may be crossing a path against those more powerful than you." Her stare locked on her Bible, her frail hand continuing to pat the cover. I could swear her cloudy eyes turned clear. "He's my son. I love him." She fell silent, peered up at me. "I can't stop him from what he does but I won't help you either. All I can say is you best be careful."

CHAPTER 13

Thursday February 20th – 12:30 p.m.

A SMALL WOODEN BLOCK HELD AMANDA JENKINS' HEAD.
It was propped up slightly above the stainless-steel table on which she lay. The teenaged girl had been waiting her turn in the morgue for a day now. There were others: an intoxicated adult male that drowned, an elderly woman who suffered a massive heart attack, a transient found behind a dumpster. The Jenkins case was different. This was a homicide, which pushed her to the front of the line.

The pathologist estimated it would take an hour and a half to perform the examination to determine when, why, and how a seventeen-year old girl was murdered. And, perhaps, the examination would reveal by whom.

Amanda had already been undressed by a deputy coroner, her clothing carefully placed in porous bags, next to the table. Typically the body is washed before processing but in this case, that would have been a mistake. If not for the dirt and dried blood covering most of her face and body, Amanda would have been mistaken for a mannequin, a plastic frame of a human without a soul. Her hair was matted, invaded by broken twigs and leaves; cuts covered her small body. It appeared she'd been abused during her capture, frantic in her attempt to escape. No one but Amanda and her abductor really knew.

Yesterday evening, she was brought to the county building in French Camp, California, in the back of the coroner's station wagon. The coroner for Mariposa was usually Stanislaus County; however, today he was unavailable. I was adamant the examination take place immediately. Bellows agreed. Waiting for answers was not an option. I woke every examiner in the surrounding counties until we found one willing to perform the autopsy. San Joaquin County stepped up.

This morning, we watched as the pathologist prepared Amanda Jenkins' body to be poked, prodded, and dissected. In an area clear of roller tables and equipment, Bellows and I stood against the back wall, waiting for the pathologist to give permission to move forward. Like our examiner, we were dressed in morgue green and latex gloves. The face-mask was optional. I took it. I never got used to the scent, the smell of life now gone, the shell of the human body breaking down to its most simplistic molecular structure, disintegrating from solid to liquid to dust. Something your senses would never forget.

"Let's get started," began the pathologist, squeezing the red button on his handheld recorder as he scanned Amanda's small frame. "Today's date is February 20th, at 10:52 a.m. We are examining a white, female adolescent, age seventeen, approximately forty-eight kilograms in weight, five feet, three inches in height . . ."

As he continued his taped reporting, the pathologist began at her head, reciting his visual examination. "Large contusion to her left parietal lobe, approximately three inches from the midline, likely caused by a large blunt force trauma." He stopped, contemplated a second before poking at the wound with a stainless-steel forceps. "In the frontal scalp, just left to the midline, there are two ragged lacerations paralleling each other separated by approximately five inches from the midline. One is five inches in length . . ."

His eyes sharpened focusing on a particular point.

"Look at this," the pathologist said as he prodded deeper into the gaping head wound. "There appears to be some type of commercial grease embedded at the point of impact. I can only assume it may have been transferred from the instrument used."

I peered over his shoulder and took a closer look. "Automotive grease?"

"My guess is packing grease," he suggested. "Used in vehicles, like ball joints and suspensions." He stopped his exam and gave me a hard look. "What was the name of your first victim?"

"Rene Walker," I said.

"Walker," he replied, pointing the forceps in my direction. "There was grease on Walker's knees, correct?"

I nodded.

"At first I thought it was dirt and grime from being exposed to the elements but now I'm thinking I was wrong."

Commonalities. We may have discovered one that helps with location.

"Maybe from a metal or mechanic's shop," I suggested.

The photographer leaned over Amanda, positioning a small ruler next to the wound and began snapping pictures to document the pathologist's finding.

"This is truck country," Bellows said. "There's a logging truck every hundred feet and a grease shop on every corner."

"Based on the width of the trauma across the right side of her head, it appears the mechanism of injury was caused by an object approximately two inches in diameter." The pathologist drew an imaginary line along the side of her head with his gloved pinky. "The trauma is just above the zygomatic arch, which is still intact. The force of the strike most likely caused her death. I'm guessing something like a steel pipe or rod."

The pathologist crouched even with Amanda's body, eyeing her from head to shoulder. "Look at the direction the blood dried." It had coagulated on her face in a downward angle, across her cheek, the same angle she was found, indicating she bled where she lay. "She was killed at the scene or close by."

Using tweezers, the examiner located and removed blowfly larvae from around the wound, carefully placing them in sterile glass containers. Rearing the blowflies allowed the forensic examiner to identify the stage of development, potentially calculating an approximate time of death.

"Located within the contusion, I find a colonization of fly larvae, indicating . . . possibly under a week of development." The pathologist clicked off his recorder. "Did anyone take samples and place them in ethanol at the scene?"

"Samples were taken by our crime scene investigators, Doc," Bellows quickly replied. "They're housed at our office."

The pathologist waved his hand without looking at either of us. "More for the bug man than for me."

He continued to remove larvae from Amanda's ears and mouth, dropping them into vials laid out on the corner of the steel table. Temperature can be a key factor in determining the time of exposure of arthropods to the deceased. Blowflies are more active around carrion at a lower temperature threshold than most arthropods; however they still require several hours of sunny weather with temperatures above fifty-five degrees. In this case, the window of time was somewhat limited even though she was found in the clearing and exposed to a portion of early day's sunlight. In this cold, a body could remain in status for weeks without much change.

"We also took soil samples under her," Bellows added. "There didn't appear to be any beetle activity or other insects. My guess's she hadn't been dead for very long."

"I'll have to agree," the pathologist said.

Her torso was scratched but there were no signs of bruising to indicate beatings, not to say she wasn't abused in other ways. She was thin and pale. Her hands, however, provided additional information about her captivity.

"Both hands indicate skin loss through the epidermal layer at the distal phalange." The pathologist cleared his throat. "Nearly worn down to bone, fingernails broken or gone. The wounds look like they had occurred over time," he hypothesized.

"She was probably clawing at whatever she was being held in until her fingers bled."

"Large deposits of dirt—maybe more grease—under the nails intact. We'll get a sample of that in a moment."

The pathologist continued down to her pubic region, examining for signs of assault. He spoke with little emotion, clinical in his pronouncement of the examination. "Vaginal and anal tearing," he commented as he rolled Amanda to her side. "There are apparent signs of sexual activity."

I took a deep breath and tried to focus. I felt the tension rising up through my throat.

He looked closely for bruising around the inside of her legs, indicate rape. Dark blotches marked the inside on both sides.

"He did a number on her," the pathologist said, monotone. He put down his scalpel and stood back, away from the examination table. His eyes slowly rolled up and down the body as he blew out a deep, exasperated breath.

I looked at Amanda and felt the weight and responsibility of what she had just become. She was no longer a young girl. She was a piece of evidence.

The pathologist peered up. "Where was the note found?"

I moved close, pointed in the area around her chest. "About here, just like the others. The note was stuffed under her shirt. I imagine the killer didn't want the note to blow away."

"What a conscientious prick," Bellows added.

"Same type of paper," I said, "same exact words. *Catch Me*. Whoever this guy is, he's not just killing. He's taunting."

The pathologist swabbed the area for residue samples, hoping the killer may have inadvertently left behind his DNA. After completing the task, he moved back to her pubic region to swab for seminal fluid. As he began his procedure, the pathologist looked closely as the overhead light reflected off Amanda's body and onto his thick-framed glasses. His eyes focused on an item of interest. He raised an eyebrow. "What do I have here? Looks like a dark brown hair, coarse. Definitely not hers . . ." He retrieved the hair. The follicle was still attached, a good chance to collect mitochondrial DNA. He placed it in a clear plastic bag for further analysis.

Now came the horrific reality of the examination.

Taking a sharp scalpel, the pathologist placed the blade along the left shoulder and began his incision, cutting a "Y" pattern from each shoulders to her abdomen. Her body opened. The smell hit me hard.

"On opening the body cavity," he dictated into his recorder, "a great gust of foul gas escaped. There is no evidence of significant trauma in the chest or abdomen, ribcage appears intact." The pathologist reached over to a steel tray and retrieved what looked like shears to trim tree branches. He opened the sharp blades and took a large swipe down the mediastinum, snapping through bone and muscle with ease. I winced as if I could feel the tool shearing her body. She was being victimized, twice. I knew it was necessary but still found myself revolted by the process. The pathologist reached inside, removed her heart, lungs, liver and kidneys, sliding them onto a scale hanging overhead.

"Her heart weighs two hundred seventy grams. The coronary vessels are widely patent. The myocardium is a homogeneous dark red brown except for some autolysis, unusual for someone her age. Her chambers are dilated."

Using a large steel ladle, the pathologist scooped out blood from the peritoneal cavity as if taking soup from a tureen. The contents in her stomach were removed and bagged to determine the time between when she last ate and when the digestive process ended. In other words: when she was killed.

I closed my eyes, squeezed them tight as if to keep it all at bay. I couldn't help but allow my thoughts to wander. Wander away from Amanda Jenkins. I thought of my daughter, Justine. I started to feel light-headed, nauseous, wanting nothing more than to leave, call Justine to reassure me she was safe. But I knew I couldn't.

Then it got worse. Without a pause, emotionless, the pathologist took a clean scalpel and carefully cut a fine line around the edge of her hair before pulling back the skin, exposing the skull. He then retrieved the bone-saw. It squealed as it touched the skull, the smell of burnt bone hung heavy in the room. Her brain was removed, and weighed.

We stood and bared witness to the examination in complete silence as the pathologist dismembered this young teenaged girl, someone who shortly ago was laughing with her friends, never considering life could be so cruel.

It was from years of practice, one-by-one, the pathologist swiftly numbered and bagged each body part until there were none.

It was more than anyone could endure. More than I could. I held back the feeling of beating on something, anything. Anyone.

The pathologist pulled down his mask. Sweat had beaded around his upper lip. He looked over at us, for the first time, speaking with some emotion in his voice, almost pleading, "You need to catch this monster."

THE AUTOPSY ENDED AND WHAT REMAINED of Amanda Jenkins was rolled back in that cold, steel vault. Cold for more than the obvious reasons. Life had departed and the chill was a void between the two worlds. A hollow universe where time stood still, an endless nothing. Those living in this space could feel the borders between that room and what's on the other side. A place only God knows. And he wasn't talking. And so, I was told to be a witness, no exception.

She would eventually be returned to her family for a formal burial. Bellows had to take a few calls, and stepped outside. I went into the locker room, making up an excuse to wash my hands, but I really wanted to splash cold water on my face and rinse away the feeling of evil and hate. I walked in while massaging the tension in my head that ran from ear to ear, for who knows how long, before grabbing a towel and sitting down on a nearby bench. The locker room was empty, quiet. The smell of Amanda's body still clung to me. I took in a deep breath and looked at the cold floor. I allowed my eyes to slowly shut, the blackness to clear all thoughts of disgust and anger. Then I felt a hand gently touch my shoulder.

Emily.

I opened my eyes and there she was.

Her face was warm, her smile comforting.

"How are you doing?" she asked.

Funny, she would always start off every conversation that way. *How am I?* She would say it like I was so much more important than whatever she had done. I never realized it when she was alive, never giving her credit for putting me first, no matter how bad of a day she had.

I couldn't help but smile at her loving face, her sweet gentle hand, her soft voice. "I'm fine," I lied.

She sat down on the bench next to me and I could sense her warmth, her skin next to mine. I could smell her hair, feel the smoothness of her dress. I wanted to close my eyes again, relax in her presence, but was afraid if I did, she would be gone the second I opened them. Her arm went around my shoulder and her head rested against my neck. It brought back memories of those days when Emily made everything better.

"The girl," she said, her voice calm and soft. "She's telling you something."

"I can't see it."

"That's because you're not ready. But you will. Give yourself time, look at it through *her* eyes." Then she added, tenderly, "This is what you do, Jack. Don't let her down."

As much as I knew she was the logical one, Emily was always a puzzle. Spoke in riddles. But once I figured it out, she was always right. I needed to experience the gruesomeness of this murder. The place, the location, the timing. The evidence. As if I'd been there with her.

I nodded, understood.

"You'll make it through this," she reassured.

"How can you be so sure?"

Emily lifted her head from my shoulder, placed her hands on each side of my face and made me look into her deep green eyes. "Because you're one of the good guys, Jack."

CHAPTER 14

Thursday February 20th – 3:10 p.m.

T HE HUM FROM THE TIRES WAS ALL I COULD HEAR.
Other than that, the drive back to Mariposa was quiet. It's never easy dealing with a murder, let alone one involving someone so young. With every other breath, I would catch the distinctive stench of the autopsy as if death had hitched a ride out from the examination room and would forever be part of me.

The items collected at the exam were important but small, curious, and Emily's words, confident that I would find the answers, played like a stuck record in my head. The one thing I was sure of: this was no way for anyone to die—an unnatural act by anyone's standards—her worn fingers, the condition of her clothes, filthy. And her body, was thin, and weak, and starved. She wasn't wearing shoes when they found her. Amanda Jenkins wasn't just killed; she was kept. Neglected and abused. I couldn't stop from envisioning a monster, hunting, keeping his prey before finally growing tired of his catch. And then, snuffing out her life. For sport. With everything that was going on in my life, watching the examination proved particularly difficult. I saw more than a dead girl. I saw a dead daughter. It became painfully apparent that no one, including me, could protect our children every minute of the day and that left me feeling weak and vulnerable. That could have easily been me crying in the waiting room, spoken to by a detective, detailing how a killer took the life of my child. I stopped myself from sinking deeper into self-doubt. I took in air and forced myself to concentrate. Working through the evidence was the only way to catch this killer, and if I was fortunate enough, find the Samuels. There was valuable evidence gathered at the autopsy. Grease and metal shaving similar to what would be found in an auto shop. A foreign hair. DNA from the swabbing. With a genetic code, I could run the samples through the two-ninety sex registrant database for a possible match or through CODIS, a nationwide databank of DNA from all types of offenders throughout the country. I just needed time.

The police radio chirped. Dispatch was reaching out, wanted Bellows to head back to station ASAP. The dispatcher's voice was high pitched. Something was wrong. A drive back that should have taken an hour took us thirty minutes. The Tahoe came to an abrupt stop in the station parking lot. Bellows didn't wait for me to exit the SUV. The dispatcher was already accosting him before I could catch up, passing along a single sheet of paper, a complaint form prepared with the information from the call no more than thirty minutes prior.

"Donald Jennings reported his sixteen-year-old daughter, Kathryn Jennings, missing." The dispatcher dipped her glasses low on her nose to see Bellows clearly. "Said he heard about a killer on TV, put two-and-two together . . ."

I moved closer to Bellows to get a better look.

"He's a mess," the dispatcher added.

Bellows scanned the report. "How long has she been missing?"

She pointed halfway down the form. "Almost two weeks."

I tapped Bellows on the shoulders. "Let's go."

THE LACK OF A FULL MOON RENDERED THE EVENING PITCH BLACK, the road to the Jennings residence curved and blending into the edge of thick foliage of scrub brush and tall weeds, no light to guide our way. Frozen pools of ice mined every crevice and pothole. Where there wasn't ice, there was slush. Bellows didn't seem concerned, foot planted heavy on the accelerator as the SUV skidded through one blind curve after another. I traced a finger along a dog-eared map page in his *Thomas Guide,* showing me the way to the Jennings' residence. GPS was useless up here where trees and mountain ranges blanket your ability to use modern advances. We came to a hidden turn. There was a wooden sign off the main highway that was posted on a stick, words in white paint hand written that read, *Jennings.*

Bellows turned up the dirt path dodging a few tree stumps and rows of over-grown bushes that were shrouded in snow, eventually coming to a clearing where we spotted a modest-sized house with a small wooden porch. A detached barn was situated to the right where a car, on jacks and beyond saving, had been laid to rest, rusting over years of neglect. The barn door was open, revealing well-used, rusted tools, car parts, and an old red and white tractor.

We pulled up to the residence. A soft light glowed in the front window. Someone was still awake.

"Dispatch," Bellows spoke into the mic. "Myself and FBI Agent Paris are 10-8 at the Jennings residence, 10576, Highway 87A."

The radio crackled back. "10-4, Hal. Advise when you're clear."

Stepping out of the car, we approached the house. A dog barked behind the closed screen door, deep and loud. The dog appeared. Large was an understatement. His nose pressed against the thin nylon mesh, no match for the two-hundred pound Neapolitan Mastiff. Were if not for the animal's discipline, the screen door never would've held. Cautiously we approached, hoping whoever was inside would see us and know we were the good guys.

"Mr. Jennings," Bellows called out as he rapped on the side of the doorframe with one hand, the other wrapped around the webbing of his gun. "Mariposa County Sheriff."

We stood at the front door, waiting for someone to corral the barking Mastiff. Donald Jennings finally appeared, backlit from the living room lighting. He looked older than his listed age of thirty-eight—a missing child will do that to you—sporting a hefty belly. A tattoo crept out from under the sleeve of his t-shirt, a Navy insignia blurred and weathered. His hair was thin, and what was there was slicked back. Jennings was definitely a smoker, the smell of tobacco becoming stronger the closer he came.

"We're here to talk to you about your missing daughter, Kathryn," Bellows said.

Jennings grabbed the dog by the collar and gave it a tug as he pushed open the screen door. The dog reluctantly complied.

"Back down, Peaches. They're okay." Peaches sniffed the air while drooling on his owner's hand. "She's okay. Got a lot of bark—"

"I know" Bellows interjected. "But no bite."

Jennings returned a muddled look. "No, detective, she bites." He yanked again on the collar and Peaches scooted backwards, following her master. We entered. Peaches lowered her large square head and stared at Bellows as if he were lunch.

I introduced myself, displayed my credentials. "The dispatcher taking the report says you think your daughter may have been abducted?"

Jennings nervously squeezed his free hand into a tight fist, then pointed at the television with his chin. "Heard there's a serial killer on the loose."

I had to ask the obvious question: "Could she have run away?"

Jennings looked down at his shoes and nodded. "She has before but never this long. I can feel it. Something's wrong."

"Does she have a cellphone? Have you called her?"

"Goes straight to voicemail."

We planned on tracking the phone, standard procedure, but doubted it would matter. The call going straight to voicemail told me the battery was dead or the phone was off. Either way, that would make it untraceable.

Jennings dropped low into his couch, finding an empty beer bottle on his coffee table to focus his attention on. "He's killing kids, ain't he?"

"Let's not go there yet," I said.

"But it's true." Jennings face was fraught with concern.

"We're going to do everything we can to find her," I said.

"We got into a fight that night," he said, as if confessing a sin only I could absolve. "But I know my daughter. She didn't run away."

"Can I see her room?" I asked.

Jennings led us to Kate's bedroom. Peaches followed lazily behind.

Stuffed animals neatly positioned on her bed and posters of teenage heartthrobs filled the walls. A small table and mirror combination was lined with nail polish and makeup containers. A half-empty Pepsi bottle sat off to the corner, forgotten. At first glance, nothing appeared out of place. No sign of someone packing to leave, the removal of things that were most important. Her backpack was still in the closet. The room typified the life of an average teenager. But Kate was no longer the average teenager. She was gone.

"Anything missing?" Bellows asked.

"Nothing I can see," Jennings said.

I wanted to be considerate, careful not to upset him, but there were questions, as an agent, I had to ask. "What took you so long to report her missing?"

Tears welled up in Jennings' eyes. "I wasn't thinking clearly when she didn't come home. I was mad . . . tired and mad about all the crap she had put me through." I saw him mouth the word "had" one more time as if subconsciously admitting the worse. He closed his eyes and held them shut for a long time. "I made a mistake."

I placed a hand on his shoulder. "Look," I said, "I'm sure you did everything you could have. What about friends? Have you contacted them?"

His response was straightforward. "All of them. Haven't heard from her in weeks."

Bellows stepped forward, spread his hands wide across the room. "Can you think of anything Kate's would never leave behind?"

Jennings opened his eyes and scanned the room. He started rubbing his hands over the furniture, eyes dull, stare far away and sullen. "She always wore this gold bracelet with a big red heart on it. Her mother gave that to her for her 13th birthday. It's not here. She must've taken it."

"That's helpful," Bellows reassured.

Jennings looked up from staring at Kate's dresser drawers, with an expression of disbelief. "She's sixteen years old, Mr. Paris. What makes a girl want to leave home at sixteen? Unless . . ." His voice trailed off.

What could I say?

Jennings shook his head while continuing to run his hand over his daughter's possessions, everything she valued.

"I'll need her toothbrush and her hairbrush," I said. "And if you could get me a current picture of her, it would be helpful."

The picture was for the B.O.L.O., in the event a patrol officer found her wandering the streets. The toothbrush and hairbrush was for DNA in case we found hair or blood in a suspect's house or car.

"I'm going to want a list of names of her friends, anyone that she may have had problems with, past boyfriends, places she likes to frequent." I took one last look around the room. "I didn't see a journal or diary. Does she have her own computer?"

Jennings shook his head. "Don't know of a diary. We share the computer in the living room but I know she hasn't touched it in months." He waited for a moment, watching us finish our search. Bellows shoved his notepad inside his jacket and started to follow Jennings out the door to pack up the computer. Jennings stopped and turned around before disappearing down the hall. "I'll go and get the stuff you asked for."

Fifteen minutes later, we were done. Jennings was sitting on the couch with a small plastic bag on his lap. Peaches lay at his feet. The bag contained a hairbrush, a toothbrush, and a few photos. He stood and anxiously handed it me. "List of her friends and their phone numbers are on a piece of paper inside. At least the ones I know."

"We're going to do everything we can to find your daughter, Mr. Jennings." I took the bag and thanked him before Bellows and I walked out of the house. Jennings, followed close behind, stopping and standing silently on the porch. He looked as if waiting for us to give him answers, words that would make things right.

I had nothing.

CHAPTER 15

Thursday February 20th - 9:30 p.m.
Captain's Lounge, Sonora, California

Bobby Rae Olsen

A T A CORNER TABLE, BOBBY RAE SAT SLOUCHED over a whiskey while the jukebox screamed in the background. He came to the Captain's Lounge alone, pissed off that his only asset in life, his pale blue Chevy Impala, was in the possession of the Mariposa County Sheriff's and the FBI.

The fucking FBI!

Bobby Rae had returned from Modesto where he was visiting an old girlfriend. Meeting her earlier in the week, she made promises she broke and that put him in a bad mood.

From the crowded bar, Bobby Rae caught sight of a friend pushing through a wall of bodies.

His guest.

Five minutes earlier, the two connected, mostly to talk about things. Things Bobby Rae needed to know. The friend found his way to the table and placed a shot of whiskey before Bobby Rae, a conciliatory gesture. Sliding the glass forward, the friend pulled back a chair and sat directly across from the somber man. Cloaked under dim lights and the haze of cigarette smoke, the figure sat quietly, akin to a priest to a parishioner.

The friend finally spoke.

"You know the FBI's looking for you, Bobby," his guest said.

"Fuck the FBI." Bobby Rae lifted the shot glass and drained its contents before setting it back onto the table.

"Do you know why they're looking for you?"

Bobby Rae sat still a moment, eyeing the empty glass. His guest signaled a passing waitress for another round.

"Bobby," the dark figure said in a low, private voice. "They're looking at you for those missing tourists from the Lodge. The place you work at."

Bobby Rae leaned back in his chair staring deep into the packed bar. The crowd grew thicker, louder.

"They think you had something to do with their disappearance." There was a brief pause. "Well . . . did you?"

He pushed forward, leaned across the table and pressed close to his company's ear. Through the hazy effect of all the golden liquor that filled his body, his demeanor became sharp, focused, like an animal on the hunt. He whispered, "You don't want to know."

His guest nodded over an empty glass.

"Everyone's got needs."

Silence.

"I hear one of the missing was a mother."

A shrug.

"Not for nothing Bobby Rae, but I thought you stuck to young girls."

No answer.

"What did you do with them?"

"You're asking too many questions."

His friend threw up his hands and leaned back in his chair.

A grumble fell past Bobby Rae's lips as he tipped his chair, rocking on two legs, demanding another whiskey.

The crowd started to spill out the back door where their table was situated. Droves of glassy-eyed drunks stumbled past, bumping into their armrests.

His friend squeezed Bobby Rae on the shoulder, said, "Now Bobby, careful what you say here. There are a lot of ears in this place and they're not all friendly."

Bobby Rae stood, thanked the man for the drinks and disappeared out the back door.

CHAPTER 16

Friday, February 21ˢᵗ – 8:14 a.m.

THE NEXT MORNING, I MET GEONETTA in front of the Mariposa County Sheriff's station. She pulled up in her government ride, a black Grand Prix. She stepped out of her car, dragged out a black sport coat and slipped it on to conceal her sidearm, a Model 23 Glock pistol. In a community of jeans and plaid cotton shirts, she looked out of place.

We were escorted to the command post where a large group had started to congregate. A dozen or so deputies stood over a large map, watching one of the search team leaders draw more red lines, depicting their advances over the expansive wooded area on the east side of Highway 120, around Tuolumne Grove and Crane Flat. Bellows towered over the deputies, studying every line drawn. We made our way over to his side as the group went quiet, preparing for the hourly update.

A man dressed in cold weather gear with a patch that read, *Mariposa County – SAR* pushed his way over. His boots were caked in mud; the hood on his jacket dripped melted snow. He circled a hand over the table, pointing at specific places along the mountain range, leading east. "At this time, we have searched everything west of the 120, traversing across the roads up and down each side." He flattened both his palms in the middle of the map. "If their car leapt over the railing and down a ravine, we'd have found it. We've canvassed every inch down to the valley. Our next step is to head toward Tuolumne Grove, continuing east. There are some steep embankments where they could have driven off the edge without anyone noticing."

Bellows asked, "What about the dam?"

The dam.

2.4 million acre feet of water held behind a 625 foot earthen wall.

"We are in the process of draining it down where we can almost see bottom. That's a lot of water and it's going to take additional approvals from the State Water Resources Department, Fish and Wildlife . . . the feds."

Bellows scratched his head with his pencil, mumbling how everything was a process. It was obvious he wanted it to be done so he could move to the next step.

"Just get it drained."

The rescue leader nodded, understanding there could be no excuses. I knew this task was more complicated than Bellows' simple demand but chose to leave it alone.

Not wanting to disrupt the meeting, Geonetta and I slipped away, walked over to a deputy manning the two-way radio. We displayed our credentials and he escorted us down a hallway to Bellows' office, the last room on the left. I had spent a lot of time there, poring over the new case files as well as the old ones. Geonetta needed to catch up and made her way over to the largest stack of reports. Bellows' desk was covered in folders, another table available on the opposite side of the room. That table was covered in more files, mostly older cases or those deemed non-priority.

"The cavalry has arrived," Geonetta called out to an empty room. She threw her briefcase onto the open but cluttered desk and began sifting through papers.

"Think any of these old cases may be relevant to your new case?"

"Which one," I asked, "Our murders or our missing tourists?"

Geonetta paused. "Either? Both?"

I shrugged.

Having a second set of eyes might prove a good thing.

She slapped her hands together, briskly rubbing them. "Okay, lawman, what do you want me to do?"

I took Bellows' seat, dug into my briefcase, extracting a binder containing Bellows' investigative notes. I opened it onto the desk and the weight of the pages fanned like bird wings.

"Start reading these. They're the reports on three teenage homicides. See if there are any similarities with your tourist case, maybe something from Hal's unaddressed work files. Find something we may have missed."

"You think there could be more?"

"Go through all the files, past and present," I said. "Tell me what you think."

Geonetta leaned back in her chair, her winter coat draped across her lap. Chilled from the cold room, she blew onto her hands before starting to filter through each report.

"How can a place so beautiful portray such an ugly picture?" she said.

I didn't have an answer. I twisted around in my chair, facing a peg-board covered with Bellows' pictorial of murderers, parolees, and molesters, lost in his morbid mural. The room went quiet, the only sound coming was from the creaking of Geonetta's chair as she rocked back and forth, now sifting through the unaddressed files.

After about an hour, she got up and went to the window, staring at the snowy mountain range. "There's a lot of land out there to be lost in."

She caught me staring out of the office window as well.

"I doubt there's enough time to search it all," I said.

It was obvious; I couldn't hide the disappointing tone in my voice.

CHAPTER 17

Kate Jennings

THE STEADY FLOW OF WATER CONTINUED to drip onto the dirt floor, echoing in the large wooden structure. The howling wind could be heard piercing through the crevices of the outside walls, shaking the building enough to bring chills to Kate Jennings' frail body. Blindfolded, her hands were tied behind her back. The rag used to cover her eyes smelled of diesel fuel and grease. If she twisted her head just so, she could glimpse a dim light under her left eye. But she was afraid to try and remove the blindfold completely for fear her captor would discover her transgression and punish her like he had done in the past. What difference did it make? Without her glasses, her eyesight was poor.

Kate had no idea where she was or what her prison looked like. She could only imagine by feel. She'd been brought here by her abductor, hogtied and blindfolded. The cold air smelled musty, sodden, like wet dirt.

Not more than a week prior, Kate was at home, making plans to sneak out of the house and rendezvous with a man she'd met on the Internet. He was fascinating, according to his bio. Funny and charismatic. Kate hoped she was meeting a young, educated guy with a great body and lots of money. Optimistic, but ready to accept disappointment. If nothing else, she'd get drunk, have fun. At sixteen, there's always time to try again.

This night was no different. Kate arranged to meet her date in town around 11:00 p.m., near the Dragon Tattoo. As in the past, she made sure her father wouldn't find out. She erased her conversations from the computer, as if it never happened.

He told her to wear a short skirt and the red cotton top, the one that she bragged so much about when they exchanged quips online. Kate was exceptional at describing herself. She was a beautiful girl looking much older than her age. From her description, there was no way this guy was going to mistake her for *just another girl.*

She told her dad she was spending the night with a friend in town. That morning, Kate left for school with the intention of heading to the Dragon afterward. Not to get any of her friends in trouble, she told no one of her plans. She flirted with danger, but life was too short to always play it safe.

But things didn't work out that evening. The hours had past and Kate was left standing alone. Stood up. The crowd had cleared and Kate could not believe the man she had just spoken to the night before would leave her high and dry.

He doesn't know what he's missing.

In the world of cybersex, this was his loss.

Not to waste the evening, she headed to the Captain's Lounge, a place she had frequented in the past. Familiar surroundings.

The street to the lounge was icy, making it difficult to maneuver in four-inch heels. She made her way down the sidewalk, two blocks from the lounge. Crossing the street, she sauntered past a darkened stretch between two buildings, an antique shop and a plumbing supply company.

As Kate stepped off the walkway, she felt a hand reach through the darkness and in a split second, grabbed her by the throat, pulling her back into the alley between the two buildings. Kate had no time to scream. The strong grip clamped down hard around her neck, preventing her from breathing. Before realizing what had happened, she felt the sting of a gloved fist slam into her face. Warm blood conflicted with the cold air. It flowed from her nose and down her chin. The twinkling light from a sidewalk lamppost began to spin. Then a second punch. The lights dimmed as she felt herself slip into unconsciousness, confused why this was happening to her.

The rope securing her hands cut into her wrists, causing pain to radiate up her arm with every move she made. Kate was too tired to cry anymore. She sat folded on her knees in wet straw that covered the caged floor. Kate slouched against the chain-linked wall, shivering. She could feel the cold, icy steel on her neck as she rested her head between the rows of metal bars and wire mesh. From the dark, a door creaked. Shuffling feet approached, a sound she'd come to recognize. Kate's heart beat rapidly in her chest, gaining speed, as her captor grew closer. Anxiety gripping, she struggled to breath.

Then, there was silence.

No more steps, no sound other than the familiar dripping water from the wet snow falling outside the building.

"Are you there?" Kate wanted to know. "Can I go now? Please let me go home."

"My dear girl," her captor replied. "I am here to save you. I am the one that has been given the power to travel this earth to save those who have strayed. And those who refuse to repent should suffer the consequences that come with sin."

Kate heard her captor kneel down and place the usual tray of slop on the dirt floor. The utensils clattered on the tray when it found its way to the ground. She moved her face to the bars and opened her mouth. As scared as Kate was, she was hungrier. She felt the spoon gently touch her lips as the soup slipped down her throat. She could taste the metal of the spoon as she took in more. It was at least warm and helped reduce the shivers.

"There you go, eat up. You'll need your strength." She could hear the spoon scrape along the rim of the bowl then back onto her lips. Each time, she could smell his breath. It reeked of alcohol.

She broke down and started to cry. "I want to go home, please. I promise I'll be good."

There was only silence.

Listening intensely, Kate heard the turning of a lock and the cage door swing open. It startled her. A strong hand, the hand that had pummeled her face several days earlier, reached under one of her arms and pulled her forward. Her breath labored. Her body shuttered, her teeth chattered uncontrollably, from the cold and fear.

"In time, Kate. In time. Remember, good girls are saved. Bad girls pay."

He stroked her hair and it made her skin crawl.

She sobbed, knowing her request for freedom was again denied.

CHAPTER 18

Saturday February 22nd - 10:28 a.m.

I HAD BEEN SITTING WITH GEONETTA IN MY VEHICLE, in front of Kelly Olsen's apartment complex for almost an hour, staring at an empty parking slot. She appeared bored, fidgeting in the passenger seat, watching tenants scramble to their apartments and cars, trying to spend as little time in the cold as possible. Every three or four minutes, Geonetta stretched her arms above her head, pressed her hands on the interior roof of the car and yawned. Her yawn made me yawn.

"Stop it," I said. "You're making me tired."

I pulled out the reports Bellows had given me on Kelly Olsen, Bobby Rae's ex-wife. A photo of Kelly was attached, showing her latest driver's license photograph. Below was a custody report for their daughter, Molly Olsen. Molly's photo was one of a young girl with a bright smile, like a school portrait.

"How could she be smiling with a father like Bobby Rae?" I flipped between the photo of Molly and her mother. Geonetta took the report and photo from my hands.

"Nothing out of the ordinary here," she said. "Just your average, run-of-the-mill single parent with a piece of shit for an ex."

I took back the report, filtered through the rest of the package and came across a list of registered vehicles. "Looks like she's got only the Ford registered in her name."

Geonetta glanced up, gave a double take, and pointed out the window. "You mean that Ford?"

Her gaze sharpened on an old Bronco turning up the steep drive-way and weaving into the parking lot of the big apartment complex. The Bronco came to a stop under a covered garage port near the entrance to unit 14, the residence listed on Kelly Olsen's DL. In the world of investi-gations, this was referred to as *a clue.*

"She's home," Geonetta whispered as she stuck her cold cup of coffee out the window and emptied it dry. "You ready?"

I grabbed a notepad, but before the Bronco's engine turned quiet, a young girl fitting the description of Molly Olsen bolted from the passen-ger side door. She skipped over to a teenaged girl who was standing in front of the unit one building down. An adult female driver stepped out and walked to the back lift-gate and began unloading bags of groceries. With her arms full, the woman struggled to balance the bags and a purse as she walked awkwardly toward the front of the building. We exited the car and headed toward the woman I believed to be Kelly Olsen.

Geonetta reached out and gently grabbed the bags in Kelly's arms.

"Please, Mrs. Olsen, let me help you with those."

She was startled by the offer, but, seeing Geonetta wasn't a threat, relinquished the bags and waited for an introduction.

"My name is Heather Geonetta. I'm with the FBI."

She managed to hold up her credentials and then pointed at me. "That is Special Agent Jack Paris. We want to ask you some questions about your husband, Bobby Rae."

Kelly's face tightened, turning a heated color before making toward her front door. She reached into her purse, pulled out a key and shoved it in the lock before scrubbing the snow off her boots. We followed her into the two-bedroom flat.

The floor was lined in blue carpet, revealing a worn path from the entry to the kitchen nook. The apartment was cold, her furnace probably turned low to reduce monthly expenses. A slight whiff of mildew hung in the pent-up air. A nineteen-inch color television was situated in the corner near the cheap, overstuffed floral print couch and matching love seat, second-hand store quality. The curtains were pulled shut leaving the rooms dark and uninviting.

"My last name now is Beckwith," she snapped. "Bobby Rae and I have been divorced for over two years." She tossed the key on the table. "I'm glad he's out of our lives." She brushed back hair that had fallen across her face.

Geonetta placed the two grocery bags on the table, stalling, trying to appear passive, helpful. Given her clear animosity toward Bobby Rae, it seemed unlikely the former Mrs. Olsen would do anything to help or hide him.

"What do you want from me? I haven't seen Bobby Rae in weeks." Kelly leaned back against the kitchen wall. "He was supposed to come by and drop off his child support check. Bastard owes me over three-hundred dollars."

She pulled a chair at the kitchen table and fumbled in her purse for cigarettes, found them crushed at the bottom. Shaking out a smoke, she dug for a lighter. Geonetta retrieved a Zippo from her winter coat. As she lit Kelly's cigarette, I studied the ex-Mrs. Olsen. A lifelong smoker, I presumed, evidenced by the ends of her middle and pointer fingers, yellowed from years of addiction. Crow's feet invaded the corners of her eyes and crease lines appeared around the edges of her mouth. Guaranteed from stress. Kelly's youth had been spirited away, years of a bad marriage leaving her the sole parent of a teenage daughter.

Kelly lowered her head as she drew in the menthol. Exhaling, she looked up at me. "What did he do this time? You know, his mother likes to tell the world her son has *found God*, but I know differently," she said, divulging a secret the world already knew. "He ain't no saint."

Geonetta pulled up a chair and sat in front of Kelly. "Ms. Beckwith, we're sorry for stopping by unannounced. We are looking into those two missing tourists."

That was true.

"And we think Bobby Rae may have information to help us."

That was a lie.

Kelly laughed in disbelief. "Help the FBI? Hell would have to freeze over before you get any help from him."

Kelly stood and walked to the front door, still opened with the screen ajar. Blowing her cigarette smoke through the nylon mesh venting to the outside, Kelly stared across the front walkway where she watched Molly laughing with a teenaged friend.

"You got to understand something: me and Bobby Rae ended when I walked out the door. The less I see of him, the better." Kelly's hands started to tremble. Ashes drifted in the air. I could see the fear in her. Fear of Bobby Rae.

"I'm not asking you to get involved," I said, "I just need to find him so I can talk to him."

Kelly started to say something but paused. Then words tumbled from her lips. "He likes young girls . . . you know, he's always liked them."

She leaned against the glossy white door jam, the cold air forcing its way into her apartment, robbing her of heat, much like Bobby Rae did with her life. She rested her head against the frame, still staring at Molly, knowing the real reason why the FBI had come looking for Bobby Rae. It was his perverted fantasies with young, preadolescent girls. Kelly turned around, stared down, unable to look either one of us in the face. She took a deep drag from her cigarette, finding courage in the nicotine.

"When Molly became a teenager, I started to notice Bobby Rae's growing interest in her friends. He would sometimes openly talk with them about sex and erotic fantasies. Sick fuck." She turned toward me now, looking me square in the eye. Tears started to well. "I was disgusted with his behavior but I was afraid to say anything." Kelly forced a half-hearted chuckle. "To do so would only mean that the problem was real and I didn't want to believe I was married to a degenerate."

"What changed your mind?" Geonetta asked.

She hesitated. "About two years ago, Bobby Rae returned home from a late night at the Captain's Lounge, drunk and stinking of sweat and vomit. It revolted me. Then he wanted sex. I pushed him away, told him to dry out but he wanted none of that."

Kelly swung her fist as if pounding an imaginary nail into a block of wood.

"He started beating me across my head and neck until I bled from both ears. I had been taking his abuse for years before that evening. This brought it to a head."

There was a pause, maybe an unwillingness to acknowledge reality before finding the courage to continue. "He dragged me by the ankles to the bedroom where he tried to rape me. I'm guessing the alcohol prevented him from getting it up, which just pissed him off even more."

Kelly shook her head and blew out angered words. "He said it was my fault." She turned away but not before her tears began to fall in a stream. "He beat me until I went unconscious."

"Did you call the police?"

Kelly tipped her chin down and closed her eyes, like the world didn't understand.

"The following morning, I packed my bags, grabbed up Molly and got the hell out of there."

I leaned against the refrigerator. "At least you're here, safe."

"Life with Bobby Rae was no Norman Rockwell painting. In the end, leaving him was my 'do over.' Didn't need any more abuse, didn't want it."

Kelly's head pitched toward her chest, the ash on the end of her cigarette broke away and orbited around her legs. "Bobby Rae had something to do with those kids that were killed, didn't he?"

I kept quiet.

"The sick bastard always wanted to have his way with young girls and I bet that's what you guys think also."

"Bobby Rae is not the only suspect . . ."

"But he's your best one, isn't he?"

Geonetta tried to remain composed. "Before we go there, I think we should talk to him to see what he has to say. He may have an alibi."

"I don't know anything about the tourists, but I wouldn't doubt he had something to do with those murdered girls."

Kelly drew heavily on what remained of her cigarette, now down to a stub. She walked back over to the table and sat down, her left leg nervously bouncing up and down, like a drug addict needing a fix. "Something else you should know." Kelly clenched her jaw and forced herself to continue. "When Molly was twelve, I caught Bobby Rae in her bedroom, tucking her to sleep. When I looked closer, I could see in Molly's eyes that something was wrong. There were tears. Bobby Rae said she had a stomachache, but somehow I knew something else was wrong. Then her friends wouldn't come over and Molly started to run away from home, staying at her girlfriend's. The first time I confronted Bobby Rae, he exploded. He beat me so bad, I ended up in the hospital. They said I had a busted spleen." There was a look of resignation. "And life never got any better. She sat at the table motionless with a distant stare.

"Have you talked to Molly about what you saw?"

"She said nothing happened, but I know my daughter. He did something to her and she was afraid of him." Kelly had a look of disgust and disbelief. "Afraid of her own father."

"Then help me find him."

Kelly nervously rubbed the back of her neck, biting down on her lower lip. I could see her weighing her options: help or hide. Helping would, at a minimum, get Bobby Rae locked up; he wouldn't be able to hurt anyone again. She relented. It was the better option.

"He's got a couple of friends," she confessed. "Real pieces of shit, but I don't know their names or where they live." She thought for a second as if trying to decide where to begin. "There is one."

Geonetta turned to a clean page and started writing.

"If he's not at his house or soaking off his mother, he could be with a guy named Warren . . . little rodent of a man. Warren has been hanging with Bobby Rae since I can remember. He treats Warren like his kicking post and Warren just takes it. Probably because Bobby Rae is the only person who pays him any attention, good or bad. Shit, he might as well be his wife. Bobby Rae certainly didn't treat me any differently."

"Do you have his full name and where I can find him?"

"Warren Kramer. He lives in a trailer park off Highway 120 and Ferretti Road near Groveland. They all live up in these secluded areas to get away from everyone. They don't want to be bothered. He's probably the only person Bobby Rae knows that hasn't ever been arrested."

Her cigarette burned low enough for the ash to reach her fingers. She was too distracted to notice.

"Bobby Rae isn't the person you think he is," she said unsolicited. "People think he's just a stupid overbearing drunk. But he's more." Kelly's hand quivered, the soot from her smoke now marking the legs of her pants.

"He's dangerous," she said. "I've seen it in his eyes. I've seen him change into another person . . . a Jekyll and Hyde. He's hiding secrets that I don't even know. And it scares the hell out of me. All I can say is you better be careful."

The same words used by Bobby Rae's mother.

CHAPTER 19

Saturday, February 22nd – 1:15 p.m.

I STRAINED TO HEAR HOSKIN ON THE OTHER END. He was at the command post and there was a shift change. Cell service was lousy as usual. When there was a connection, the commotion from the returning search teams, ringing phones, and barking dogs was deafening.

"Tell me something." I was heading back with Geonetta to the station.

Hoskin cupped a hand over the mouthpiece to block out the background noise; it made him sound like he was talking into a sock. "No luck at Olsen's home in Tuolumne. Doesn't look like he's been there for a while. Malloy's keeping two deputies on the residence in case he shows. Hal is applying for a search warrant as we speak." I could hear Hoskin checking his notes. "I contacted the maintenance staff at the Junior High. Several janitors confirmed Olsen volunteered there, but hadn't seen him in over a month. Said he liked flirting with the young girls but was pretty nondescript."

"What about the car?"

"We were able to lift a number of prints belonging to Olsen and several unknowns. The ones so far don't match your vics but we're still working through the lifts. There's some possible DNA on the handcuffs. I've sent that back to the lab for analysis."

The DNA would have to be matched against known samples. That meant pulling the forensic analysis reports of our victims, hairbrushes and toothbrushes for the Samuels.

"We also found notes and receipts. An agent is combing through them. We're in the process of building a timeline."

"And the ground search?"

"We drained the dam down five feet. Lot of debris and garbage but no car. Dogs are still out searching, but it's slow. Our next initiative are the old mines."

I heard Hoskin clear his throat.

"There's literally thousands."

I let the phone drop to my side with Hoskin still talking in the background.

"You there, Jack?"

"Yeah," I replied, placing the phone back to my ear. "We don't have that kind of time."

"I wish I had a better answer," Hoskin said.

After the call, I updated Geonetta and drove directly to the command post. I wanted to get started on my search for Warren Kramer. Fifteen minutes later, I pulled into the parking lot that was now filled with large vans and Uplink trucks, satellite dishes high on telescopic poles. News crews were starting to set up camp, preparing to cover any major development on either the murders or the missing tourists, whichever broke first. It was national news. I dodged the news camera, shot through the lot, and parked on a side street. I tilted my head low and walked toward a back door, Geonetta following close. Hoskin came outside and herded us in before the crowd saw us. Rain started to fall.

Hoskin glared at the media. "It's getting cold outside. Give it time and they'll be running for shelter like rats in a rainstorm."

There was a CLETs terminal in Bellows' office. I pulled up a chair in front of the keyboard and started typing. CLETS stood for California Law Enforcement Telecommunication System and it allowed me access to driver's licenses, car registrations, wants, warrants, and criminal histories of people of interest. It was my start in finding Warren Kramer.

The walls in the small office space were now sectioned by cases: exhibiting evidence from the homicides on one wall and the missing tourists on the other. A large topographical map hung in between. As it related to our missing tourists: red hatch-marks continued to advance across the map, denoting areas searched and cleared. A line of yellow yarn, pinned to various points, signified witness sightings of the two tourists. Blue yarn nearly parallel to the yellow represented telephone charges and cell phone traces, supplying a timeline from when they arrived in Mariposa until they disappeared. Numbered green dots showed chronologically where money was spent, either cash or credit cards for food, trinkets,

gas and entertainment. Pictures of the Samuels were also posted, showing the last-known photos taken. For our murdered victims: red dots
marked where they were found, yellow where they were last seen. Cell
tower triangulation also tagged from calls made, if any, the day of their
disappearances. This was where we looked for commonalities. With our
murdered victims, our information was limited but growing.

"I spoke with the husband, Harold Samuels," Geonetta said, "while
you were out with Hal."

She opened her notebook. "He's staying in a hotel in Sonora. We
showed him these two photos from the hotel room his wife and daughter
were in." She pointed at the last two photos posted on the wall.

"Look here," Hoskin said. "In these photos, you can see Judy wearing
a small pair of gold earrings. Mr. Samuels said those are her angel-shaped
earrings, purchased for her junior high graduation. We contacted the
maker in San Francisco and received a close-up photo of the design."

Hoskin handed each of them an 8x10 color photo of the earrings.
Solid gold, with large, shiny gold wings, they looked less like angels and
more like dragonflies.

"Now, Maria has a big diamond wedding ring, platinum setting,
twelve posts, three-carat heart-shaped diamond. Samuels says Maria
never takes that off."

"Okay, so we are looking for a large rock and angel earrings," I said,
sliding back in my chair, melted snow puddling around my boots.

Bellows walked into the office, his demeanor cranky. I scooted my
chair back, giving him access to his desk. He pointed at the pictures of
the Samuels, a big finger indicating the jewelry. "I've dispatched two
investigators to all the pawn shops in the surrounding counties. I've
already posted a TRAK flyer online for all western states to have the items
checked in their areas. Cross your fingers. With a little a luck, something
will show up."

"We could use a little luck right now," I said.

CHAPTER 20

Saturday February 22nd – Late Evening
Outside Bobby Rae's Residence

Mariposa Deputy Bud Carroll

SAVE FOR THE DULL, YELLOW FRONT PORCH LIGHT, the rest of Bobby Rae's house had been dark for the past week. The term "house" was generous. It was actually a dilapidated mobile home. A double-wide, sitting atop a strip of sloped dirt, buried next to a wall of evergreens. A rotting cedar trellis enclosed the structure, a chalky commercial white, heavily spotted with reddish-brown rust marks, the result from pooled rainwater. A poorly constructed wooden ramp led to a weathered front door.

Tall trees shook in the wind. Clumps of snow fell from branches, pelting the metal roof. Two deputies sat in a patrol car across the street, keeping watch for Bobby Rae's possible return. Both deputies were pulling back-to-back shifts. They welcomed the opportunity, eager for the overtime pay.

Deputy Bud Carroll was in the driver's seat. He grabbed the coffee cup perched on the dashboard.

"Crap, it's ice cold," he complained after taking a swig.

His partner, Deputy Kyle "Skip" Martin offered a sympathetic grin, before he hunkered down in his seat, pulling his Stetson low.

Carroll set the cup back on the dash, and stared at the empty mobile home across the road.

"Skippy, I gotta' take a piss," he said.

Martin didn't flinch, Stetson still tipped over his eyes.

Carroll gazed back at the forest behind him. "Back in a sec." He stepped out the car door and a gust of cold quickly filled the interior of their patrol car.

"Don't go pissin' on your shoes," Martin mumbled.

Carroll shuffled out the door and slid down the steep hillside opposite the residence he had been surveilling. Like many rural areas in Tuolumne, the nearest residence was a quarter mile away. Seclusion was the primary objective for the citizens of this town and Deputy Carroll quickly took advantage of it. He slipped into a thick cluster of trees and bushes and disappeared for a while.

Bobby Rae Olsen

Behind Bobby Rae's Trailer

In the dark tree-lined back slope of the rental property, Bobby Rae slid off the snow-covered hillside, moving stealth so the officers didn't see him. But wet, wild grass accelerated his decent, his boots skating over the slick slope. He collided and flattened against the back wall of his trailer.

Thump!

He peered around the edge to see if the cops had heard the noise. It appeared they did not.

Water soaked through his dirty, brown down parka. He reeked of body odor from days without showering, which should attract every animal within a mile. His stench hung in the air and stuck to everything he touched.

He was aware the FBI was looking for him. Being accused of a crime was not a concern to him. He treated the accusation like a challenge issued.

Carefully, he pulled away a section of the old trellis and dropped to his belly. He slithered under the trailer, something he had done in the past to conceal movements. Cops or drug dealers were often on the lookout. Following alongside a drainpipe, which was dripping water in the mud, he pulled through a trapdoor in the bathroom, lifting himself into the cold and dark trailer.

Grabbing a large, green military duffle bag from his bedroom floor, Bobby Rae began to open drawers, emptying them of clothes, socks, and underwear. He crept into a second room filled with abandoned boxes, broken furniture scattered about. Retrieving a cardboard box from under a bed, Bobby Rae transferred the contents—a folding knife, several watches and bracelets, and wallets, both men's and women's—into the duffel. Things he may be able to pawn, or trade for favors. Digging deeper, Bobby Rae removed a handful of clothing: women's panties and bras in various colors, sizes and styles. He stared at the clothes, considered what to do with them. Leaving them would only give the cops something to use against him. He shoved them into the bag. He'd deal with getting rid of them later. There was another reason for his return.

On his knees, he slid his hand under a cheap wooden chest-of drawer, raked back-and-forth with his fingers until he touched the blue steel .357 Magnum revolver.

Bobby Rae tossed the gun into the bag, then stocked up with ammo from the lower drawer. He knew there were other things he should take, things far more incriminating than old clothes and jewelry. But the longer he stayed, the greater the chances of getting caught. The risk was too high. Better run now.

Sweat poured down his gritty face, even with the meat-locker temperature. Bracing himself on both sides of the opening, he lowered himself through the floor and onto the cold ground. From there, he pushed the duffle bag forward, crawling out from under his home, disappearing into the dark thickness of the forest from where he came.

Mariposa Deputy Bud Carroll

DEPUTY CARROLL, FINALLY FEELING RELIEVED, STOOD at the side of his patrol car, arranged his duty belt and checked to see if he had zipped his fly. Something caught his attention, something out of place. A creak from a branch, an unnatural whisper in the air. Peering over his shoulder, his eyes scanned the hillside behind the trailer as he opened the door of his patrol car. "You hear something, Skippy?"

Deputy Martin hadn't moved an inch, still slouched on the passenger side, trying to stay warm, eyes remaining hidden. His tone was flat when he responded, "Shut up, Bud. Get in and close the door. It's cold outside."

CHAPTER 21

M OST OF THE SNOW IN FRONT OF THE MOTEL, cleared by trucks and plows, had been replaced with dirty slush. The early-morning sun provided some warmth, unless you were stuck in the shade. A thin sheet of ice formed across the patches of earth the sunlight hadn't touched, making the walk to the car a crapshoot. We'd spent the previous evening reviewing case files, searching for similarities while checking in hourly with the rescue teams for an update. Bellows had been preparing a warrant for Olsen's trailer, something we wanted to search if Olsen didn't return by this afternoon. By the time we called it quits, it was one in the morning and nothing new had been discovered.

"For you, Jack." Geonetta handed me a large cup of black coffee. She opened up her other hand exposing several pink and blue packets. "How do you take it?"

"Like my partners . . . bitchy."

"That's not very original."

"Sue me."

She shoved the packets of sugar into my jacket pocket and left me alone.

I shuffled up alongside her and we made our way across the icy parking lot together, dodging the sporadic foreign tourist, unfamiliar with our driving laws, their vehicles drifting onto the wrong side of the road. We drove back to the Sheriff's office and returned to the same spot from last night. Before turning in, I had located a couple of addresses for Warren

Kramer. A few I knew were outdated. His driver's license was still active but there hadn't been any citations or field contacts by law enforcement for over a year. Today, I planned on checking out the newer addresses and, hopefully, get a chance to interview him. While I was pulling the paperwork, Geonetta headed to the command post to get an update on the Samuels. She returned shortly, her face forlorn.

"The search and rescue teams are moving along." Geonetta stepped up to the map, spread her hand and swept left to right. "But they're looking at months, not days, to finish up. That includes every cave, mineshaft and riverbed. Accident or malice, it could be spring before we'll have an answer."

With all that needed to be done to locate Maria and Judy Samuels, there was still the matter of Kathryn Jennings. So far there was nothing of value coming from our examination of the home computer, but that's not uncommon. Histories and hard drives get erased to conceal activity, and it would take a while to recover that information. Officers jettisoned to interview her friends had come up empty, just as her father said they would.

My jaw tensed as I stared down, ice particles shedding from my boots. "She's not a runaway. Not this time." I mulled over the evidence: the murders, Kathryn Jennings, the missing tourists. The more I thought, the more I was convinced of a common denominator.

"Someone," Geonetta said, "has put the *habeas grabus* on her."

I nodded in agreement. "Reminds me: A killer, an abductor, and a child molester walks into a bar. What does the bartender say?"

"Drinking alone?"

I pointed a finger at her and winked.

During the silence my mind trailed back to Bobby Rae Olsen.

The simplest answer is usually the right one.

"I better let Frank know what's going on," I said, reaching for my phone. "I'll tell him we got a person of interest."

Geonetta added, "Tell him we're going hunting."

A LITTLE PAST NINE A.M. AND BELLOWS was already on his fourth cup of coffee, reviewing late night's reports from his deputies. The warrant for Olsen's place was prepared and submitted to the DA's Office for their review. Bellows was waiting to hear back but the truth is, if we don't get it, we're still going in.

Hoskin had arrived an hour earlier, sitting in front of a heating unit, trying to stay warm while perusing the receipts found in Bobby Rae's Impala. There were a lot of receipts. He decided to take them over to the large conference table. Bellows lugged his stack of papers, while Hoskin toted evidence sealed in plastic sleeves. By the time Geonetta and I returned to the command post, Hoskin had spread out the receipts in a chronological order that told a story.

"What does all this tell you?" I asked.

He methodically moved scraps and receipts taken from Bobby Rae's car, arranging them like chess pieces. Prominently in the middle of all the evidence, Hoskin displayed three wadded up business cards from an establishment called the Dragon Tattoo, listing an address in East Sonora. Turning over one of the cards, Hoskin pointed to a note written in pencil: *Candy*.

"The Dragon is a biker tattoo parlor that caters to meth distribution and teenage hookers," Bellows said as Hoskin continued laying out more items.

"Here is a paystub for the week ending February 7th, for $135.78, made payable to a Robert Neumann."

"I'm guessing that's Robert Rae Olsen," I said.

Geonetta picked up the paystub. "You can change your name, but we can still see your snake skin."

I took the stub from her hand. "Where's he working?"

Hoskin spoke up. "Mountain View Lodge, Jack. Maintenance worker." *The victim's lodge.*

"I went through all the reports taken by my deputies." Bellows scratched his chin. "Strangely enough, we never made contact with Olsen in this case. He was never interviewed."

Even though Olsen evaded the initial contact, I could now track his movements by pulling his timecards from the school and the lodge, see if his time was unaccounted for during our murders and abductions, the difference of having a strong alibi or being a suspect.

A deputy entered the room, shot a thumb over his shoulder. "Got a person here. Says he's got some information about your missing tourists."

"Well, get him in here," Bellows barked at the deputy.

He turned away, returned in a minute with a short man with sullen eyes.

Bellows worked his way around us, aiming for the man.

Geonetta's eyes went wide, her pupils dilated. She jabbed a finger forward and shook it. "I know you." Geonetta pushed open a folder and stabbed at the middle of the enlarged DMV photo.

"You're Warren Kramer."

Kramer nodded, looking almost embarrassed at the pronouncement. He stepped up to the nearest chair, placed a hand on the backrest while holding tightly onto a purple knit cap he had taken off his head with the other. His hair was a mess, tangled and matted. Nervously, he released his grip on the chair and brushed back his limp hair with his fingers. His whiskers were stubbly gray.

"I came here because I wanted to tell you about a conversation I overheard at the Captain's Lounge. I thought it might interest you."

Bellows pointed down the hall to a private room, a place where we would be able to conduct an interview uninterrupted.

"Let's all take a walk."

Down the hallway, we entered a small room with a table situated in the middle, surrounded by four metal chairs with cheap, black cushions. Kramer chose the seat at the end. His eyes were locked on the three of us, studying as we placed notebooks, pens and folders on the table. I pulled out my case folder marked OLSEN, ROBERT RAE, placed it in front of me. Kramer looked nervous. Bellows tried not to stare as Kramer fumbled with a pull-tab hanging from his jacket.

He sat quietly, patiently, waiting for someone to say something. Then he twitched as if remembering something he had forgotten to do. He reached down and retrieved a small, black Bible situated on his lap. Paperback, curled at the corners with gold leaf foil along the edges. A red tassel hung from the middle as a book marker. He placed the Bible on the table and rested his right hand on the cover.

"My name is Warren Kramer." The words spilled out of his mouth like marbles falling from an open bag. "There's this guy I know, his name is Bobby Rae Olsen, and I believe he had something to do with those missing tourists."

CHAPTER 22

"WHERE CAN I FIND BOBBY RAE?"
It was the first of many questions I wanted to ask, hoping this would be the break in the case.

"I don't know," Kramer said. "He skipped out yesterday. Not too long ago, I overheard him talking to some drifter at the Captain's Lounge. He came over to my place late last week . . ."

"The day?" I interrupted as I scribbled down everything, verbatim.

"Wednesday . . . I think this was Wednesday night."

Kramer's eyes fluttered in a spasm. Head was beaded in sweat, he was tense, still wearing his heavy leather jacket, which even made me feel over-heated. He shook his head. "I . . . I want to make sure that I don't say the wrong thing, get somebody in trouble because of me." Kramer stood and shook his right hand, tapping his forehead with his knuckles, trying to shake lose his memory.

I softened my tone, tried to calm his nerves. "Warren," I said his name like we were close friends. "Just tell me what you came here to say. We won't assume anything until you're sure we understand."

Kramer took a deep breath and sat back down. He wiped the sweat from his forehead with an open hand and wiped it dry on his jeans. "Last week I was waiting for a friend at the Captain's Lounge in Sonora. It's a bar where most of us locals go to get away from the tourist crowd."

"I'm familiar with the place."

"I'm sitting at a table waiting for this friend, just minding my own business, having a beer, and I look over and see Bobby Rae." Kramer started to fidget in his chair, rocking forward and wiping the spittle from his mouth that was building around the corners. "Bobby and I go back a ways . . . he's a friend, sort of, and once in a while we go drinking—I usually end up paying because he's always broke." Kramer's eyes bounced between the three of us, angling for any indication of acceptance. "It's been about a month since he and I went out drinking together. He owes me fifty bucks from the last time. Well, the other night, I see Bobby sitting with this guy. I don't recognize him."

"Can you describe him?"

Kramer paused for a moment. "The guy or Bobby Rae?"

"The guy."

"Oh, yeah." Kramer closed his eyes and thought for a moment, then shook his head. "I can't really say. It was dark. I remember he was clean cut 'cuz I thought it was strange for a guy like that to be associating with Bobby Rae."

"What else?"

"I can tell Bobby Rae was hammered because the more he drinks, the louder he gets. And he was pretty loud. If it hadn't been for the music box and the crowd, you could have heard him across the street. I didn't want him to see me 'cuz he'd ask me over and I'll get stiffed for another fifty."

"What did you hear him say?" Bellows asked.

"This guy he was with starts talking about the missing tourists and that the FBI was looking at him for it. I hear Bobby say that maybe he did have something to do with them."

We all went quiet.

Kramer raised a hand. "His words. He starts laughing with this guy and then they all of a sudden get quiet."

Kramer looked at us in wonder. "Why would anyone say something like that if they weren't involved?"

"Did he say where they were? If he harmed them?"

"No, nothing like that. He just said that he had something to do with them."

"Did you hear anything else?"

"No. I got scared and took off out of there. I wanted to tell you sooner, but I wasn't sure I heard Bobby right and didn't want to get him in trouble."

"Do you think you would be able to recognize his friend if you saw him?"

Kramer thought for a moment, squeezing his eyes shut, trying to remember what the shadowy figure looked like. "I don't know. It was dark and his back was to me. I never got a chance to look over and I didn't want Bobby to see me."

Geonetta jumped into the questioning: "You saw Bobby Rae the next day? Where?"

"Yeah . . . the next day. Wednesday. I was at home . . . in Groveland. I got a little place. It's enough for me since I split with my ol' lady couple years back. The kids, they come see me every so often. Raley, my oldest—she's sixteen, almost seventeen. She comes and stays because she can't take the other kids all the time. You see, my other two—Josh and Amelia—I call Amelia "Squeak" because she so quiet. They're a handful. I think that's why me and my wife split up." Snow slid off his jacket and pooled onto the linoleum floor. "They moved up deep in Calaveras County to get away from staring eyes and judgmental folks. I bought a plot for them and built them a small cabin. She likes it up there. People here just like to be left alone."

How many times have I heard that expression since arriving here, I thought. It must be a rural philosophy to want isolation, never to be contaminated by city life or modern convinces. Own a truck, a shotgun and a wood burning fireplace and you can live your life almost entirely in seclusion.

"Bobby Rae . . . Warren." Trying to get him back on the subject matter. "Why was he at your house?"

"I'm sorry. I didn't mean to get off track. Wednesday night, Bobby came knocking on my door, all nutted-up and sweatin'. He tells me that he needs a place to crash for the night and would it be okay. I tell him okay and asked him what was wrong. He says that the heat's on him and he just wanted time to lay low."

"Do you think he was talking about the murders or the missing tourists?" I asked.

Kramer paused like he was caught off guard. It was the first time in the conversation the murdered teenagers were mentioned. "I don't know. Maybe." Kramer started chewing on his thumb, rocking back and forth. "The missing tourists . . . one was the daughter, right?"

I nodded.

"A young girl, wasn't she?"

"Yes, she's seventeen."

Kramer closed his eyes, face sagged with the look of resignation.

"Look, I don't know if this is important or not but he likes young girls, you know. When he's drunk, I've seen him pick them up for sex. He likes them *real young*. I think he's sick. Left his wife because he was fucking teenagers." Warren's face reddened as he looked over at Geonetta and began to apologize.

Geonetta smiled. "That's okay, Warren."

Kramer nodded nervously before continuing. "Bobby Rae left the next morning, late. He had a large green duffle bag with him that he slept on, almost protective of it. When he left, he told me that he would be in contact soon and could he borrow some money. I gave him forty dollars, which was all I had at the time. He said he was going up into the hills until it cooled down. Then he left. I was too afraid to ask about his conversation at the Captain's Lounge."

Bellows leaned forward, "Warren, do you think Bobby Rae could be involved in the murder of those teenaged girls?"

"He can be violent for sure, but I can't believe he would kill. Not that he'd ever tell me. That's something he'd keep to himself, even when he's drinking. He's been known to shoot off his mouth, but he's a survivor. That's why I was shocked when I heard him say he was involved in those tourists' disappearance."

"Do you have a way of getting in touch with him?" I asked.

Kramer shook his head. "He usually just shows up."

I passed along my business card. "My cell phone and office numbers are on it. Day or night, please call me if you hear from Bobby Rae."

Kramer took the card and carefully studied it as if he was trying to memorize the information. "I won't testify, not against Bobby Rae. I can't."

"I'm not asking you to."

At least not yet.

Kramer shook his head. "I won't. I got a family, kids. Bobby Rae finds out that I've talked, we are as good as dead."

"He can't harm you if he's in jail," Bellows said.

"No disrespect but I beg to differ. Bobby Rae's got friends. Got a lot of enemies too, but it's his friends that I don't want to come looking for me."

"Could any of these friends have helped him?"

Kramer shrugged, leaving the possibility open. "Like I said, he's got friends that I don't know but what I do know is that they're dangerous." Then his face went tense. "Look, my daughter stays at my place, on and off. I just don't want her to know we're talking, say anything to my ex. It will just make matters worse."

"Our secret."

Warren Kramer just became an important key to this investigation. Although what he heard that night at the Captain's Lounge was hearsay, it was the only link between Bobby Rae and the missing tourists. And a disappearance just may have turned into an abduction. Without Kramer, it would be difficult to find and interrogate Bobby Rae. And without Bobby Rae, I may never find the whereabouts of Maria and Judy Samuels.

"We'll keep you in confidence. I promise."

Kramer let out a deep sigh.

"You got to promise me the minute you find out where Bobby Rae is, you'll call."

He placed his right hand on the book he brought with him and started to rub it in a swirling motion. Nodding his head in agreement and in full cooperation, Kramer acknowledged the order, "I promise you, I swear."

Bellows chuckled under his breath. "You don't have to swear on the Bible."

Kramer looked at Bellows with a puzzled gaze, eyes wide and his mouth slightly agape before realizing the misunderstanding. "Oh no . . . no, I'm not swearing a promise on the Bible. I brought this for you. I found it." He carefully handed me the book. "It fell out of Bobby Rae's duffle bag. I thought you might want it."

Warren's face clearly displayed the look of a man who had betrayed his best friend. "It may be a coincidence. You know, he worked there. Maybe they're the throw-aways and he took it for his mother. She's very religious, you know."

I quickly slipped on a pair of latex gloves, opened the front cover of the worn Bible and read an embossed stamped notation on the first page:

Mountain View Lodge, El Portal, Ca. Rm <u>309</u>.

From the Samuels' room.

I looked at Bellows, knowing we may have stumbled on to something positive. This, along with Kramer's information, was just more for our probable cause statement to get a search warrant on Bobby Rae's trailer. I instructed Bellows to pass along the newly acquired info to the DA for the pending warrant. Like I said, probable cause or not, nothing was going to stop me from getting inside Bobby Rae's trailer.

I weighed my options. Kramer provided our best opportunity to gather information about Bobby Rae's possible involvement, in either the missing tourists and/or the teenage murders, and I needed his continuous cooperation. To use the Bible in any affidavit would eventually *single source* Kramer as the person providing the evidence, and at some point might require his identity to be disclosed in court. To disclose him as a cooperating witness would only cause those who may be involved to stay clear. Or worse. But I wasn't going to let that happen. A good informant is too valuable. They are what make cases. They're goldmines. And like goldmines, you don't ever disclose their whereabouts.

I watched Kramer leave before Bellows said, "I can't guarantee his confidentiality if it means stopping a child killer."

"I wouldn't have it any other way."

Bellows accepted my answer knowing it was more complicated than that.

We watched Warren through the entrance window as he disappeared into the rows of parked cars in the station lot.

Bellows gave me a suspicious look and said, "I think it's the money that boy's after. Reward money."

His remark didn't set square with me. He never mentioned money, never even hinted but I wasn't going to argue the point. "Whatever his motivation, we better take advantage of it now before people find out he's talking."

Bellows grunted, his jaw working double-time. "I hope he understands the people he's talking about don't cotton to double-crossers. That could get him a fast ride to the morgue."

I didn't say a thing after that. I just knew, Bellows was right.

CHAPTER 23

Sunday February 23rd – 5:07 p.m.

THE SKY BEGAN TO DARKEN, TURNING STEEL GRAY. A chill ran down my arm. I was unsure if it was from the cold or anxiousness. I waited down the street from Bobby Rae's trailer with a couple of uniforms. Bellows called to say he had just left the judge's chambers with the signed warrant. Geonetta stood by her car wearing her bureau parka and a dark blue ski cap. She danced in place trying to stay warm, her breath escaping her mouth, clouding her face like cigar smoke. Thumbs hooked on their belts, three deputies stood guard like sentinels to ensure no one got in. Or out. Not until we executed our search. Bellows wanted this to be a low-key entry, minimize the chance of drawing the media's attention. I agreed.

Walking up the hillside, I studied the front and side view of the trailer, angling for the safest route in. Working my way around back, I maneuvered up a slope, noticed a loose trellis panel with a large pile of snow and mud pushed in front of it. I slid down and positioned myself at the backyard's edge, trying to gain better access. The snow was in the form of a horseshoe, indicating it was man-made. Upon closer inspection, I observed bare spots where snow would have fallen over the past day or two, meaning the panel had been recently removed. The mud in front was further proof of a recent disturbance. And based on the curvature of the pile, it had come from under the trailer. Which meant someone had come and gone. And that would be Bobby Rae. And more than likely, he would've taken any incriminating evidence with him.

Geonetta trudged to where I stood, dropping to a knee in the snow.

"Looks like we're a little late," I said.

She raised an eyebrow. "I think you're right, gunslinger."

She tossed a handful of snow, stood and started toward the front of the trailer.

"Let's see if Bobby Rae was dumb enough to leave anything behind."

We walked off the hill as Bellows' Chevy Tahoe pulled up onto Bobby Rae's wet, pine needle covered driveway.

"I got the warrant. Let's go inside."

Three deputies fell behind Bellows, jogging up the walkway, guns drawn. Bellows tried the doorknob. Locked. Without further notice, he kicked the door in with his size thirteen steel-toed Red Wings. The flimsy aluminum door easily gave way to the force, banging against the wall before flying back, slamming Bellows on his left shoulder. Bellows pushed forward with an S&W Model 27, .357 Magnum, looking like a hood ornament on a land yacht.

From inside, the trailer was actually larger. The hallway led to three rooms. It was dark, dirty, and smelled of mildew. I followed Bellows, his gun aimed down range, high-powered Maglite illuminating the path. Geonetta was close behind covering our blind spot with her Glock. We moved quickly.

"*Clear!*" Bellows yelled as he swung through the door to his left. He waved an officer to search for anyone hiding.

"*Clear!*" Bellows shouted again, this time pushing through the second room, quickly painting the room, shafts of light scouring for figures hidden in the darkness.

Entering the last room in the trailer, Bellows panned the cluttered space, stopping before backtracking, locked on something that caught his attention. He stood motionless, staring at figures suspended from the ceiling, pictures stapled to the walls.

"What the hell do we have here?" he said, voice filled with disbelief.

I holstered my weapon and cleared the doorway. The room was dark, lit only by an officer's flashlight. A lamp lay askew beside a nightstand, bulb shattered on the floor. Bellows scanned the perimeters as I stepped around a deputy holding the flashlight. My eyes followed his beam, gave it a second look, trying to make sense of what was before me. Pictures of children, some clothed, others not, cut from magazines, plastered like wallpaper. There were items of clothing, some jewelry, trinkets, also pinned.

"A trophy room," I said while sliding on a pair of latex gloves.

Bellows held out his hand, displaying a stack of Polaroids he had taken from a small wooden desk drawer. He shuffled through them like trading cards. Grainy snapshots of teenaged girls.

I tapped at the photos. "I'm guessing Bobby Rae's the cameraman."

Young girls tied up, violated. The deeper I went into the stack the more disturbing the photos grew and the angrier I became. I had seen enough to know the dark side of guys like Bobby Rae. They crawled from holes that had no bottom, no light, no restriction. In the brightness of day, they preyed on the unaware, the susceptible.

Bellows made another pass through the stack. "Can't tell if they're minors." This was a critical element in charging Bobby Rae. I had to show these girls were underage to violate federal laws.

"Any of these look like someone you've arrested or had contact with in the past?"

Bellows' face drew tight from the perversion of it all. "Don't recognize them." He tossed the photos on the table." Let me get them over to vice in Tuolumne. Bobby Rae's a Tuolumne resident, could be Tuolumne girls."

I swept up the photos and gave them one last look.

Trophies.

I turned over each picture, imagining what he had done to these girls, and it made me shudder. But there was now hope. I realized what these photos meant. It meant we had something on Bobby Rae.

Find one victim in that stack, confirm she was a minor, and I'll have a chargeable offense. Not impossible. Just time-consuming. Sooner or later, though, I'd find Bobby Rae and with this evidence, he'd be under my control. More importantly, no one else could be under his. That made me feel better, almost euphoric. I was finally getting some traction. I took the stack and placed them in a plastic sleeve, labeled and sealed it with a strip of evidence tape. I looked at the photos as I dangled them in the air, each face looking back at me as if calling for help.

"You're going to be mine, motherfucker," I whispered. "All mine."

CHAPTER 24

Sunday February 23rd – Late morning

The Truck Driver

MELTED SNOW DRIPPED FROM THE ROOFTOP of the old wooden structure onto the uneven parking lot comprised of dirt and broken blacktop. The regulars had just pulled into *Ivan's Restaurant* to have their usual breakfast of coffee, scrambled eggs, bacon, and hash browns. America's comfort food.

Ivan's Restaurant was a standard place for breakfast. 1950s steel tables with cheap marble-designed Formica tops, yellowing from age and chipped from over use. The interior consisted of a small dining area and an L-shaped counter for those who preferred watching the cook throw thick slabs of bacon onto an ancient black iron grill, the grease flowing into bubbling scrambled eggs.

Suspended high in the corner of the restaurant was a tiny color television, giving everyone the opportunity to catch up on world events. The local news was on, the reporter standing in front of the Mariposa County Sheriff's office.

"We are here live where we have just been told that an all-points bulletin has been put out on thirty-six-year-old Robert Rae Olsen of Tuolumne County. Olsen is being sought for questioning involving the disappearance of Marie and Judy Samuel, from Phoenix, Arizona. The two were last seen February 14th at the Mountain View Lodge where they had checked in to spend their vacation. Officials are not speculating what happened to them but are concerned because of several unusual sets of circumstances surrounding their disappearance. Anyone

with any information pertaining to the missing tourists or Mr. Olsen are asked to contact the Mariposa County Sheriff's office or the FBI Office in Modesto."

A picture of the Samuels flashed on the screen. Then, a mug shot from a previous arrest photo of Bobby Rae's, somewhat younger, but still with the same disheveled look. The customers at Ivan's sat captivated by the report, gulping large porcelain mugs filled with hot black coffee while pushing around remains of their breakfast.

"I betcha' that boy has got somethin' to do with those missin' tourists," remarked an old man sitting at the corner table. "He looks like a killer."

Two other customers sitting nearby nodded in agreement. Low, muffled *uh-huhs* and *oh yeahs* could be heard resonating throughout the small café as the sound of clanging metal and sizzling meat crackled in the background.

The truck driver that had come in from the rain, stood at the front counter, ordered a large cup of coffee to go. Taking in everyone's remarks, he pointed at the TV still showing the picture of Bobby Rae Olsen. "You think there's a reward for him?"

Ivan handed the trucker his coffee in a Styrofoam cup. "Oh, I would think the police would pay handsomely a person who helped capture this hooligan."

The trucker pulled out a wadded five-dollar bill from his pants pocket and handed it to Ivan. Making change, the trucker gave Ivan a dollar tip.

"See you around," the trucker said as he headed out the door to his eighteen-wheeler parked in the open lot.

CLIMBING UP INTO HIS RIG, HE placed his coffee on the dash, dug around in his vest pocket looking for his cell phone. Finding it next to his cigarettes, he held the phone up into the air. No bars.

"Shit, just my luck."

The trucker sat impatiently for a second, contemplating his next move. He tapped his fingers on the steering wheel, thinking. His load of soccer balls, baseball gloves, and warm-up suits destined for Big 5 in Visalia, California, was already a day behind schedule. His boss had already told him if he once more missed a scheduled date, he'd be out of a job.

The driver decided to get his precious load down Interstate 5 in a hurry. "They'd probably just screw me out of any reward."

His truck started up with a loud growl, only to be overwhelmed by the screech of the PTO gear and disengaging brakes. The truck lurched toward the exit of the parking lot. It started to rain, the snow turning into slushy puddles on the pavement. Before exiting the lot, the trucker looked to his left for any oncoming vehicles and seeing none, crept the big-rig forward. Just in front of his view, he spied a single public telephone booth planted alone at the edge of the parking lot being pounded by buckets now falling. The truck continued to creep, the large diesel engine rumbling, competing with the sound of the rain now hammering down on the forty-foot cargo box he was pulling. Focused on the payphone, he bit his lip. Then the trucker threw the transmission into neutral and jammed on the emergency brake.

"Oh, what the hell . . ."

The driver's door flew open as his boots fell hard along the side of his rig. He stepped out, the rain now falling in sheets, like shards of glass hammering off the bill of his well-worn red ball cap. He moved quickly to the public phone, and jumped inside to protect himself from further abuse by the elements.

Picking up the receiver, he punched on the keypad.

"911 Operator . . . what is your emergency."

Trying to hear over the noise of the wind and rain, the trucker stuck a finger in one ear and pressed the receiver tightly onto his other. "Yeah . . . uh . . . I think I got some information on the guy you've been looking for—Olsen? Can you connect me with the guy at the Sheriff's Department who's looking for him? I recently picked up a hitchhiker. Just now, I saw a picture of your guy Olsen on TV. I think it's the same guy."

"Stand by," the operator said. Silence fell over the telephone line. A series of beeps let the caller know that the conversation was being recorded. A moment later, the trucker could hear the operator breathing and tapping quickly on a computer keyboard.

"I'm connecting you now."

A click, then ringing. The trucker heard a voice on the other end.

"Mariposa County Sheriff. Officer Halverson. Can I help you?"

"Is there a reward for information on that guy you're looking for? Olsen?"

The voice on the other end responded, "There is, but it depends on what you have to offer. Why don't you tell me what you know and then we'll talk about the money."

He let out a deep sigh and began his story of traveling south on highway 49 when he picked up a hitchhiker with a large green duffle bag. The deputy listened to the trucker as he provided the details and directions about where he dropped off the hitchhiker, a small cabin house just off the highway, in Calaveras.

CHAPTER 25

Two Nights Earlier

Him

He didn't bring Kate her usual bowl of soup. The only thing he delivered tonight was a gold chain with a cross dangling on the end. Reaching into his pocket, he retrieved a silver key. Carefully, he slid it into the padlock that secured the large barn doors. Lock removed, dangling off the latch, he entered into the dark, cool building. Kate lay asleep in the cage. She was still blindfolded, fearful of being punished if she tried to remove it. Her hands had turned blue from the bite of the plastic ties and the chill in the air, breaths sounding strained and labored. He approached the cage, knelt down to get a closer look at his prisoner. He pushed his nose into an open area between the rusty bars and sniffed the sleeping girl. He could smell it.

Repentance.

He could smell the difference between a lie and the truth. And for that reason, he was the one to determine who had sinned and who had atoned. Keep the clean; cleanse the earth of the failures. He had learned of the dark perversion that lay within these teenaged girls. They were the ones that sought out others, men and women, speaking casually of immoral ways. They were the ones who fed their promiscuity like a devouring beast, never getting enough of their deviant behavior. They were bent; they were broken.

Their scent gave them away.

"Are you awake?" Whispering into the air, his breath trailed, a mist hovering above Kate's face.

At the sound of his voice, Kate awoke and immediately began to shiver.

He sniffed at the cage, taking in every heartbeat, every breath.

"I thought of what you said," Kate responded, pushing herself blindly to the back of the cage.

She almost sounded convincing.

"I have changed. I have repented . . . honest. I won't do the things you say I did. I will be good . . . really."

He paused for a moment, gave her words some thought, said nothing. She fidgeted, anxiously listening for a reaction.

"Please? Do you hear me? Please believe me. I am better. I did the things you told me. I can be good!"

Still he remained silent. He watched her body shivering, mouth quivering, until she started to cry. "Please, I just want to go home."

Curiously, he hovered to her side of the cage, watching her cower in the corner. Bowing his head, he knew what he had to do.

The smell.

He unlocked the cage door, reached in and led Kate out by the hand. His touch made her jump at first, resisting his pull, but she quickly surrendered. She was barefoot and dirty, jeans unbuttoned and torn.

Her captor closed his eyes as he ran his hands down her body, feeling every curve, imaging those that had touched her in the same way, at her willingness. It offended him. He found it ironic that his touch was met with such indignation.

He wrapped his arms around her chilled body. "I have failed you," he confessed. "And for that, I am sorry."

He guided her with a gentle hand, down to the floor. She knelt onto cool dirt, sobbing. He stroked her hair, offering comfort, weeping for her soul. With swiftness, he raised a steel pipe he brought with him above her head, took a quick short swing and struck her hard.

The explosive strike rang out, sounding like the fall of a massive building, a devastating mountain slide. Her body sagged as she fell motionless.

Time had stopped.

Like the others before her, she couldn't have heard the strike coming; she felt no pain. He towered over her with the blood and bone matted, pipe dripping crimson on scattered hay. Her blood seeped from the gaping wound until there was none. The bright red fluid that flowed was Kate's life departing her body. He knew she had not been saved. God knows, he tried. She had to pay because of her misguided ways.

He could smell it.

"This was your fault! I had no choice."

The man reached into his pocket, took out a piece of paper. Two lines of words were scribbled: *Kate Jennings* above, and below, *Catch Me*. He folded the paper and tore, separating the two halves. *Catch Me* was placed under her blouse, the other returned to his pocket.

Outside the building, the wind cut a deep path of cold and with it took Kate's soul far away.

Jack Paris

MY EYES POPPED OPEN AND I struggled to breathe.

It was a bad dream. There was a young girl, a barn. It was cold. I felt her cold. And there were tears, quiet voices, and then a heightened sense of anxiety, pain, helplessness. Then a sinking feeling of blackness. I was still drowsy, confused. It took me a second to remember, I was in my hotel room, in bed, safe. I was covered in a cold sweat, my heart pounding a staccato rhythm, like the girl in my dreams.

I looked out my hotel window. It was too dark to make out anything other than the parking lot lights. The clock read 3:24 a.m.

I fell back onto my pillow and closed my eyes. It took almost an hour to find calmness. The dream faded but the feeling remained.

Is that you, Emily? Are you telling me something?

Falling into a twilight haze, I whispered, *"Please, no more dreams . . ."*

CHAPTER 26

Monday February 24th
Morning – 7:26 a.m.

THE HUNT FOR BOBBY RAE STARTED EARLY. While one group set off to locate and interview those on our sex-registrant list, we had divvied up the names of the employees at the Mountain View lodge, and once more, began to re-interview the staff, hoping to gain new information that would help generate new leads. Bellow called earlier that morning and said he was following up on a lead from last night—a trucker with information. He said he would get back with me if it panned out.

A lot of the staff came from Mexico, and many had returned home for the holidays. Such trips weren't uncommon for immigrants in the region. The timing was unfortunate. The chances of finding a witness became increasingly difficult.

I needed to know more about Bobby Rae's associates, where he stayed, whether anyone noticed anything peculiar about his sexual proclivities.

The interview process with the remaining potential witnesses was long, arduous, limited. Some spoke English, most did not. Using an interpreter gummed up the works, a lot lost in translation. Mostly, I grew sick of the same answer, shrugging shoulders, eyes that intimated confusion, the words that flowed like a rehearsed line, *No se, No se.*

I flipped through the pages in my notebook as Geonetta grabbed a chair from another room. We'd taken over the manager's office at the Mountain View Lodge.

"How many more employees do we have?" I asked.

Geonetta leaned down over the desk, covered in loose papers, a large outdated calculator and a bowl of fruit. She dragged a finger down a notepad. "Fourteen. That's if you include the contracted landscaping workers."

"How many are actually here?"

Geonetta shrugged. "We're going to find out." A second later, there was a knock.

A Hispanic man gently tapped his knuckles against the wooden door-frame. My gaze shifted to the man. Slight build, tan, gray shirt, slacks with the word *MAINTENANCE* embroidered above the shirt pocket.

I looked over my notepad for my next scheduled interview. "You must be Jamie Navarro."

He nodded.

I gestured toward the chair in front of the desk. "Please, sit."

Navarro sat down, crossed his legs and placed his hands on his lap. He was thin with a dark tan. His hair, thick and black I could see his hands were rough with calluses. His knee started to bounce. His arms dropped to the sides of the chair, bracing his weight like bridge supports.

"Mr. Navarro, how long have you been working here at the lodge?"

Navarro pursed his lips. In a moderate Spanish accent, he said, "Almost eight years, on and off."

"What do you mean by 'on and off'?"

"I work during the busy season, then go home to Mexico for holiday."

"What's your responsibility here at the lodge?"

Navarro placed a finger on the table and tapped as he described his job duties. The last was the one that drew my interest. It was entering the rooms to make repairs.

"Tell me the process of accessing the rooms," I asked.

"The manager calls me on the radio." Navarro pulled a small walkie-talkie from his belt and held it up. "I go knock on the door and tell the guests I am there to do repairs."

"What if no one answers?"

Navarro stiffened. "I use the passkey."

"Passkey? You mean a master key?"

"Si."

"Where do you keep the master key?"

Navarro pointed toward the front lobby. "In the drawer."

"Is the drawer locked?"

"No."

"Who has access to the master key?"

Navarro's shoulders went high. "Any worker."

Then I asked the important question: "Jamie, do you know a man by the name of Bobby Rae Olsen? He worked at the lodge and the local high school as a maintenance helper."

Navarro turned away before answering. "No Olsen."

"How could you not know him? He worked at the lodge. Are you sure?"

"Sí. I only work with my crew and the manager. There are many others I don't talk to."

I perused through Navarro's original statement given to the Mariposa detectives a couple of weeks ago. "You told the detective that you were not here the evening the Samuels came up missing."

Navarro nodded. "That's right. After work, I went home, then out of town."

"Where did you go?"

"With friends." Navarro's mouth twitched with a nervous energy.

I repeated my question. "Where?"

"Around, just around."

"Who were your friends?"

"Just friends."

"Look, help me out here," I said. "Tell me their names, where I can find them and what you were all doing."

Navarro scratched his head, his thick black hair tangled into the configuration of a bird's nest. "I was with a girlfriend, in Modesto."

I looked at the list of names again and noted a Maria Navarro also working at the lodge. "Maria," I said. "Is this a relative?"

"Wife."

"Oh. Well then, what is the name of the 'girlfriend' and how can I reach her to confirm you two were together that night? In confidence, of course."

Navarro drew a grin, like we shared an understanding. "Lorena . . . Lorena Sandoval. But she has gone home to Michoacán."

"Is there a way to reach her? Is she coming back soon?"

Navarro shook his head. "No, we got into a fight. She said she wanted to go home . . . to her husband."

I placed my pen on top of my notebook. "Mr. Navarro, I don't want to get into your private affairs but we have two missing persons and I need to confirm where everyone was that night."

Navarro remained silent.

"Can anyone else verify your whereabouts?"

Again, Navarro shook his head. "Just Lorena." He hesitated for a second then added, "She has no phone."

Geonetta walked up with a stack of yellow cards in her hand. She filtered through three or four of them, then handed me one. It was Navarro's timecard for the week in question. "Mr. Navarro, you said you went home first, then out with Lorena sometime after the Samuels were believed to have come up missing?"

"Sí."

"Your timecard said you worked up until 7 p.m. the night they disappeared. Is this your regular work schedule?"

"No, I worked late because of bad plumbing in the building." Navarro pointed out the window toward a block of rooms east of the main lobby. It was next to the building where the Samuels stayed. "Leaks in the ceiling."

"Did you work on anything in room 309?"

He thought, then rubbed his lips with his left thumb and finger. "No, but I was in there a few weeks ago, fixed the toilet."

"Did anyone see you leave work that night at 7 p.m.?"

"Sí. Maybe Maria."

"Maybe?"

"Sí . . . yes."

"She's outside in the lobby," Geonetta spoke up. "I can get her."

Navarro's eyes widened, a concerned look cast across his face. He stood up and started walking toward the door. "I'll get her."

I made my way around the table and stopped him, placing a hand on his side.

"No problem, Mr. Navarro. Agent Geonetta will get her." Geonetta turned and went out the office door. Navarro sat back in his chair, his eyes bouncing between me and the door. A few seconds passed and Geonetta appeared, escorting Maria Navarro into the room. I introduced myself and went through the story her husband had just told. She looked at me, then at Geonetta, weary.

"Just tell 'em, Maria," Navarro said, agitated. "Tell 'em I was with you after work."

Maria's head bobbed back and forth, picking up speed as the words fell from Jamie Navarro's lips. I leaned in close to Maria, blocking her view from her husband.

"Maria, it's important you tell the truth. Otherwise, if I find out that you are not, we're going to have a problem."

She strained to respond, her English failing her by the second. "No trouble, please. He was with me. All day."

"No Maria, his time card showed he worked till 7 p.m."

She shook her head. "I mean night, at night. After work."

I pressed. "Are you sure you were with Jaime after 7 p.m. that night? He said he was out with a *friend*."

Maria paused, checked with Jaime, then back to me. "Si, yes, yes, yes. He was out with a friend for only a short time. After that, he was with me. Honest."

Jamie Navarro looked at me, the grin still holding tight on his face. "See, like I say, we were together."

Command Post - Mariposa County Sheriff's Office

WE FINISHED THE STAFF INTERVIEWS—AT LEAST with those that were still in the country. Tomorrow, I planned on getting with Bellows to compare notes, see if there were any conflicting statements. Navarro was one of them. Until then, it appeared no one saw the Samuels on the night of their disappearance and no one knew Bobby Rae. Somehow, I found that hard to believe.

It was getting late. The search teams planned on staying out as long as there was light. It was still very cold, snow turning to slush, turning to ice. The search dogs needed rest. After days of sniffing, their noses became desensitized, making them almost useless. The search was still the priority and the media made sure it would stay front and center on their newsfeed.

Hundreds of tips from concerned citizens reporting sightings of our tourists were called into the command post. By the end of the day, I completed another five interviews, all dead ends. Hoskin and Geonetta took off to follow their set of leads, all with the same results.

At sunset, everyone returned cold and dejected, having made no progress. At least it was warm in the station, heater cranked, hot coffee brewing, courtesy of the local Chapter of the VFW.

We hung our wet coats on an old wooden coat rack that was already over-taxed.

I found two chairs in the corner, away from the ruckus, where Geonetta and I could decompress, elevating our legs on an old metal safe. A young deputy saw us and brought us each freshly brewed coffee. The warmth from the steam felt comforting. I closed my eyes allowing the vapor to engulf my face and suddenly I felt exhausted. I needed sleep.

"I have to ask you something," Geonetta asked, dragging me back into consciousness. "What are doing here?"

Where is she going with this?

"Because it's my job."

Geonetta paused. "You don't have to be here."

"I want to be here." I raised an eyebrow, now catching her meaning. "I'm fine."

"I didn't mean it like that."

"Like what?"

"Like because of what happened . . ."

She stopped mid-sentence. I sensed her regret starting down that road. "I'm sorry about your wife," she said, softly.

I stared into my coffee. Geonetta put her hand on my shoulder.

"Is that why you're here?" I asked. "You think I need someone to keep an eye on me?"

She smiled like I was being stupid. I was. "You shouldn't work alone."

"Why's that?"

"You can fall and break a hip."

"Very funny."

Her eyes relaxed. "How are the kids?"

My throat went tight. I massaged my jaw, tension pushing up from my neck. Over the years, Geonetta and I had spent long days and nights working together. We shared a lot but seldom did the conversation get into our personal lives. "They're great." It was all I could think to say. "What about you?" I asked. "Anything?" Truth was, I had never asked about how her dating life was going.

She kept the smile but raised a hand and pointed her thumb down. "Nah."

Then she rotated her hand up and snapped her fingers. "Let me see them."

"See what?"

"Pictures of the kids."

I hesitated. Then gave in. I reached into my briefcase, retrieved a wallet containing personal identification, credit cards, and family photos. They were separated from my Bureau property.

I pulled out a few shots; Michael's high school football picture, Justine at the prom, a couple others that meant a lot to me. There was one of Em.

Geonetta held still, looked at the spread for a long moment as if her eyes were taking in something more than just pictures. She leaned in, gently pressed her shoulder against mine. That touch. I felt her warmth radiate through me—and wanting it more than ever—but I pulled back, enough for her to notice. Geonetta straightened. I felt like shit, didn't seem to understand why.

But I did.

I've never opened up to anyone, never allowed a stranger into my personal world let alone, someone I knew as well as Geonetta. You try to be tough, can take on anything that life throws your way. But that ain't the way life is. Life comes in drips and drabs, then like a tsunami. It slams you to the ground, pulls and pushes you in every direction, especially the direction you don't want to go. It's then that you need to find a hold, something to ground you in place, know which way is up. Otherwise, you get washed away. I tried finding it when Em died. But what I grabbed onto was nothing more than a false tether to a fictitious world. Just a dream. And now I find myself being washed away while pretending everything is all right, down a spinning torrent into a deep gorge, and unless I find someone to help me through all this, there won't be a way back.

It was wearing me down.

So I leaned back in.

"I like this one," she said, filtering out another photograph from the stack.

It was an old Polaroid, taken by a neighbor when Michael was just five, Justine three. It was special. The yellowing photo, creased from accidentally being bent, captured Michael standing in a newly planted front yard, holding hands with the neighbor's six-year-old girl, Jordan. Justine, dressed in her *Little Mermaid* pull-over top and blue stretch pants, stood nearby chewing a wad of gum, waiting impatiently. Big smiles from Michael. Attitude from Justine.

The picture was my escape from reality. Secretly, it was the one thing that gave me balance. I found solace in the photo when my world trembled. In every spinning day, I would find a window back in time when life was calmer and under control. The white border was a framed view, the illusion of having the ability to reach through it and touch their young faces. I could feel the blue cotton shirt Michael wore and Justine's sticky hands. I felt the heat from that summer's daylight, even thru the yellowing tint of the picture. I remembered the exact time that photo was taken, the sun's warmth on my face, the love of their innocence. Of family. I still remembered.

Geonetta carefully handed back the Polaroid with a sympathetic smile knowing what it meant to me. I slipped it back into my wallet, careful not to further damage the weakened edges.

"Your turn," I said. Why are you here?"

"I needed more in life." She said it matter-of-factly. "Went to law school because my brother was a lawyer, my sister was a lawyer, Dad was a lawyer, his dad was a lawyer . . ."

"I get it."

A slight frown. She straightened up and turned to face me, her eyes locked on mine. "I felt disconnected, left outside of a world that moved faster than me. I didn't want to wake up one morning and question what I did with my life."

I looked down at the floor, thought about what she said and she looked into the distance and smiled. "Stories," she said. "I want my life filled with stories."

A deputy walked up with a small note in hand.

"Detective Bellows asked me to come get you two. He's talking to a guy who says he knows where Bobby Rae Olsen is."

Relaxation time was up. We launched our tired bodies out of our chairs and out the door, looking for Bellows. I started to get the sense: the hunt was back on. As we pushed ourselves out the command post doors, I whispered into Geonetta's ear, "Okay Heather, you just might get those story you're looking for."

CHAPTER 27

Monday February 24th – 7:36 p.m.

W E CAUGHT UP TO BELLOWS AND JUMPED INTO HIS SUV.
The speedometer quickly reached eighty as we sped up the road heading north on 49 to Calaveras. Without any moonlight, I could see no further than the high-beams. Beyond that was anyone's guess. Having driven these paths enough, Bellows reassured me he was in control. I trusted him—kind of. Hoskin and three ERT members followed close behind. A patrol car with two Mariposa deputies shadowed us. If Bellows was right, tonight we'd be transporting Bobby Rae back to the local lockup.

"A truck driver called in," Bellows said. "Last night, while driving southbound on 49, he saw a hitchhiker thumbing for a ride. Cold and foggy, he said the guy looked like he could use a break. So he picked him up."

"Why did he call?"

"Said the guy acted suspicious, could tell that he was hiding something. Then he saw the news article on TV. That's when he recognized it was Olsen. He didn't want to see more kids hurt."

"A responsible citizen."

"Also heard there was a reward."

"And considerate."

A message flashed on my cell. *Missed call.* Coverage was bad as usual. Nothing got through with everything going straight to voicemail. I'd have to wait until returning to Mariposa to retrieve the message.

After a few twists and turns, we eventually pulled down a dark road overlooking the residence, a dull illumination coming from the kitchen window. Smoke billowed from the fireplace chimney. The house was secluded deep in thick trees, miles from anyone else. My senses said I had been here before.

Using only his running lights, Bellows pulled high on the ridge and to the right, to observe from a distance. Seeing his lights go out, everyone followed suit. The cars went quiet, crawling to a stop. The wind gently rocked our vehicle.

Bellows was finally able get through on his cell. A deputy at the station was trying to wake the judge, authorize a verbal search warrant.

"Are we good?" Bellows asked into the receiver. There was a moment of muffled response, before he again spoke. "Okay. Call me when you get the approval." He shoved the phone into his jacket. "They're still trying to get a stenographer on the line with the judge to document the call. Another thirty minutes."

Hoskin's voice broke over Bellow's radio. "What's your plan?"

"A verbal warrant is being obtained," I responded.

As we waited, everyone began gearing up, sliding on their level IIIA ballistic vests, low-slung holster, additional magazines, handcuffs, an ASP collapsible steel baton. Geonetta prepped her MP-5, 10 mm submachine gun while Hoskin removed the Remington 870, 12-gauge shotgun from the overhead rack. They covered their vests with the traditional dark blue windbreaker, "FBI" in large yellow letters displayed prominently on the back. Whoever was inside, it was important they knew who we were. I was too familiar with rural areas concealing marijuana farms, raids on houses by fake law enforcement officers whose only purpose was to do a *drug rip*. This gave reason for the groundkeepers to shoot first and ask questions never. Clear identifiers showing us as law enforcement and placed everyone in the house on notice: we were not there to steal their drugs.

Hoskin stood next to Bellows' Tahoe as he racked the action of the shotgun, chambering a round before topping off the tube.

My cell phone vibrated again displaying the notice, *Missed 2 Messages/ Voice Mail*. I waved the phone above my head, and was able to retrieve the last message sent.

"It's me. Warren. I've been calling you for an hour! He's here! He's here at my ex's house. I came by to pick up Raley and I find him here. Call me. I want him out and away from my kids!"

I sat up, gave the area a hard look, now realizing where I was. "We can't hit the house," I said. "That's Warren's ex-wife's. He's in there with Bobby Rae."

Bellows shook his head. "I can't let him get away."

"I agree, but we need to protect Warren."

Bellows peered through his night vision goggles. "Well, whatever you want to do, it may not matter. We got people coming out."

Bellows steadied the binoculars through the rain-soaked windshield, relayed what he was seeing. Bobby Rae had stepped out from the cabin door.

"And here comes Warren," Bellows continued. "Jack, you need to make a decision."

I stared through the windshield as the rain began falling in splashes. Objects appeared to blur until I started seeing star-crossed flashes on the misty glass. A puff of smoke exploded from the back of Warren's car.

"They're in and moving. What do you want to do?"

I knew I couldn't let Bobby Rae leave. A fuzzy sight of Warren's car departing the driveway. It wouldn't take much time before they were long gone.

"Take him."

In unison, our engines cranked over and roared to life, catapulting our caravan down the muddy road. We tailed each other through the narrow path, bumpers nearly touching, headlights searching for Warren's vehicle, a tan 1995 Ford Taurus. Bellows swerved across a large patch of gravel, causing his SUV to slide. The vehicle behind fish-tailed, jerked back in line then straightened. Any second, we would come head-to-head with Warren, a collision most likely unavoidable. Bellows blindly approached a sharp right hand turn at high speed. I blocked myself against the front dash with a stiff arm. Covering his brakes, he performed a controlled skid around the turn, hoping if Warren was there, he would have time to swerve away. But luck was against us. Headlights blaring on high, Warren's car suddenly appeared out of control, swerving to the right, his bald tires floating above the mud and ice that spotted the trail. Bellows slammed on his brakes and the back end of his Tahoe broke loose, drifting to the front. Geonetta braced herself against the back of my seat using the stock of her MP-5 to stop her from flying through the windshield.

Bellows' rear lights glowed red, his foot pressing the brake pedal nearly through the floor. The two cars behind us followed in our path of uncontrollable skidding, sliding sideways, spraying mud like a rooster's tail. The Tahoe slid to a stop but not before crunching Warren's front driver's side panel. Glass fragments scattered through the air, flying in every direction like shiny nail as the rain began to pound heavier from the cold sky.

Bellows' large body lurched forward from the impact, held back only by his shoulder restraint. Before all the vehicles could stop, Warren's passenger door flew wide and Bobby Rae leaped out, running back toward the house. I threw open my door and rolled out, drew my Glock, steadied by my flashlight, hunting for Bobby Rae in a sea of black. I sprinted down the hill, knowing if Bobby Rae cleared the trail, he would be gone forever. I could hear Geonetta running close behind, the strap of her MP-5 clattering against the metal frame. Hoskin took up the rear, clearing the trees and bushes that lined the road in case Bobby Rae was hiding along the way, setting a trap.

We moved quickly down the hillside, approached the driveway of the house below. I ran to the left side of the garage, pointing my flashlight downward as not to give away my position then, sidestepped around the corner, leading with my pistol held at eye level, concealed in the dark. I painted the side of the house with a burst of light, catching a figure skidding into the backyard. Geonetta, with her MP-5 covering forward, shuffled behind me as I cleared the way ahead. Turning the corner, I saw Bobby Rae running down the back slope into a large patch of Manzanita bush. Geonetta beaded Bobby Rae with a small red dot from her Aim-Point infrared laser. The beam bounced on and off her target as she fought to steady her aim. I shouted at Bobby Rae to halt, knowing I didn't have the ability to close the distance before he could reach the woods. He heard my command, looked over his shoulders before tripping on a stack of dead branches at the bottom of the hill.

"FBI! Hold it right there, Bobby Rae!"

From the corner of my eye, I spotted Geonetta's finger slide onto her trigger, a pound short of double-tapping two 165 grain hydra-shock hollow point bullets down a path to Bobby Rae's chest.

Bobby Rae struggled to his feet, stumbled twice, trying to maintain his balance on the uneven terrain. Spit flew from his mouth. "What the fuck do you want with me?"

I held out a hand trying to de-escalate the situation and stop him from making a bad decision. I needed him alive. "I just want to talk."

"I don't have anything to say."

He went low, like a sprinter in his block. I could see he was preparing to make a run for it.

"Give me a chance to convince you otherwise."

Bobby Rae rose, slowly, breaths heavy, a fog masking his face every time he exhaled. "Not a chance."

"You don't mean that," I said, moving forward, trying to close the gap.

Bobby Rae scanned the expanse between him and the woods. It was short. If he made it, he would be swallowed up. With a look of boldness, Bobby Rae gave a wide-eye stare then turned back at his escape route.

I lowered my pistol, lifted both hands away from my side. "I can't outrun you from here."

Bobby Rae started to find balance and grinned, stepping backward.

"But that weapon can," I shouted, pointing at Geonetta and her MP-5. "I doubt you can run faster than 1300 feet per second."

On cue, Geonetta zeroed the deadly red laser dot on Bobby Rae's forehead. The bright glow of the beam struck him in the face and he flinched.

Bobby Rae contemplated his options. Could he clear twenty-five yards to freedom before being hit by a speeding bullet? Is she that good? Even though he was full of bravado, fueled by the alcohol in his veins, running would only result in a large gaping hole through his head. His shoulder fell slack, and he mouthed an exasperated response. *"Fuck!"*

BELLOWS BENT OVER WARREN'S FRONT FENDER, examining the damage sustained in the crash, the rain pouring buckets. "I guess it could have been worse." Water drizzled off the brim of his Stetson.

We huddled, waiting as deputies secured Bobby Rae in the back of their cruiser.

"Has anybody checked the house for his personal belongings?" I said.

"One of the officers spoke with Warren's ex." Bellows shook his head. "Didn't appear to be anything there."

Strange. The truck driver mentioned a large duffle bag, said he was being protective. "Check again," I ordered.

Bellows nodded, flagged over an officer and sent him back to the house.

"Let's keep him and Warren separated," I said. "Make Bobby Rae think Warren just got caught up in this."

"All set, Jack. I got Warren cuffed and strapped in the back seat of Hoskin's car. Warren's playing along. He's okay, just a knot on his head from his steering wheel."

The two deputies placed Bobby Rae in the back of their cruiser, cuffed, wet and cold. He was filthy, his jeans embedded with soot, grit and dirt from hiding in the woods. Someone took pity on him and tossed a blanket over his shoulders. His shirt was torn, his arms and chest tattered in bloody cuts and scrapes from being dragged through the Manzanita brush. The sweat on his face had mixed with the grime and rain that emulsified into a cakey-film.

The rain continued to spill in sheets, flowing down the steep dirt edge, creating its own inlets and rivers. Our headlamps illuminated the downpour, exhaust billowing from tail pipes. We had returned to our cars knowing Warren was safe, Bobby Rae now under our control. One by one, we maneuvered onto the main road, heading back to the sheriff's station in anticipation of an interview. I was anxious to hear what Bobby Rae had to say.

CHAPTER 28

House of Warren's ex, Post Arrest of Bobby Rae

Josh Kramer

WARREN'S TWO YOUNGER CHILDREN, JOSH AND Amelia, stood by the front door, watching as their father and his friend were handcuffed and placed into the backseat of the patrol cars. Their mother ran into the house after being confronted by a deputy—twice—asking a bunch of question she couldn't answer. After telling them there was nothing here for them to take, she shut herself in the bedroom.

As the vehicles finally departed, Amelia dashed out the front door, heading down a dark road to the west. Dressed in a pink sweatshirt and jeans, she had shoved her feet into her black rubber boots and grabbed a small umbrella, knowing she would be running in the cold rain and icy-snow as soon as the police left.

"Squeak, get back here! Squeak! Mom's gonna be furious with you!" Josh screamed into the night air but certain it was useless. He knew where Amelia was going but dared not tell anyone, for it would potentially ruin their secret. His to keep. Every child has secrets from their parents and this one was Josh's and Amelia's. He slowly closed the door, reluctant to take his eyes off the direction she'd gone. Knowing she would be back soon, he left the door unlocked so Amelia could return without their mother ever realizing she had left.

CHAPTER 29

STARK WHITE WALLS ENCASED THE SMALL INTERVIEW ROOM, a single metal table surrounded by four mismatched chairs in the middle. The door leading into the room had a viewing window with non-breakable glass, embedded with thin crisscrossed wires. The florescent lights above hummed.

Bobby Rae slouched in the chair, furthest from the door, handcuffed. The leg irons attached to his right ankle was tethered to a heavy eyebolt on the floor beneath the table. Outside the room, Bellows approached the entry as I stared at Bobby Rae through the small window.

Bellows handed me a fresh cup of coffee. "This should help." My hands immediately warmed.

I thought about how important this interview was. A chance to find our missing tourists and hopefully stop this string of killings. The problem was, aside from his perversion and desire for young girls, there was no direct link or hard evidence to either the murders or the Samuels. With little to go on and nothing but circumstantial evidence, this situation required finesse.

Bellows leaned in and poked his head next to mine as if we were observing a poisonous snake in a reptile house.

"Bobby Rae's been through the system all too many times to be fooled," Bellows asserted. "He's not giving up anything unless it's to his benefit."

I turned away, against the outside wall. "You may be right."

Bellows dipped his head and lowered his voice, removing an old-style blackjack from his coat pocket. "Give me five minutes alone with him. This 'ol fashion lie detector of mine usually gets results." He slapped the leather against the palm of his hand. I could tell it had enough weight to cause damage. He held back a smile. "Nothing cures a problem better than a *leather Demerol*."

"Don't you mean a wooden shampoo?"

"Nope, this is more like a prescription drug." Bellows shrugged. "There are side-affects, though."

"And that would be?"

"Swelling."

Geonetta's eyes widen, pupils went large. Then a quiet nod of agreement. I couldn't fault her. The reactive part of me wanted to turn this over to Bellows and his confession tool. But giving Bobby Rae a tune-up was an answer guided by raw emotions, I confessed. There was no compassion in me for a person who found pleasure in harming others but getting what I needed didn't mean becoming one of those that I despised.

Besides, I knew Bobby Rae had secrets and more than likely, even a beating wouldn't get him to confess. Hell, he'd probably enjoy it. Having little to work with, I needed to rely on my intuitions and a great deal of finesse laced in bullshit.

"Thanks for the offer," I said. "But let's try my way first."

Bellow gave a look of indifference.

The three of us entered the interview room. We all jockeyed for chairs but I wanted to be the one in his line of sight. Bobby Rae refused to look up, staring down at the table, grunting and mumbling under his breath.

"I'll cut right to the chase," I said without any introduction. "I have evidence showing your involvement in the kidnapping of two tourists, Maria and Judy Samuels." I waited for his reaction. There wasn't one.

"This is what I think: I think they're still alive."

I waited for any indication I was correct.

Still nothing.

"Whatever the reason why you took them, it's more important we get them back. If you know their whereabouts, saving them could help save you."

Bobby Rae looked up, eyes like black stones, sunk deep in their sockets. His hair swayed like seaweed adrift. "Wish I can help you, Chief." He bent forward, twisted his neck and raised his left eyebrow, slid his chained hands across the table. "Is that why you're chasing me?"

His tone was condescending. My body tensed. Bobby Rae was drawing a line and dared me to cross it.

"You think I had something to do with those missing tourists?" His
pupils expanded, looking endlessly dark. His voice boasted a confident
tone.

I countered by leaning inward, hands folded in front, meeting him in
the middle. "Word has it you got an affinity for young girls."

Bobby Rae slouched low in his chair rubbing an invisible spot on the
table but was taking in every word.

That's what predators do.

"You're a survivor, Bobby Rae, I can see it."

A nod of understanding.

"Let me help you. Giving me back the Samuels will go a long way."

He took a moment to absorb the words, grabbed at the corner of the
table with his left hand, polishing the shiny metal edge with his thumb as
the chain on his ankle clattered below the table. He lifted a hand, made a
surrendering gesture. "Wish I could help."

Don't let him end the conversation.

"You worked at the Lodge under your mother's maiden name. Was
this to hide the fact you are a registered sex offender?"

He held back a grin. "People are so judgmental. No one wants to give
a man a break."

"The job gave you access to the master keys. That gave you access to all
the rooms. Access to *their* room. Robbery's one thing. Murder's another."

He sat still, unbothered by the accusation.

"I can place you in their room."

That was true.

"And I was able to lift blood and skin DNA from your car."

That was half true.

"Their blood."

That was a lie.

Bobby Rae didn't respond.

"I don't believe you meant for things to go bad. It just did, right?
Help me rescue them and I'll help you find your way out of this predica-
ment." I pulled the Bible from my briefcase and placed it on the table. It
was sealed in a clear plastic bag and marked "*Evidence—Hold for Latent
Prints.*" I was betting he wouldn't remember where he left it. It was a gam-
ble that could backfire, revealing Warren's cooperation, so I lied again. "I
found it at your trailer . . . on the floor. My guess is you dropped it before

you could get it out. I also have your prints all over the Samuel's room."
I paused to see his reaction. "People say you have been known to be violent. Even capable of killing."

Bobby Rae held still, began to speak slow and methodically. "I changed my name . . . to get the job. I needed the work. Yes, I used to be violent, but I'm not any more. I found God."

Big grin.

"And yes, I took that Bible, but not from the room. I took it from the storage closet. For my mother."

He straightened and looked away like he was uncomfortable talking about her.

"She loves Bibles. As for my prints, I'm sure they're in the room. I'm the maintenance man. My prints are everywhere in that lodge."

I pushed. "What about that room of yours, the one with the cut-out pictures of kids and all those sex toys. All those photographs. Photos of minors. That's a bad look."

"My personal life is not your business."

"It is when minors are involved. That's a federal crime."

"Who says they're minors?" A slight shrug. "They're just young."

Geonetta interrupted, "How young?"

Bobby Rae's eyes widened then he softly laughed at the three of us. "Go ask them yourself."

He was taunting us like a bully on a playground. I tightened my fist into a ball, gently rapping my knuckles on the edge of the table, thinking about Bellows' offer.

"Experts will attest to the girls in your photos as being minors. That'll get you fifteen year, minimum."

Bobby Rae folded his arms across his chest. Nervously, he started twisting his long, greasy hair around his fingers. He grabbed his left leg and squeezed it tight, stilling a nervous twitch. He was holding back something, but he wasn't going to relent. With each passing minute, I felt the Samuels slipping through our grasp.

I forced myself to appear calm, but inside I was anxious, getting enraged. "If the Samuels are alive, I can help you explain what happened, that it wasn't your intent to cause them harm. But if they die before we can do anything, you're looking at capital punishment."

Bobby Rae closed his eyes and gave a half-hearted shrug.

I placed my hands on the table, pressed them hard and flat. "Where were you the night the Samuels went missing?"

Again he shrugged. "Can't seem to remember."

"Did you work that day?"

"Can't remember."

"Drive anywhere memorable?"

"Can't remember."

"See anyone?"

"Can't remember."

"Kill anyone?"

Quiet, then a smile.

I stuck out a hand, trying to hold back my anger. "Wait, let me guess. *Can't remember.*"

Bobby Rae ran his hands back and forth along the edge of the table, rocked his chair back on two legs. His stare was distant, his mind disbursed into a lost thought.

He took a few moments, drew in a deep breath and exhaled a long, hushed sigh as he sat up straight. With both hands, he glided his fingers through his hair, tugged his disheveled shirt smooth then folded both hands in front. The chain on his ankle swayed and rattled between his legs and the wall, a reminder he was still secured to the massive bolt in the floor. He gazed up. "I'll bet you, more than likely, they drove off a cliff, like a bad accident." He shifted his focus to Bellows. "Don't you think, detective?" All four legs of his chair touched ground. "Folks not familiar with the park should be more careful."

Bellows' face went cold, his expression clearly readable.

"Maybe the husband is a wife beater," Bobby Rae continued in an animated tone, "and she just wanted to get away and hide. It's not that uncommon."

I pulled close, inches from his face, getting into his personal zone of comfort. "You don't want to find out what electricity strapped around your head and body feels like. It's time to cooperate because you're not going to get another chance."

He smirked. "Me working at the lodge is far short of proving murder."

"Who said I'm accusing you of murder?" Then I add, "Yet."

"Unless you charge me, you can't hold me forever, Chief. And you got nothing."

"Maybe I should ask your ex-wife what she thinks," I said.

Bobby Rae became edgy.

I hit a nerve.

He looked irritated, more fidgeting in his seat. The chains from his restraints followed his every move as they rattled and clanked louder against the table, agitating him even more.

"Now that wasn't nice, Chief. I'm starting to think I really don't like you." His teeth grinded, and his jaw went taught. "The detective here has been dogging me for a long time, like a man who likes kicking a lost mutt. Well, I'm still around and I don't plan on leaving."

"It's not a game, Bobby Rae."

"You're wrong," he shot back. "It's just like a game." He dropped his stare to the ground. "I suggest you play."

Bellows muttered, "You are one genuine 24-karat asshole."

My voice steadied, caught his eyes as he looked up. "No game. And I'm holding you until we find the Samuels." I reached into my briefcase and pulled out the photos of our two victims taken from the hotel room, plus the one I received of Kate Jennings. I slid the pictures in front of him, hoping to dredge up some hidden pocket of sympathy.

"Look at the photos, Bobby Rae. We've got kids here. They don't belong in your game. I'm not asking for a confession. I'm asking for your help in finding them, so I can bring them home alive. It's your way out of this mess."

Saying nothing, he picked up the photos, shuffled through them, spending little time on any one in particular, his eyes dull with indifference, void of any humanity. "It's really a game, Agent Paris. There's a winner and a loser. And I don't play to lose."

"Today, you do," I said. "You're under arrest for the production of child pornography." I walked around the table and pointed at Bellows. "And he's holding you for failing to properly register as a sex offender." I jabbed a finger into his bony chest until I could hear the contact.

"If you had anything to do with those missing tourists and you do nothing to help save them, you'll spent the rest of your miserable existence locked in a concrete box. That's if they don't strap you to a chair and end it."

"You've got nothing," he replied, doubling down, "and sooner or later, I'll walk out of this place. Let's face it Chief, you're not playing *this game* too good, and because of that, you're jeopardizing the lives of your tourists. That's if they're not already dead."

I felt my skin crawl. "What do you want?"

"What do I want?" The muscles in his jaw relaxed and tightened, back and forth. "There are days when the law comes down hard, puts a hurt on you." He pointed his chin at Bellows. "Because they can." His eyes went sharp, pupils pinpoint. "Today, it's your day to hurt." He kicked out a leg, the chain on his ankle snapped hard against the wall. He looked away. "Like I said, Chief, you kick a dog enough times, it has no choice but to bite back."

He stopped talking and I knew there wasn't anything else I could do to keep the conversation going. Bellows called in his deputies, ordered them to take the prisoner back to the holding tank.

Everyone stood. I turned and ripped the photographs from Bobby Rae's hands.

He reached out, touched my arm. "Time's running out," he said, then leaned close and whispered, "You may have just killed your tourists."

CHAPTER 30

THE FIRST ROUND FAILED.

It was a long shot getting Bobby Rae to confess, to give up the Samuels without solid evidence. But I had to try. I was angry and frustrated. Mostly anxious. Worse, I let him get under my skin. I needed more to put the squeeze on my primary suspect.

Geonetta crossed the parking lot from the holding cell, back to the sheriff's station. I followed. We entered the room where Hoskin and his crew were, preparing their reports on today's events.

"How's Warren?" I asked.

Hoskin approached with a stack of reports under his arm, fighting to adjust his glasses. "A little shaken but I think he's okay. He called his ex-wife and told her that he was detained because of Bobby Rae but that the police were going to let him go. I offered to give him a ride but he said he didn't want the police to show up at her house again. Said it would be too much for the kids."

"Where is he now?"

"In the back. Hal's office."

Hoskin gave me a look that held my attention.

"I got some interesting news from the lab," he said. He removed an electronic communication report known as a "bureau EC" from a folder and laid it down on the conference table. Atop the maps and drawings, Hoskin placed the photographs of the notes taken from the bodies of our murdered girls. Each one enlarged and appearing next to a ruler for size comparison. "The first note shows two sharp edges with two rough or torn edges, indicating it was taken from the left corner of a sheet of paper. The next one shows three rough edges, the same with the third. Lab concludes they all came from the same sheet of paper."

"Do they know who manufactured the paper? Points of sale?"

Asking a lot, but I needed a break.

His shoulders dropped. "There's a lot of similar paper out there."

So much for my break.

"It's not necessarily the paper as much as the torn edges," Hoskin went on to say. "Find the pad and we may find a match. That'll identify your killer."

"How about paper at Olsen's place?"

Hoskin shook his head. "Nothing that matched." He pointed at a file folder sticking out of his portfolio, tapped it like it meant something. "Then there's the indented writing."

He pulled photos from within and laid them out. Using side lighting to illuminate the shadowed lines and indentations, faint but clear: letters, words.

"*Dragon Tattoo* and *pretty thing*," I read it out loud.

Hoskin pointed at the edge of the first note. "There's a number before the tear but they can't tell if it's a 5 or a 9."

Bellows ran a finger over the letters, said he was familiar with The Dragon Tattoo, a place in Tuolumne. "Same place shown on the back of those business cards found in Bobby Rae's Impala."

He described it as nothing short of a dive.

"Drugs and hookers. I'm guessing it's where he hunts for his victims."

Made sense.

"I'll phone Sergeant Malloy," Bellows added. "See if he has any sources inside the parlor. Maybe we'll get lucky."

Bellows went off to place the call so I thought I'd check in on how Warren was holding up. I found him standing near Bellow's desk, quietly staring at the wall papered with pictures of our three murdered victims. He was fixated on the school portraits, slowly turning his gaze toward the graphic crime scene photos, ending with the autopsy pics. It was as if he was reading a story.

"They're all so young," Warren said.

Bellows appeared at the door, cellphone in hand. "You shouldn't be in here."

Warren looked hurt, but kept his feelings to himself.

I stepped up next to Warren. "I don't want to see another person on that board."

His eyes grew large. "Look, I've done everything you've asked, but I can't help but think that if Bobby Rae finds out I've been helping you, he'll kill me." He faltered in his thought, fought to find the right words. "Look, I don't know if you're understanding me but just so we're clear; I'm scared as hell." He let out a deep sigh, long until his lungs went empty. "Not just for me," he added, "but for my wife and kids." I saw his jaw clench and he turned away. "What the hell was I thinking, coming here." He turned back to me, eyes fixated. "He killed those girls . . . and those tourists, didn't he?"

"I'm hoping the Samuels are still alive." I got up close to Warren, forcing him to take a step back. Then I pressed. "I need you to start thinking of every place Bobby Rae may have talked about or stayed. I need to know who his friends are and where they live. I need to know everything about him before it's too late."

I needed him to dig, find answers, knowing his help could get him killed.

Warren turned his eyes downward as if he had already failed at the challenge. "I can't."

"You will."

"And if I don't?"

"If you don't, I may have no choice but to compel you to testify."

Warren's mouth fell wide open as he choked on a deep breath.

"You can't! I won't! That wasn't part of the deal." He jabbed a finger forward, his voice raised to near desperation. "He'll kill my family."

"Then help me. Get me answers."

His eyes flooded in desperation as he barked back his response. "You can't bring yourself to admit that it may already be too late."

Even Warren knew too much time had passed. It was unrealistic to think otherwise.

I ran a hand through my hair and felt the tension in my skull but I wasn't going to show that to Warren. "I won't give up."

We collapsed into chairs on opposite ends of the room, each feeling caught in a position with few options and little time.

"What are you going to do with him?" Warren meant Bobby Rae.

"We're going to keep him locked up as long as we can. I can't risk letting him out." I leaned forward, hands clasped together. "If he's our killer, the abductions will stop. If not, we'll soon know."

"You're not so sure yourself, are you?" His voice reduced to a whisper. "It's inevitable, isn't it? He's going to get out, hunt me down, and kill me."

CHAPTER 31

Tuesday February 25th – 7:12 p.m.

I CALLED MICHAEL.

It's rare that I do. I never liked bothering him, whether at work or at school. Today I needed to hear his voice.

The phone rang three times before Michael picked up. I could hear a television in the background.

"Hey," I said. "What're you up to?"

"Nothing, just watching a movie."

"You want me to call you later?"

Michael voice cracked a bit. "No, it's fine. What's up?"

I stalled. I hadn't thought of what to say, make it halfway interesting. How could I tell him I just wanted to hear his voice? Not like me to be unprepared, but in the case of Michael I never seem to get it right. Not like his mother. She was the queen of conversation—made the kids feel engaged, important. "Nothing much," I said. "Just had a moment to say, hey."

"That's cool," he said.

There was a long pause. "What are you working on?"

I felt a moment of hesitation—all those years, talking about murderers and death to Emily and how it affected her. Now, it was as if the burden was being inherited. That was the last thing they needed; being drawn into the dark side of my world. So I hedged the truth. Hell, I lied. "Nothing out of the ordinary, someone lost in the woods."

"The news is reporting about a series of murders in Yosemite." He knew I wasn't being honest and he was calling me on it. "They also mentioned missing tourists too."

That last sentence sounded more like a question.

"Is that what you're working on?"

"What are you, the news media?"

"Maybe I should be."

We both laughed.

Michael's a bright kid, lots of street smarts. Even at an early age, there wasn't a puzzle or problem he couldn't unearth the answers to. More importantly, he found questions no one else thought to ask. That's the difference between a good investigator and a great one. Michael would have been the latter. But secretly, I never wished for him to take on this life. After Emily died, I was even more sure of it.

"What's happening in your world?" I asked, turning the conversation back to him.

"Work sucks."

"Boy, don't I know it."

Again, we both laughed.

Another voice came through the phone, in the background. A woman asking if he wanted anything to drink, the refrigerator door being pulled open. I heard glass bottles clink. He had a guest over and I was interrupting.

"I should go," I said. "Don't want to cramp your style."

"Cramp my what?"

"It's an old expression." I chuckled. "Go. Spend time with your friend."

Michael pretended he didn't hear my insistence. "Tell me about the case? Are you making progress?"

"I'm trying," I said. I gave him a quick summary, kept out the dark parts. He listened, asked a few questions—good ones—knew I was downplaying the severity. He knew better. I could tell though, he too, just wanted to talk.

We rambled a bit longer about the case, school, work, until there wasn't much else to add. "Justine called," he said, changing the subject. "She's stressing over her class schedule." Justine just started her sophomore year at the University of Washington. "She's worried about you."

That hurt.

After Emily's death, Justine took time off to stay with me but returned to school following winter break.

"You tell her to hang in there," I said.

"And you do the same," Michael replied. "Remember the mantra you always tell us to live by: *Keep the living, living and the memories of those that are not, alive.*"

I felt my breath catch deep in my chest. My son, the adult in the room. "Thanks for the reminder."

We both knew there was nothing else to say. So, we said our good-byes, and I told him I loved him—something I didn't do enough of when he was younger.

I looked over at the television. It was old and boxy, sound turned down low. Some black and white movie from the '40s or '50s was on, the only distraction in the room. I stared blankly at it; my mind drifted between Michael, Justine, the case, until they all blurred. I closed my eyes, resting my head against the headboard.

Then the hammer of three thumps at my door. I got up, peered through the peep-hole and saw a fish-eye view of Geonetta standing in her winter coat, hoisting a pizza box in one hand, a six pack in the other. She pushed forward the beer with emphasis and grinned. I pulled the door open. A gust of cold air followed.

"Thought you might be hungry." She breezed past. "Besides, I hate eating alone." Geonetta tossed the pizza box on the bed and cracked open a beer, pushed it in front of me. "Doctor's orders."

Thirty minutes later, we had talked through the case, what we had learned, where we needed to go. Half the pizza had been eaten and the beer all gone. Geonetta slouched in the cheap hotel chair, legs resting on the end of the bed.

"You know, I can get use to this," she said. "Traveling from hotel to hotel, eating out of a carboard box . . . alone. Go to sleep, wake up, work all day and do it all over again. God, I'm becoming just like you."

I knew she was joking, but the reality of her remark stung. This was how I spent the most important time of my life, when Em was alive and kids were still young.

"You okay?" she said.

"No, I'm fine, just tired," I again lied. I made a move back to the case, my fears. "I got a bad feeling, Heather." I sat against the headboard, peeling the label from my beer bottle. "They're dead."

Keep the living, living. . . . Isn't that what Michael just told me to remember? I was having a hard time keeping the first part of the promise.

"It'd be a miracle if they weren't," I added, "after two weeks . . ."

The frigid elements, a kidnapping, either way, statically, the odds were against them. Geonetta didn't have a response that could dissuade my suspicion. She sat quietly and turned away.

"And the girl?" she asked. "Kate?"

I felt the heat in my face, my head being hammered away with a chisel. "If Bobby Rae is holding her, we just killed her."

"*We* didn't kill anyone." Geonetta tossed her empty bottle into the trashcan.

She reached over and grabbed the bottle from my hand and placed it on the nightstand, pulled up a chair and trained her eyes onto mine. "Bobby Rae was right about one thing. You're in a game whether you like it or not, Jack. And you better focus on winning. Because if you don't, he's going to get away with murder." Then with emphasis, "And he'll kill again."

The hotel phone rang. It was Bellows.

"I spoke with Malloy about The Dragon Tattoo parlor," he said. "If you're looking to get high or laid, that's your spot. The place is known for hookers, young ones."

"Is there anyone we can talk to about Bobby Rae?"

"That's why I'm calling," he said, sounding more upbeat. "Got someone who might be able to help."

I heard Bellows shuffling papers on the other end. "Candice Barton, aka Candy.

The name on the card.

"Apparently Candy used to party with the clientele that included overnight stays. Arrested several times in Tuolumne. The detectives there said she's harmless and has actually been a pretty good source of information when it comes to drug dealers and PALs. She told the detectives, drugs and fugitives ruined her business. Go figure."

More papers shuffled.

"One of his detectives remembered talking to Candy about a guy the girls were complaining about. 'Bout a year ago."

"Get a name?"

"Nope," Bellows said, trying to sound positive, "but the description fits our suspect, Olsen."

"Rumor was, this guy picked up a young girl at the Dragon and beat her up pretty bad. The girl said something about a barn off of the 49, near Vista Point, one night after they had a couple of drinks. Thinks the guy may have slipped her something. When they got to this barn, the guy started to get aggressive. She decides she wants out." Bellows paused. "He wasn't going to take no for an answer. Gave her a real bad tune up."

"Did she report it?"

"No. These girls are too afraid. Besides, half these kids still live with their parents. Telling the cops would only make it worse."

"Do we know who this girl is?"

"We do."

Long pause.

"You going to tell me?"

"Kathryn Rene Jennings. It's our girl, four."

I felt a jolt of energy. "This may be our break."

"I hope you're right because I don't want to see five."

"Get hold of the detective in Tuolumne, find Candy. Maybe she can help confirm Bobby Rae, help us find that barn."

"Already in the works."

I hung up the phone and summarized the call to Geonetta. "Hopefully, with some luck, Candy will get us our answers."

She jumped up, gathered her belongings. "I'll let you know what I find."

"Where are you going?"

"I got this," she said, holding out a stiff arm. "Look, Lawman, you talk to the boy witnesses, I'll talk to the girls."

She was right. I shouldn't be the one doing this interview. It's humiliating enough for a woman to recount an assault, let alone provide it in graphic detail, to a male investigator. Geonetta was a better fit.

"Do the interview," I acquiesced. "But I want to hear what you find out as soon as you're done."

She slipped on her jacket, holstered her weapon and grabbed her car keys before bolting out the door. I stepped outside, stood at the railing and watched her drive off. She didn't look back.

I stood there, unprotected in the winter night. The chilled wet air seemed a bit edgier than earlier. The misty air made my clothes heavy to the touch, damp and cold the longer I stood outside, but I couldn't pull myself back in. My knuckles whitened as I gripped the frosted steel railing even tighter, the sting of the cold penetrating my hands, like razor-blades slitting every finger. Even through the pain, I wanted to stand and wait—no matter how long it took—for Geonetta to return. With good news. Good news would be great.

CHAPTER 32

Tuesday February 25th – 8:07 p.m.

Heather Geonetta

B ELLOWS CALLED.
He told Geonetta where to meet Sergeant Malloy; said Candy was willing to meet.

She pulled over at the darkened street corner where Malloy would be waiting, caught sight of him standing next to his SUV. Gingerly, she stepped out of her car, trying not to draw attention from the late-night street crawlers. The frigid wind whipped at her clothes as she quickstepped toward Malloy. She pulled up the collar on her wool winter jacket and tucked her hands under her arms to stave off a chill.

Malloy smiled and took her hand when offered, holding it just a little too long, oblivious she was shivering.

"Candy is in the parlor," he said.

Malloy pointed down a dark street toward a building with the lights still burning bright. "Place is owned by an ex-con by the name of Royce Shelby, tattoo extraordinaire. He's old and harmless now, call him Poppy. Patrons gather at his shop to drink, socialize, whatever."

Geonetta glanced over, nodded.

"Basically, it's a pick up joint."

She checked her watch, feeling a bit anxious to get started.

"She'll be here," Malloy said. "Better than talking in the parlor. Less headaches."

"I brought a photograph of Bobby Rae," Geonetta said. "I'm hoping she can tell us something about him we don't know."

"Well here's your chance." Malloy jutted his chin in the direction of The Dragon.

The street glistened like an oil spill as the light streaming from the lampposts reflected off the icy blacktop. Candy wore a puffy pink parka that made her look like a female version of the Michelin man. She was smoking one of those thin cigars, advancing in high heels. The smoke trailed behind her, dissipating as it drifted in a light breeze. As if they were old friends, she gave Malloy a bear hug, smiling.

"Hey there, Malloy," she said. Then she looked over at Geonetta, sizing her up. "Who's the girl?"

Malloy stepped to one side and motioned with an open hand. "Candy, Special Agent Heather Geonetta."

Candy looked at Geonetta and, except for a slight grimace, barely acknowledged her. "You gonna invite me into your cop car or what? You know it's cold out here." She threw a finger toward Geonetta. "Look at her, she's turning blue."

Malloy again smiled, then opened the back door of his Jeep Cherokee, waved them inside. Climbing in, Candy held onto her skirt as it hiked up high on her backside. Geonetta slid in beside her, Malloy to the front.

He turned around with his right arm over the backrest. "Thanks for coming out to meet with us, Candy. Means a lot." Malloy was pleasant, especially since she was cooperative and willing to meet.

"Agent Geonetta is with the FBI. She has some questions about the assault against that girl, Kate, you had mentioned to my officers."

Candy blew out a high-pitched whistle. "That was a while ago. A real tragedy," she said.

"I wanted to hear the story from you," Geonetta interjected. "Maybe there was something left out. It could be helpful."

"You know, I do what I can to take care of the girls that come around here." Candy made a fist and pumped it twice. "Anyone tries to hurt them, I let Royce know and he'll get some of his friends to fix the situation."

Geonetta softly smiled. "What do you remember about Kate?"

Candy flicked the ash from the tip of her cigar through a crack in the window and lowered her eyes like just the thought of what happened brought her pain. "Just ugly," she said. "When I was young, there were a lot of freaks I got sideways with, but when she told me about this guy, it just made me sick."

Candy began describing what had transpired that night a year ago in front of The Dragon. She told it as if it happened yesterday:

"It was summer," she started out saying. "The Dragon had always been a magnet for the lost. I think that's what attracted her there. One night, the place was packed with bikers who had come to town, looking for a place to get drunk and raise hell."

Candy's eyes grew distant, like she was reliving the conversation. There was fear in her voice.

"I believe Kate was just turned sixteen." She looked down and her face fell into the shadows. "She was a pretty girl."

Geonetta put down her notepad because somehow she knew, listening was going to be the best way to understand what really happened.

"She told me she wasn't there too long when she met him."

Geonetta knew who Candy was referring to. Candy shook her head in disgust just thinking about him.

"He approached her, bought her a drink, and struck up a conversation. Real smooth like," she adds. "Like a predator."

"Then what happened?"

"She was charmed," Candy said. "From that moment on, he had her in his spell. Said they spent the entire night talking until the placed closed. That's when he took her."

"Where?"

Candy's face went dark and Geonetta knew the story was going to turn dark. "By that time, Kate was pretty liquored up and the guy knew it. He coaxed her into his car, said he would take her home. But that's not what happened. He took her to the barn."

The barn.

Geonetta leaned forward. "Did she say where the barn was at?"

Candy shook her head. "Nah, her head was in such a fog by then."

"Please," Geonetta said. "Go on."

"All she remembers is the drive was long. Up hills and dirt roads. She did say she remembered the barn was red. And old. That when they went inside, it was dark and musty smelling."

"Anything else about the place?"

"She remembered smelling gas fumes. Like a power generator running."

So, the barn must be somewhere that doesn't have access to power, Geonetta thought. Somewhere rural.

"She said they sat on his bed and talked for a moment." Candy's lower lips started to quiver and her voice shuddered through short breaths. "That's when he took her, held her down so she couldn't move, couldn't leave."

Candy didn't have to described any more. It was more than enough to fill their imaginations.

"She tried not to anger him," she said, "but he was getting rough, causing her pain, to the point she had no choice but to fight him off."

Geonetta and Malloy continued to remain silent.

"She punched and kicked and scratched. . . ." Her voice grew painfully heavy, her face filled with disgust and defeat. ". . . but he was just too strong. She told him she wanted to go home."

Candy looked away so we couldn't see the tears well up in her eyes. "That fucking monster took away her innocence and scarred her for life."

CHAPTER 33

Tuesday February 25th – 8:42 p.m.

Heather Geonetta

WHEN GEONETTA FINALLY PICKED UP HER NOTE BOOK, she noticed her hands were shaking. She folded them together and squeezed, trying to steady her nerves. She took in a lung full of air and forced herself to focus because what she just heard could be crucial in confirming who their suspect is. Geonetta returned to her notes to make sure she had every detail right.

After regaining her composure, Candy finished her recollection of that evening.

"It took a week before she told me what happened. Poor girl was broken, head-to-toe. She told her parents she fell in a ravine while walking home late at night. I took her to the clinic to get checked out. Thank God she didn't get some disease or, worse, pregnant. I can only imagine how many other girls he'd done this to."

"Why didn't anyone—"

Candy cut Geonetta in mid-sentence. "Tell the police? Who's gonna believe a sixteen-year-old who's labeled a runway?" She looked over at Malloy, who turned away leaning back into the darkness of the interior cabin, silent.

"Did you ever learn the man's name?" Geonetta asked.

"Kate told me his name was Rob or Bob. I'd seen the guy at The Dragon before. Loud talker. He liked the young ones. What a jerk. Haven't seen him since he beat that poor girl."

Geonetta removed a six-pack photo spread from her briefcase and handed it to Candy.

"Take a look at these. Recognize any of them?"

Candy studied the photos, biting at her polished nails, studying each one. She froze, tapped a finger on the picture marked number three. "That's him. That's the son-of-a-bitch."

Geonetta's head started to buzz. The ID was good. She picked Bobby Rae Olsen.

"Any idea where this guy lives, other places he frequents? Was she able to tell you how to get to the barn?" Geonetta wasn't interested in where Olsen was now; she already knew. She wanted to know where it all happened, where he might be holding the other victims.

Candy shook her head as she lit up another smoke. "Don't know anything about the guy. I just knew him from the tattoo shop. No other details about where he took her. She was too out of it to remember where it was."

"Check around if you would, please," Geonetta said. "Whatever you can find out could make a difference."

"I'll do what I can," Candy responded with a spark of enthusiasm.

Geonetta handed over her business card and Candy slid it in a glossy green handbag.

"I'll drive her back," Malloy said.

Geonetta shook Malloy's hand and returned to her own car, the photo-spread and notes clutched tightly in her hands. Exhilarated at what she had learned, Geonetta retrieved her cell phone and punched in the number to the motel. Paris would want to hear her story. Good news can never travel fast enough.

She looked at the cell's screen.

No signal.

Geonetta waved the phone above her head, hoping it would magically connect. After a few orbits, she gave in, tossing the phone onto the empty passenger seat. It was late and, besides, Paris needed to rest, re-energize. As much as she wanted to share the news, it would have to wait until the morning.

CHAPTER 34

Tuesday February 25ᵗʰ – 7:45 p.m.

Warren Kramer

WARREN KRAMER STOOD AT THE EDGE of the stairwell that led to a row of businesses in the middle of downtown Sonoma. The corner lamppost flickered in unison with pulsating bursts of cold wind that sprinted down the dark alley behind him. He pulled back a sleeve, peeked at his watch and noted the time. He then wrapped his arms tight around himself to fight a shiver.

Arrangements had been made. A meet-and-greet in five minutes with someone who had information about Bobby Rae. Earlier, Warren made several phone calls, spoke to a person, who led to another, which led him here. He did as Agent Paris ordered: identify Bobby Rae associates and their whereabouts. He fought off his fear of retaliation if it were discovered he was cooperating with law enforcement. But his success would help Agent Paris find his missing tourists and hopefully, keep Bobby Rae behind bars, forever.

He was set to meet a guy by the name of Roy Ganz, a parolee. Ganz had become fairly close to Bobby Rae, having shared a cell for a burglary conviction back in '92. The one that gave up Ganz said he could probably be of some help. Warren couldn't believe he had never heard of Ganz, especially if they were that close. Word on the street was Ganz was nothing but trouble, a real shit disturber. The notion Warren had stumbled on a righteous lead made him anxious. He took Ganz' number down, called it and the two spoke. After twenty minutes of not saying much, Warren was able to persuade him he was just trying to help his friend. Ganz didn't want to talk on the phone, said people have a habit of listening in, so Warren asked to meet and reluctantly, he agreed.

Warren's cell phone vibrated deep in his jacket pocket. He pulled it out, hit the talk button, and put it up to a frozen ear.

There was a slight delay, typical of crappy cell coverage. "It's me, Ganz."

"Where are you?"

"I'm checking to see if you're there already."

"Of course I'm here," Warren responded, frustration leaking through each word.

"Then I'll be there."

"How will I know who you are? I don't know what you look like."

There was a pause. "Don't worry. You'll know."

The call terminated. Warren shoved the phone back into his pocket.

Five minutes passed and Warren was still alone. Three dark figures approached from a distance. Warren sharpened his stare, wondering if Ganz brought back-up. They came into view, lit up by the lamppost. Two men and a woman, bundled in thick winter clothes, faces buried deep in wool scarves. They were laughing, the woman holding onto one of the men. Warren blew out a sigh and fell back against the stair railing. The three disappeared down a side street.

A second later, he felt a tug. At first, he thought he caught his jacket on the railing, then realized someone was holding him back. As he tried to pull away, Warren felt a sharp blow between the shoulder blades, dropping him to the ground. In a daze, he tried pushing himself up but a boot slammed against his left side. The pain jolted through him like a bullet, his lungs deflate of air. He flattened onto the street, rolling over a crust of jagged ice.

A robbery?

Then he saw the black outline of a face and a crowbar high above his head.

Shit!

He forced himself to the left, just in time to hear the explosive thunder of the crowbar smashing pavement. Ice chunks flew, ricocheted off his face and neck. Scrambling to stand, he slipped and stumbled, unable to gain traction. The sharp bite of the crowbar gripped his right ankle, dragging him toward his assailant.

A boot fell heavy on his back and Warren wailed in pain. This time he felt the cold steel of the crowbar pressed against his neck. The pressure increased until his face compressed against the ice-covered pavement.

"I hear you're gathering information about Bobby Rae. You shouldn't be doing that, Warren. Could get you hurt." The man bent low, close. "You don't remember me, do you?"

Asphyxiated, Warren could barely speak, choking out a response. "No . . . I . . . don't . . ."

"At the bar. You were watching us that night."

The man talking to Bobby Rae.

"It's not safe talking to cops. You could end up dead."

"Yeah, I hear ya."

His attacker pushed down harder on the crowbar. "So can your family."

Warren froze as the words soaked in. His throat tightened.

"So, can I count on you to listen?"

"Warren responded, "Yeah . . . I'm listening."

"So first, I think you should forget my name."

"Yeah . . . forgot it already."

"Good. Now, maybe a little tuning up will make the memory disappear, permanently."

Warren cringed, prepared for a few hard thumps on the head.

A voice screamed out.

"What the fuck are you doing?"

Three figures stood a ways away, facing their direction. It must have been the group that had passed earlier, backtracking. Warren glanced up at his attacker, who was momentarily distracted. It gave him the opportunity to make his move. His foot found the corner of the walkway, pushed off, propelling him to his feet. He bolted down the street, his only thought: gain distance.

"You're a dead man, Warren!"

He kept running, never turned around to see if he was being pursued. Into a dark alley, he dodged through a maze of side streets before bailing out onto a major road leading out of town. He took no chances of slowing down.

The glow of the town's lights was a half mile behind him before Warren slowed and took a breath. He leaned heavy on his knees, sucking in air through his mouth, blood dripping off the right side of his head. He pulled a handkerchief from his back pocket and wiped his forehead. He was too pumped up with fear and adrenalin to notice how much pain he was in. By tomorrow, he would be in a world of hurt. Slowly, he started to make his way home, wondering how he was going to explain this to Agent Paris.

CHAPTER 35

Tuesday February 25th – 9:05 p.m.

Warren Kramer

WARREN CLEANED UP, WASHED OFF THE DRIED BLOOD on his face, and then put on a clean shirt to cover up his bruised body. The cold chewed through his boots as he stepped from his mangled car and walked down the path toward his ex-wife's home. It was late, dark. The snow crunched under his soles, as he labored through the slush that had frozen into hardened chunks of ice.

He needed to explain to his ex, Helen, what happened that night, why the FBI came, guns drawn, arresting Bobby Rae Olsen, his friend. Helen had left numerous messages on Warren's answering machine, furious. She said he'd frightened the children, frightened her. Warren needed to think of an excuse without disclosing his cooperation with the FBI. He didn't want her involved any further.

Before reaching the door, Warren took a rag from his pocket and wiped his forehead one last time, making sure he didn't miss any blood. He was shaken from the attack but wasn't going to tell her about that. It would only make for more questions, more trouble.

Warren knocked on the door. Although he helped her build the cabin, he no longer had a key. The door cracked open with Amelia standing in her nightgown. Warren smiled; a feeling of warmth swarmed over his entire body. He reached down and ran a hand through her hair. "Hello there, Squeak. Where's your mom?"

Amelia took her father by the hand and led him into the living room. It was warm inside. Hot embers glowed that tumbled off the logs in the fireplace. Warren pulled off his ski cap, ice rained like sprinkled diamond chips from his jacket onto the area rug. Helen stood in the kitchen, watching him enter the room. Their eyes met. Warren thought how beautiful she looked. Thirty-seven years old, still slender with short brown hair, not much like when they first met. She acknowledged his presence with a slight smile.

"You look cold, Warren. Take off your jacket. Let me get you something to eat."

Her smile faded when she noticed the scrapes and bruising on his face.

"What happened to you?" She reached up and gently touched his cheek.

He pulled back but took hold of her hand, softly. "Stupid me, just fell. Ground's slippery."

"You okay? You want me to take you to the doctors?"

"No, I'll be all right."

Helen kept quiet, walked to the sink and soaked a cloth towel in warm water. She placed it on Warren's cheek and neck. He nodded his appreciation.

"I want to explain the other night. I hope it didn't scare the kids too much."

He had Helen's attention.

"I had no idea the cops were looking to arrest him."

She didn't look convinced.

He rambled on with a few more excuses, much of which made little sense; Bobby Rae mixed up in this and that, something about his work schedule at the hotel and that it could just be a big misunderstanding. He talked fast, hoping she wouldn't catch his involvement in it all. Helen listened but was overwhelmed with his rambling remarks. She glided a bowl of soup in front of him, sat down at the table and watched him eat. Warren could see the tension in her body anytime he spoke—no different than when they were married, especially near the end of their marriage.

Helen's jaw went taught, her right hand cupping her chin, elbow planted hard on the edge of the table. "Bobby Rae said you asked him to come over."

"I never told him that!"

Helen placed both hands over her eyes and rubbed.

"I'd never have him come over and endanger you and the kids."

Helen's hands fell to the table. "Endanger? What do you mean? What did he do? Is he involved in the disappearance of those missing people?"

Warren started to squirm.

"I don't know. I mean . . ." He grabbed his head with both hands, squeezed his eyes shut. "I think he may have something to do with them."

"What about that missing girl? And the others? You think he had something to do with them too?"

Warren didn't look up, kept his focus on his empty soup bowl. "He's a predator." His gaze turned toward Helen. "I don't want him around Squeak."

"He's in jail," she said. "He's not getting out." She placed a hand on Warren's arm. There was a brief silence before she sat forward, eyes wide, "Is he?"

Warren contemplated for a moment before responding. "No . . . no, I guess not. I just want it make sure you and kids are safe." But Warren was worried. As much as he wanted to trust Agent Paris, there was little evidence linking Bobby Rae to the missing tourist or the murders. And with little else, he feared Bobby Rae would be a free man in short time. Then, he would come after Warren and his family.

"Did Bobby Rae leave anything here?" Warren asked.

Helen stood up from her chair and walked into the living room. Warren followed. She pulled out a large green duffle bag from behind the couch.

"I didn't realize it was his." She took a step back, the mere sight of it repulsed her. "In all the confusion, I thought it was yours." She waved her hand in the air as if to say, *how could I be so stupid?*

"The police came back twice looking for Bobby Rae's belongings and I told them there wasn't any." Helen walked away, massaging her forehead. "What should I do with it?"

Warren reached down and pulled it next to him. He rummaged through the opening, pulled at wads of clothing and small trinkets, junk, seeing nothing Agent Paris might find interesting. "I'll get rid of it."

Helen took a deep breath, relieved.

"You better say good-bye to the kids, especially Squeak. You know how irritated she gets when you leave without her knowing."

He placed the duffle bag near the doorway before walking back to the bedrooms. Opening the first door, Josh was sitting on his bed with a set of headphones on, reading a textbook. He nodded at his dad, continued listening to his music.

Further down the hall, Warren gently rapped on another door, creaking it open. Amelia was already asleep but Raley's bed was empty. The lamp between the two beds had been left on. Amelia never liked going to sleep in the dark. Her mother turned it off after she had fallen asleep.

Warren quietly knelt by the front of the bed and stroked his daughter's fine hair. He leaned down and kissed her on the cheek. "Good night, Squeak."

Amelia didn't wake. He tucked her arms under the covers before heading out.

"I forgot to tell you Raley's at a friend's," Helen said when he came back. "I'll let her know you stopped by."

He slung the green bag over his shoulder, nodded a silent goodbye, and he stepped outside to his car. Warren trudged across the driveway in the dimly lit path, shuffling boots through the ice and snow. After he unlocked the car door, he turned in time to see his ex-wife step inside and close the door, the dead bolt banging shut. He surmised she would return to her kitchen, picking up where she left off as if he had never come.

The light was off in Amelia's room. She was safely asleep, room bathed in soft blue from the moonlight shining through the cotton curtains that hung across her windows. Like most kids, Amelia's nightstand overflowed with toys, a half-filled water glass, a crumpled juice box. If you looked at the items long enough, you could see the progression of her day. A preoccupied girl who neglected to finish one drink as she played with her toys before getting another drink because the old one was too warm. She was no different than any other child, like having secrets. Amelia had a secret. A special secret. She dared not share it with anyone except her brother, Josh. And her imaginary friends. They didn't tattle. Behind the lamp, entangled with her toys were treasures. Hunting in the deep woods, Amelia discovered things that excited her. Like her latest discovery. On her table, glistening atop the mess, lay a single, shiny golden earring. It had fairy wings in the shape of an angel.

CHAPTER 36

Tuesday February 26th – 7:38 a.m.

IT HAD BEEN THE SAME RITUAL each morning; breakfast and a briefing. We had become familiar faces at the local restaurant. Curious stares followed us as we made our way to a secluded table in the back. Geonetta would nod a morning greeting. Hoskin kept his eyes on his notes. Bellows mumbled something incoherent under his breath. I thought about the Samuel.

The sun was out, a blessing, although illusory. The temperature hovered around thirty-two degrees. It was like working in an icebox.

Geonetta and I sat at one end of the table, Hoskin and Bellows at the other. We started out with the Candy interview. Geonetta sifted through her reams of notes as she spelled out every detail. Afterward, everyone ate without comment.

"Everything points to Bobby Rae," she said breaking the silence.

Encouraging, the evidence was overwhelming, but I was still frustrated; it didn't get us any closer to finding the Samuels. As much as we were moving forward, we weren't moving fast enough. With all our effort, rescuing our missing victims was still beyond our reach.

I looked around the room, thought about the people going on with their lives, clueless of the evil just beyond these doors. A young girl walked outside, unaccompanied, maybe to meet a friend. I nearly stood and chased after her until I saw her parents follow close behind. Still, it made me uneasy.

Was I sure I had the right person? That the killings would stop?

"I reviewed the reports from the forensic examiner," Hoskin said, putting down his fork. "Based on the larvae and maggot colonies found on all our victims, they were killed fairly recently before being discovered. My guess is a day or so, not much longer. Lack of ground insects under the bodies fits in our PMI timetable. Although in this cold, I doubt there would be much activity."

As we listened to Hoskin, I watched everyone—one at a time—push away their plates. I pushed mine forward and wiped my mouth. Breakfast was over.

Hoskin continued. "Most of your victims were reported missing for a couple of weeks before being found. With what I just said, I could only conclude they had to be held captive for some period of time. Find the place and I'll bet we'll find items belonging to our victims."

"Trophies," Geonetta added.

"Trophies are big ticket items with abductors," Hoskin agreed. "Constant reminders of their conquests. Allows them to relive the moment over and over."

"What about DNA?" Bellows asked.

Hoskin shook his head, looking embarrassed as if any indication of bad news was his fault. "Not good. It was apparent there was sexual activity but we found no semen or blood. Dilution, degradation over time, could have been a number of reasons."

"My money is still on Olsen," Bellows said.

"Something's still bugging me," I said, "We got these brutal murders and people disappearing and yet, at all the crime scenes, we have little evidence left behind."

Bellows leaned in. "What'd you saying?"

"Just this: our victims were old enough to know better than to be taken away without a fight. Yet we find no blood, sweat, or skin samples. What about something thrown, kicked over or broken? In a small town like this, don't you think someone would have heard or seen something?"

No one spoke.

The stillness made me question our focus only on Bobby Rae. He was a violent criminal, a predator, but was he slick enough to kidnap, kill, and clean up all by himself?

It had been gnawing at me for a while.

"Maybe he had help," I said.

That could change everything.

"An accomplice?" Geonetta said. "Maybe someone to lure our victims into a false sense of security."

"Someone that knows how to plan, clean up, and hide the evidence," I said.

"Like who?" Bellows asked.

I was hesitant expressing my thoughts but knew I had no choice but to put it on the table. "Like maybe a cop."

Bellows pushed back from his chair and crossed his arms, eyes piercing.

I tried to convince him to have an open-mind to the potential. "Warren saw him meeting someone at the bar that night. If not a cop, what about a former cop? Even a PI. Someone familiar with law enforcement. I just don't think Olsen is smart enough to pull this off on his own."

A mash of words tumbled out from Bellows' lips, deep under his breath, something that ended with the word *bullshit*.

I could tell the group didn't like what I had to say but couldn't deny the plausibility.

A deputy approached and informed us Olsen wanted to speak, then pointed a gloved hand at me. "To Agent Paris."

"Has his lawyer showed up yet?"

"Said he didn't want one, would represent himself."

An opportunity opened and I wasn't going to let it pass. There wasn't much time to plan but agreed an interview would have to focus on the Samuels and Kate Jennings.

I stood from the table. "I say we take advantage of that decision."

Everyone started gathering their belongings but then, stopped Bellows half-way out of his chair.

"Let's hold off a moment," I said. Everyone froze, wondering why the sudden shift in immediacy.

Rushing in would be a bad idea. I didn't want to appear desperate to talk. Doing so would show weakness. His request to meet was really a demand, a power play. It was time to turn this into a psychological fight between combatants. Slow down the process, make him understand who's in control. It was better to raise his anxiety level. I've always said a fair fight was one in my favor, so I made him wait.

BELLOWS AND I STEPPED INTO THE SMALL INTERVIEW ROOM nearly an hour after Bobby Rae requested our presence. He was clearly agitated, fumbling with the chain securing his wrists. He looked tired and disheveled, his chin hovering close to his chest, hair resembling a dirty mop.

"Sorry." Bellows apologized but with no sincerity in his voice.

Bobby Rae twirled a finger on the table, fixated on each rotation. I leveled my attention at his sour-looking face hidden under thick strands of matted hair. "What did you want to talk about?"

Straightening, he folded his hands in front and stared directly at Bellows.

"Have you found that missing girl yet?"

I leaned across the table into his view. "Why?"

In a flat tone: "She dead?"

"Is that a question?"

Bobby Rae smiled, his voice excited. "So, you haven't found her?" He pushed back his chair, stared at a blank wall before closing his eyes. "Poor, poor Kate."

"I don't recall ever telling you her name."

A smug look, like he just gave away a secret.

"Her name's Kathryn Jennings," I said. "Only her friends call her Kate."

"Kate it is . . ."

I cut him short, "I said her friends call her Kate."

This time, a look of indifference.

"I got a witness that says you raped her. Also said she was ready to give a statement to the police. That's motive in her disappearance."

"You accusing me?"

"The assault and rape? You bet. Her disappearance, I'm coming close."

"Prove it, Chief."

"If you know where Kate Jennings is, I'm asking you for your help in saving her. I know you don't want to see a young girl die."

"Why would I care?"

"Because I'm willing to speak with the District Attorney for consideration for her safe return."

Bobby Rae waved a dismissive hand, "Twenty years instead of thirty? What's the difference?"

"I'm talking about murder."

"Like I said, prove it."

Bellows had enough. He shot up, his chair catapulted away from the table. It ricocheted off the white cinder block wall like a child's playset before landing on its side. With the speed of a man half his size, Bellows closed the gap, his face a hair's breadth from Bobby Rae's, his voice a low roar as he waved a thick, pointing finger. "I got a better idea. How about you tell me where that girl is and I'll think about not kicking your balls up into your throat?"

Bobby Rae turned his head and looked in my direction. "You don't intimidate me."

"I'm not." I pointed at Bellows. "He is."

Bellows' jaw clenched, the cross-hairs of his focus falling directly on to Bobby Rae's jugular.

"Don't waste this moment," I said. "Kate has been missing for almost two weeks. I'm hoping she's still alive and finding her will go a long way for you."

"The game, Agent Paris . . . don't you want to play the game?"

"There is no game. She's sixteen."

Bobby Rae's eyes ascended toward the ceiling. "Tell me something compelling before my arraignment and maybe we'll talk. Otherwise, I'll wait it out."

The interview continued but was going nowhere. I again asked about his whereabouts when Jennings came up missing, same about the Samuels. Like before: he couldn't remember. I even brought up his mother, asked how she would feel if he helped "rescue" a missing child— redemption, forgiveness, acceptance. But Bobby Rae refused to cooperate, refused to give me anything that would help me find them, help find his morality. That was the end of our conversation.

One thing Bobby Rae was correct in assuming, though: there was little to hold him on without direct testimony and hard evidence. Candy's recount of Kate's assault could be used to file a complaint but most likely would be inadmissible at trial. Without Kate's personal testimony or corroborating evidence to the crime, it would be doubtful the District Attorney's Office would consider filing charges. As to the child pornography, I still needed to show the victims in the pictures were clearly underage. If I couldn't, the child porn case could certainly go away as well. My worst nightmare: knowing I had caught a predator only to have little choice but to let him go. And I feared, like all predators, he would hunt again.

CHAPTER 37

Wednesday February 26th – 9:41 a.m.

WARREN WAS SMOKING A CIGARETTE at the entrance of a parking lot in Groveland. Not wanting to be seen talking to the law, he asked to meet at the Crane Flat lookout deep inside the national park. At 6,200 feet, the area was blanketed in thick snow, tall evergreens covered in powder surrounded the entry, shading the area and locking temperatures far below freezing. Bundled in a down parka, hood up, Warren stood alone, awaiting our arrival. He spotted our SUV as we drove past, panning up and down the highway to make sure no one was following. No one was.

Bellows pulled into the first open spot. A large, green duffle bag leaned against Warren's leg. He was shaking all over and I don't think it was from the cold.

"Why so urgent we meet?" Warren asked. "Is something wrong?"

I looked at his face. One eye was swollen half shut and his head showed thin crevices crusted in blood. "What the hell happened to you?"

He cupped a hand over his cheek and right eye, used his other hand to pull down his hood. "Nothing, just took a fall. I'm okay."

His excuse fell short of being convincing, but I decided to let it go.

"I just learned of an assault that took place about a year ago," I said. "On our missing girl, Kate Jennings. We got a positive I.D. confirming it was Bobby Rae."

I summarized what Geonetta had learned. But as good as the information was I said to him, it was hearsay. It was up to Warren to get me more. "To keep Bobby Rae in jail, I need to find that barn."

The words struck Warren hard, his face twisted up with confusion. "What do you mean *keep in*? You told me he would never get out." With each word, his tone grew unhinged, climbing an octave. "You can't let him go. If he finds out I've talked, he'll kill me!"

"He's not going to find out," I reassured him. "Do you know anything about this barn?"

"No!" His shoulders slumped, the air gushing out of him like a deflating balloon. "He's going to get away, isn't he?"

"It'll be okay," I replied. "I need you to ask around, see if anyone knows about the barn, any other place Bobby Rae may have stayed, talked about. Anything."

Warren stared off into space, a look of an immeasurable heavy burden suddenly pushing down on his shoulders. I added more to the load.

"One other thing," I said.

Head slumped, Warren peered up, eyes meeting mine. "What now?"

"Do you think Bobby Rae could have had an accomplice?"

"Why would you think that?" He seemed aggravated at the mere suggestion.

I held up a hand. "I'm not saying he did. Just exploring all possibilities."

"You got someone in mind?"

I took a moment to respond. "Like maybe a cop?"

The cigarette in Warren's mouth fell to the ground. "Are you fucking kidding me?"

"I'm not saying he broke bread with the police, I'm just wondering if *by chance* he had a friend that *may have been* a cop at one time."

"Agent Paris, the only contact Bobby Rae had with the police was at the end of their nightsticks."

"What about the guy you saw that night at the bar?"

"I already told you: I didn't get a look at his face."

I had to acknowledge the absurdity of the suggestion. "Look, just think about it."

"So now I not only have to worry about Bobby Rae coming after me, I got to worry about dirty cops?"

"Focus, Warren. I'm not saying there's someone else, I'm asking you to keep it in the back of your mind when you're checking around." I placed a hand on his shoulder, hoping to quell his anxiety. "Understand?"

He took in a deep breath, held it and tried to concentrate on my request. "Yeah all right, let me ask around."

I patted him on his shoulder. "If I get anything else, I'll call, okay?"

"Don't do me any favors."

Warren pulled another smoke from his pocket to replace the one smoldering in the snow. I saw his hands were shaking.

He lit it and after taking in a deep drag, pointed at the duffle.

"This is for you," he said. "Bobby Rae left it at Helen's the other night." Warren pushed the bag forward with his foot as if he didn't want to touch it. There were shirts and musty smelling jeans protruding from the opening. Warren turned and walked away, his head tilted down to protect his face from the freezing air. He disappeared behind a row of trees, heading back to his car. I picked up the bag and placed it in the SUV. Bellows jumped in and cranked the engine over. As we drove away, I could see Warren sitting in his car, his stare still and distant. The smoke from his cigarette was hazing the inside of his cabin to a point where he was nothing more than a soft blur. With what I just asked of him, all I could hope for is that Warren could hold it together long enough to get some information that may help me find Kate Jennings and the Samuels. Long enough without getting himself killed.

CHAPTER 38

Wednesday February 26th – 8:00 p.m.

Warren Kramer

THE SUMMER SCREEN ON WARREN'S FRONT door rattled as the visitor softly knocked on the splintered wooden frame. He had been waiting for his guest for at least an hour. This time, he knew who was coming. It wouldn't be a trap and his friend promised not to breathe a word of their contact to another soul.

He barely heard the knock. Warren put down the hot cup of tea he had been nursing and moved toward the entry, stopping a few feet back, quiet and apprehensive. "Who is it?"

A small voice responded, barely audible. "It's me."

He held a deep drawn breath reaching for the door. Slowly, Warren twisted the brass handle and pulled. Winter moisture had soaked the wooden door, causing it to swell and tighten around the frame. It creaked. The dim porch light was on, barley giving enough to illuminate the front step. Seeing no one, Warren peered deeper into the darkness, looking for his guest. As his eyes adjusted to the moonlit driveway, he saw her, a young girl, standing ten feet away. The figure held still.

"Are you coming in?" he said.

The girl took a step back.

"No, wait," he begged. "Please don't go." Searching for the right words, he stuttered out his plea, trying not to scare his visitor away. "I need answers."

The figure took one step forward, still shrouded in the dark.

She spoke: "I asked her. At first, she wouldn't say. She was afraid. But I got her to tell me."

Warren felt a rush of anxiety, suddenly overwhelmed. "Did he take her there? Did he take her to the barn?"

"Yeah . . . he did."

Suddenly, he could no longer stand, his legs weak, gravity taking over. He sat down on the ice-covered cement porch step. His visitor began describing in detail the directions to Bobby Rae's barn. Warren visualized in his mind each turn, every road sign and landmark. He committed each to memory. Tomorrow, he would meet with Agent Paris to relay what he had learned. It was difficult for Warren to comprehend the ramification of what he was about to do. Helping law enforcement meant betraying a friend. But Warren knew that the friendship had come to an end. It was one-sided, at best. Bobby Rae was demanding and without reciprocity. Prior to this moment, the mere fact that Bobby Rae called him *his friend* was enough, considering the few friends Warren actually had. For that benefit, he gave Bobby Rae tremendous leeway. It wasn't until Bobby Rae abused something he considered personal—more than that—something he considered sacred.

The small shadowy figure turned and began to walk away.

"I know this was hard for you," Warren called out. "I promise you, I won't ask you again. Thank you."

The shadow stopped for a moment without looking back, then continued down the driveway, swallowed in the black hole of the night.

CHAPTER 39

Thursday February 27th - 7:15 a.m.

THE DAY STARTED OUT SLOW, OUR DRIVE, cautious and deliberate. At the lower level, the snow was thin, the roads slick. Exposed to the sun, the soft powder melted during the day, only to transform into an invisible sheet of ice by evening. Cars descending from Big Oaks Flat onto the 120 Highway found themselves creeping around sharp corners, the fear of being catapulted off a one-hundred foot embankment a great deterrent for speeding.

The search team consisting of fifteen volunteers and two cadaver dogs mapped out a trail, taking them southwest on the 120 toward Moccasin, just north of highway 49. The ground was drenched and soggy, hindering their ability to maneuver through the sloping hillsides. Most had been working since the beginning, almost three weeks ago. The long, cold days had been hell on each volunteer. Tired with little sleep, injuries from razor-sharp foliage and tripping in potholes, their numbers began to shrink.

I knelt down in a shaft of sunlight to catch some heat, listening to Hoskin on the cell phone talk about the morning's search.

"We're down by the 49 and 108. It's cold but we're at a low enough level where there isn't much snow." He was walking around the Vista Point parking lot, overlooking Don Pedro reservoir. "Waiting for a briefing. Hoping to get started soon. Depending on the weather, we may get put off a bit. Until then, you got anything for us?"

"Warren came through with a possible location of the barn. It seems very close to where you're at."

Hoskin said to sit tight while he grabbed a map to trace the route.

"You'll see a road to the west of Highway 49," I explained, "blocked by a chain fence. Couple hundred yards down from Vista Point. If you pass Old Priest Grade, you've gone too far. The gate is locked, but according to Warren, it's not secured. It's a dirt road up the hill that will bend for a mile or so. What you're going up is Moccasin Peak. You'll be up around 2,400 feet, so be aware that you're going to run into deep snow and nasty conditions. It's an old horse grazing area. The barn is located on the north face of the peak. I'm coming out to join you. You're in Tuolumne territory so I notified Malloy. He may join us if he can break away."

"We'll clear you a path," Hoskin said.

After ending the call, I jumped in Geonetta's Pontiac. Bellows followed in his SUV.

"We took the items in Bobby Rae's bag to a sterile room," Geonetta explained while trying to concentrate on her driving. "Laid the items onto a clean tarp. We did what we could without taking a chance on losing any evidence for the lab—ALS lighting, hemasticks, and florescence for blood and DNA. Nothing remarkable, unfortunately. No blood or grease stains. We did find several pieces of women's clothing and some cheap cosmetic jewelry but nothing matching what we have been looking for. The items were photographed and will be shown to the parents of the victims as well as to Mr. Samuels for possible identification. I re-bagged everything and sent it off to the lab, FedEx."

Fifteen minutes later, we reached the turn off, just past Vista Point overlooking the north fork of the Don Pedro Reservoir. From my vantage point I could see the search team congregating below. Trucks with camper shells lined the path up to the parking lot while sheriff vehicles blocked the entry to sightseers and curious onlookers. Dogs on leashes were prancing and circling the lot, barking at each other, while handlers strained to hear their conversations with other search members. I saw a crew deployed up the ridge, poking the ground with metal rods, looking for a possible burial site, I imagined. I was glad their search had started. Hopefully, we would have a second location shortly.

We pulled into a small gravel-covered turnout that led to a dirt pathway wide enough for a single vehicle to travel. Bellows followed close behind. A chained-link fence blocked the entrance, with a hand-painted sign that read, *Private Property*. Bellows stepped out of his SUV with a set of bolt cutters. He knelt down near a side-post set in concrete and snapped the lock.

"He was right," Bellows yelled, referring to Warren's directions. "It's not secured." He tossed the lock in a tall clump of weeds, then pulled open the gate and jammed a large rock in front to prevent it from being blown closed. Geonetta crawled her car forward as Bellows waved us in. The Pontiac started to bottom-out from the jagged boulders and potholes along the path. The sloping walls to the hillside edged closer as we continued. Bare thorny branches from shrubs and trees sprouting from the slope began to scrape along the side of our vehicle. As we ascended the peak, the road continued to narrow.

The wind started to gust as we cleared the adjacent hill that provided cover, exposing us to a cold, icy hailstorm. The hardened particles unleashed from the sky ricocheted off our cars; balls of ice piled up on the wipers. Hard rain danced on the hood of the vehicles but it didn't last long. As we turned a corner leading to a level plain, the hail subsided, the wind calmed. We pierced through a misty haze as an abandoned building came into view perched within a secluded enclave in the middle of an open field. I became anxious, tapping a finger on the dashboard. "That's got to be it."

The view cleared but left the sky filled with thick, dark gray clouds looking ready to unleash another wave. The sun broke through a gap in the rolling mass, lighting a pathway toward the large wooden structure. Our vehicles lumbered along the rough road, coming to a stop at the entrance.

The large barn was, for the most part, structurally sound. Strips of red paint curled away from the long wood panels that made up the exterior. The giant doors on both sides were framed in thick white borders, also peeling. Exposed wood showed the sign of wear and old age. Fast growing weeds had infested the paneling, growing between the slats and forcing the boards to separate.

The only noise that could be heard was the sound of the outside walls expanding and contracting from the warmth of the sun's rays.

A thick layer of hail crunched under our boots. Bellows dragged out his bolt-cutter and easily sheered the shiny hard-cased Masterlock. The steel latch split in two before falling to the ground. I picked it up and studied it. Too new for an old abandoned barn. Someone had just been here. Geonetta and I each grabbed a door, swung them open. Sunlight spilled over moldy stacks of forgotten hay and feed. Immediately the warmth from the sun stirred the inside air, causing dust particles to flurry, evoking a musty smell. Insects cartwheeled, tumbled in the air.

Slowly, we entered the building, cautious not to contaminate poten-tial evidence. We panned the dark interior with our lights, looking for items typically found in abduction cases: restraining devices, duct tape, rope, maybe a holding cell such as a well, or cage. We also combed for human remains.

"It's just as Candy described," Geonetta commented. She pointed her flashlight up toward the back corner of the barn as a shaft of bright light hit the ceiling. "Up top . . . that's where he raped her."

My heart began to race, knowing this could be the break we were looking for, maybe even lead us to a rescue. I pointed at Geonetta, instructed her to take one corner of the building while I took the other.

"Look for any hidden trap doors, ventilation pipes coming out of the ground. Pound on the walls. Make sure, if someone's in here, they hear you."

Bellows took the outside, looking for bunkers or burial sites. We all set off in different directions, calling out for someone to respond. Anyone. Twenty minutes later we returned to where we started, having found not a living soul.

CHAPTER 40

FBI Supervisor Timothy Ashton

A SHTON WAS UNENTHUSIASTIC, knowing his morning would start with the daily ritual of reviewing the incoming mail. Stacks of it. *Fan Mail*, as he liked to call them. It would build up over the weekend and, as the supervisor of the office, it was his job to give each item his full attention. He stared at the stack, glanced at his watch, and forced himself to tackle the task. At least an hour.

Opening one after the other, Ashton read the legible ones and scanned the rest. A few were marked and indexed into the database. The others went directly into the trash. After the fifth letter, he felt his eyes strain, squeezed them shut, and decided to take fifteen before returning to the remaining indecipherable heap. Hand-drawn diagrams of how Kennedy was really assassinated, another one describing psychic visions of the location where Jimmy Hoffa was buried.

But when he returned there was this one:

Ashton sliced through the sealed flap of an unassuming white envelope addressed to the *Special Agent in Charge of the Modesto FBI*. His eyes ascended skyward, head tilted up, hoping for something at least entertaining. Inside he found a plain white sheet of paper, folded in thirds, edges exactly matched and neatly creased. The message was short and to the point. Written in child-like penmanship, and in pencil: *You will find your girl here. Catch Me.*

No one except a handful of investigators knew those last two words.

Above the written statement was a crudely drawn map of the Vista

Point area near Moccasin. The author placed a large X above two crooked lines representing the intersection of Highway 49 and Jacksonville Road.

Before taking over the Modesto resident agency, Ashton had been an agent for almost twelve years working violent crime cases. He knew this warranted a search crew, stat.

"Ah, shit!" He looked at his bare hands, fingers firmly pressed onto the letter like the other fan mail, without gloves, potentially compromising a key piece of evidence. He dropped the letter, opened his lower desk drawer where he maintained latex gloves, and pulled out the box. Hating the fact that he made such a sophomoric mistake, especially if the letter was authentic, he slipped on a pair before continuing.

"Just what we need," he cursed, "a killer trying to taunt us. And I'm contaminating evidence." Ashton reached into his drawer again, this time retrieving a clear plastic folder.

He called out for Special Agent Brain Crews, one of his violent crime investigators.

"Crewser, get in here!"

Crews had just passed Ashton's doorway and was about to receive his next assignment.

With a load of file under his arms, Crews quickly spun 180 degrees, back toward Ashton's door. He stuck his head in, cocked past the doorjamb. "What's up Tim, somebody die?"

"Got a letter in the nut mail."

Crews walked around next to Ashton, dropped his files onto the corner of the desk. He took hold of the plastic, lifting it eye level and gave it a good look.

"I'm afraid it may be legit," Ashton said.

"It's happened before. These psychos like seeing and hearing their work on TV. Kind of a freak/glory thing."

Ashton rocked back and forth in his chair. "What's the name of the missing girl Paris is looking for?"

"Kate Jennings. Sixteen, seventeen years old."

Ashton's brow wrinkled above a tense jaw. "Awfully young. Photocopy the note and get it out to the task force. Let's see if they can get a search crew out there, ASAP."

Crews nodded at Ashton as he bolted for the door, note in hand.

"And Crewser . . ." yelled Ashton. "Get your damn files out of my office."

CHAPTER 41

A GUST OF ICY WIND SLAPPED ME ACROSS THE FACE.
I stood outside the barn, waiting for Hoskin. Geonetta and Bellows were still inside, double-checking we didn't miss anything. Anyone. I cupped my hands and blew in a breath of warm air. It was still early, but up here, the sun fell quickly, and if Hoskin couldn't start his search soon, we'd be facing mountain darkness, something I'd rather avoid.

From a distance, a Suburban crested the ridge, then broke in my direction. Another followed close behind, bouncing high over the rough terrain. I imagined, Hoskin had his foot to the floor, a half a million dollars' worth of forensic gear bouncing like grocery bags. The large black vehicles made it to the barn, nosing next to Geonetta's Pontiac and Bellows' Tahoe, parked next to a clump of tall weeds. The crew baled from all doors and immediately started to unpack their gear.

Tarps were laid on the ground for everyone to suit up, each carefully stepping into their white nylon Tyvek coveralls, booties and hoods. Congregating under a free-standing canopy, the crew awaited orders from their team leader.

"Sorry we're late," Hoskin said, eyeing the open barn door.

"Hal and Heather are still inside."

He motioned his crew to get ready to start processing the scene.

"Photograph the exterior area," he commanded, "then the interior."

He leaned his head through the barn door, ordering Bellows and Geonetta out so he could get started. He turned back to me and hooked a finger. "Stay with me so I know what I'm looking for." A crew member handed me a pair of Tyvek and booties.

Two of Hoskin's agents entered the building. Agent Chad Gilliard took overall photos of the scene while Agent Bart Williams jotted down the frame number with a short description. Gilliard had been with the team for over five years, Williams six. It took them thirty minutes to work their way through the barn and to the janky ladder leading to the loft above.

"Get a replacement," Hoskin instructed. Two agents dashed back to the Suburban, returning with a portable aluminum ladder. They began to disassemble the wooden one, now evidence, wrapping each section in clean, brown butcher-type paper. Tomorrow, it would be on its way back to the FBI laboratory for fingerprints, DNA, or residue that could be compared with evidence found at our other crime scene.

With a flashlight wedged between his teeth, Agent Gilliard ascended the aluminum steps, gear and camera dangling off his shoulders. As he reached the loft floor, he froze, his flashlight illuminating two pairs of red dots swaying in the darkness before coming into view. The eyes of rats caught in the brilliant light, mesmerized before scurrying back into the shadows.

He returned his focus to the landing. Balancing himself hands-free, Gilliard lifted his camera and began snapping pictures, capturing the scene before any human intervention.

Four teams of two made their way into the barn, ready to conduct their examination. I took position from behind to watch and see what they would find. The last agent to enter pulled the barn door closed. Hoskin handed out light-wave-filtering goggles, while another agent shifted the ALS source to scan for prints, fibers, and fluids. An amber-colored light clicked on. A yellowish beam struck the back wall, revealing spatter marks that streaked in all directions, typical of farm chemicals, cleaning products, even animal urine. Maybe human blood.

We moved deeper into the loft. In the middle, there was a rusty, metal-framed bed and mattress that sat between a stack of milk crates and an old wooden nightstand. Gilliard studied the bed, which was being examined by a half dozen flashlights. With the rest of the room black, the bed was now the center of attention. In my mind, I couldn't help by imagine Bobby Rae and Kate Jennings here. How he lured her here, what he did to her. It made my face itch in heat and anger.

Hoskin ordered all flashlights off then instructed an agent to maneuver the ALS wand slowly across the blanket that covered the stained mattress. The agent positioned the wand on bright white. Scattering of fine hairs glistened across the blanket, betraying the transference of a person's mitochondrial DNA, from head to bed. Gilliard squatted, his eyes level to the mattress. With a set of plastic tweezers, he began lifting hairs that glistened in the bright light. Each item was bagged with a note describing where exactly it was found. Location is critical in understanding what happened at the scene and in corroborating witness statements.

Moving further up, Gilliard trained his focus on a pillow. Blurry brown and tan rings stained the cloth cover. He tried to lift it off the bed but it stuck to the mattress. A wadded cotton rag, dried and crusty was the cause. Gilliard pulled, then tugged side-to-side. They separated. The underside of the rag appeared to be covered in dried blood. And there was weight. The rag was wrapped around a long cylindrical object, a heavy piece of metal.

"I got something."

I repositioned a lamp. He moved closer, placing the rag under the bright shaft of light to give himself a better view of what was wrapped inside the bloody cloth.

Agent Williams rolled out a clean sheet of butcher paper on the bed. More lamps were brought over, their power cords snaking their way to an outside generator. I moved closer to the bed and Gilliard put on a new set of gloves. The pipe and rag were photographed at every angle to ensure nothing was missed. Carefully, Gilliard lifted the rag and placed it on the butcher paper. With a pair of tweezers, he gently peeled back the corners to expose what was hidden inside: a galvanized steel pipe, approximately two inches in diameter. The pipe was threaded on both ends and was spotted a rust brown. Rust can give that appearance. Not this time. I was sure it was blood.

"We have our murder weapon," I said.

"Bingo," Gilliard replied.

He cautiously removed the pipe from the rag and proceeded to place it in an evidence bag when something caught my eye.

"Wait!" I called out.

That's when I saw it.

I pointed my flashlight at the pipe, got close and placed a gloved finger on the rim.

"Right there, Chad. Something is inside."

Gilliard lifted the bag higher and into the beam of overhead lamp. The plastic container dangled inches from his prescription glasses, and that's when he saw what I saw: a sliver of paper.

"I'll be a son-of-a-bitch!" Gilliard exclaimed. He removed the pipe from the bag and placed it back on the butcher paper. With the tweezers, he grabbed a small corner and tugged. The paper flared, sliding clear of the pipe. I could see words scrawled on the small white sheet.

A note.

An agent's camera began to flash, the automatic winder advanced a quick staccato beat.

The note, measuring two by five inches, was carefully unraveled, laid flat on the butcher paper. I looked deeper into the pipe and saw others. Carefully, Gilliard retrieved three more small notes.

"*Failed . . .*" was the first word scribed on each. I placed them side-by-side and read. Just below the word "Failed," above the crease on each, I read out loud:

Rene Walker, Anna Taylor, Amanda Jenkins.

I stopped.

"Is her name there?" Geonetta asked.

My heart sank.

Kate Jennings.

I said nothing but I saw it in their stare. They knew. Kate Jennings was victim number four.

THE REMAINDER OF THE SEARCH CONTINUED IN SILENCE but the feeling of failure and loss palpable. I tried to focus but struggled, my mind forced to see visions of Kate's body, sprawled in an empty field, alone, just like the others.

I could only hope we caught the right person and the killings would end.

We finished collecting and bagging our evidence, enough to fill a warehouse. And if we were lucky, connect Bobby Rae to the homicides. But it may be days if not weeks for the lab to return with their findings.

I walked past the evidence bags lined against the wall, ready to be shipped, and wondered if any of this stuff would mean anything. For Kate Jennings, it was irrelevant. She was dead and no amount of evidence was going to bring her back.

HOSKIN AND HIS CREW STRIPPED OFF THEIR TYVEKS before placing their discarded garments into large paper bags for disposal. Nothing was left behind; no spent gloves, torn tags, or remnants of lunches. Everything was taken away as if they were never here. The canopy was disassembled and loaded back into the Suburban. The evidence was boxed for immediate transport to the lab.

"We've got to go," Hoskin informed as he peeled away his coveralls. "Ashton is having us meet with one of his agents down below. He received a map in the mail that pinpoints a place where we may have a body. Maybe your fourth victim. Ashton wanted to make sure you were in the loop on this one."

I nodded. "We'll finish up and meet you down the hill."

Hoskin wiped the sweat from his forehead with a handful of cheap paper towels. He waved an arm, signaling the crew to pack up and get prepared for their next examination. He dropped behind the wheel of his Suburban and slowly pulled away.

GEONETTA SHIVERED FROM A BURST OF cold air. She pulled her collar high, before sinking her hands deep in her jacket pockets. The building creaked and the door banged against the side. Her hair floated loosely as she made her way in my direction. Bellows was close by and had just ended a call on his cell phone. We all met by the car.

"I just spoke with one of my investigators," Bellows said. "He interviewed the owner of the property, said he hadn't been up here in a year or so. He was unaware of anyone using it and doesn't know Olsen."

For us, the news was good: explained why there was a shiny new lock. It told me Bobby Rae was a trespasser, which meant in a court of law, he had no standing to the property. What evidence we find, he could not challenge.

It didn't take long before we were ready to head out. The rain had stopped, and Geonetta was thankful for the reprieve. She found her keys, gestured for me to get in. Soft music filled the interior of her car. My head fell back on the passenger side headrest as we sped off the mountain without speaking. With one eye barely open, I heard the music on her radio turn to static, and spied the bars on my cell phone slide in and out of coverage. I must have caught a momentary signal as my phone started to vibrate. I answered the call but it didn't come through clean. Every so often, a word would punch through the static but was able to recognize the voice to be Hoskin. There was a sense of urgency in his tone.

"We're at Vista Point . . ."

More garbled chirps and tones, nothing but digitized computer garbage.

"Sorry Chris, I can't make out what you're saying," I shouted back. More noise screeched over the speaker. I was ready to give up before I heard: "a body . . . a young girl's body."

Then the line went dead.

CHAPTER 42

M ANZANITA HAS A VERY DISTINCTIVE SMELL, one I'll never forget. Like an herbal mint. The first time I smelled it, I was sliding, feet first down a crumbling slope that fell onto a bend in the road that snaked to the upper ridge. The brush collided with my face as I hit the prickling wall of thorny growth. It hurt like hell.

Its scientific name is *Artostaphylos* and, according to Sunset's New Western Garden Book, there are over seventeen varieties of manzanita brush. An evergreen shrub, it's low growing ground cover typically found in loose, heavy soil, like a thick rug. The bark smooth and reddish, the leaves gray and green. Winter months produce heavy, snow covered-shrouds over wet soil, the prickly branches darkened to a deep maroon. An invasive plant, manzanita crawls across the terrain, encasing the landscape with its dagger-like thorns, razor wire on a battlefield. Carpeting much of the national forest, the vicious plant made it difficult for Evidence Recovery Team members to do their job without succumbing to severe cuts and puncture wounds. But that's what we had to do in search of our victims. The national forest was not going to make the hunt for Kate Jennings or the Samuels easy.

THE LINE OF CARS IDLED MOTIONLESS at the Vista Point entrance.

Drizzling rain fell as uniformed patrol officers donned heavy, yellow rain ponchos, confirming everyone entering was authorized. No media allowed. We waited in line, pushing forward slowly, anxious to park so we could get briefed.

"We're moving," Geonetta said, the red emergency lights coloring her dash blood red. In front of us: a motor home being used as a makeshift command post. Geonetta inched forward, where an officer with an amber-coned flashlight waved us through. Rows of vacant patrol cars, parked along the path, led to a narrow opening, where ERT vehicles crammed tightly together. Search crews funneled up a clearing; evidence tape hung loosely on both sides. This was the beginning of the interior perimeter. An officer stood guard, granting clearance.

Walking toward the ERT vehicle, I saw Hoskin by the path. He waved us over.

Bundles of power cords and cabling slithered across the parking lot, snaking away, feeding electricity to flood lights, radios and work equipment. Hoskin rocked back and forth on his heels, arms crossed in front, anxious to start his examination. He pointed up the hill that was nothing more than a dark outline. "Search dogs found a body, two hundred yards up. I had everyone pull back because I didn't want the area contaminated."

"Is it Kate Jennings?" I had to know.

"I can't confirm it's her, but it's definitely a young teenager." He started walking as he spoke. "Let's go find out."

BELLOWS, GEONETTA, AND I FOLLOWED HOSKIN up the unlit dirt path that wound around manzanita and tall evergreens, flashlights our only source of illumination. We had to side-step large patches of ice puddles, a product of the afternoon rain and dropping evening temperatures. Soaked, wild grass grew along both sides of the path, covering the hillside, dark green and slippery. We trudged up the trail, maybe fifty yards, before reaching a plateau. I was the first one up top, Bellows, just behind me, huffing heavy from the climb. Now exposed to the elements, the cold wet wind pierced my protective clothing making me shiver.

Huddling under a wide oak tree, Hoskin pointed down the other side of the hill. A circle of floodlights and muffled hum coming from a power generator.

"Down there," Hoskin said. "I got the crew prepping the area before we enter."

Dashing in and out of the lighted area, I watched forensic agents carefully maneuvered around the body, carrying clear plastic containers, vacuums, and preservation chemicals. There was Gilliard, his camera flashing away, igniting with machine-gun speed.

"We're clear from here to the south edge of the crime scene. I'll take you in."

We followed Hoskin down the rain-drenched slope, the dirt and wild grass getting slicker with each step. It took some time to the bottom and everyone was exhausted. Gathered behind Hoskin, behind the second row of tape, we studied the crime scene. There she was, her body, twenty feet in front, beneath a group of portable lighting stands. Illuminated with such intensity, I could see her clearly; we just couldn't approach quite yet. She was positioned in a downward slope, face turned toward us, her lifeless eyes open and hazed. She had been here for a while, I presumed, pushed up against a large oak tree.

Hoskin slipped on a pair of Tyvek booties. I did the same. We advanced, Hoskin first, to assess the surrounding terrain. The path was nothing more than a dirt trail, cut from years of pedestrians walking between hidden spots to smoke dope and drink beer. The hill sloped up and then down toward the body. The area was a blanket of green wild grass, matted down from the heavy rains. Hoskin pointed at a series of small, triangular yellow flags attached to thin metal rods stuck in the open area.

Hoskin swept a hand left to right. "If you look at the hillside at an angle, you can see the grass is brushed in the direction of our victim. That means to me she was rolled or dragged to her resting spot. My guess is, she was rolled. Look closer and you can see shapes in the grass from the trail to her landing. Those are shoe prints, walking down to the body then, back up."

I stared at the impressions, imagining our killer walking through the area the night Kate Jennings was taken, brought to this location. The direction of the bent grass blades, the shoe prints, it all made sense.

Cautiously, Hoskin continued sidestepping a few feet down the slope, pointing to another yellow flag flexing on its wire post. "This is interesting." Next to the flag was a cigarette butt balanced on top of a matted area of wild grass in the shape of a shoe. The cigarette was clean but wet.

"The cigarette is *above* the matted footprint," Hoskin said. "Possible it could have been blown in by the wind, but I'm thinking our killer dropped it after rolling her body down to the bottom. If someone else left it, maybe they saw something, someone."

DNA. The results could be checked against the CODIS database. The cigarette was left in place for Gilliard to photograph.

Hoskin took his first step into the inner perimeter, waving me in. I unfolded my coveralls from its bag, slid into them and took up a position next to Hoskin. It wasn't more than four steps before we were over the body.

Hoskin knelt to the left side of her head. I was to the right. Both of us had a clear, unobstructed view. Her eyelids were dried open, pupils staring though cloudy white corneas. The body was contorted, her lower half resting on her left side, exposing her stomach and pubic region, while her chest was flat to the ground. Her skin was splotchy with the lower half a dark purple, gravity causing her blood to sink and pool. Her hair was tussled across her face, large black clumps of dried blood streaked throughout her head and neck. A gaping hole was clearly visible through her matted hair where blood had once flowed freely across her cheek. Her shoulders and neck show signs of edema, caused by her downward angle, giving her body a tinted yellow and brownish hue. I stood up and took a step back, taking in the entire scene.

Her clothes were torn, one shoe missing, exposing a bare right foot that was now an opaque white. She had on a skirt that was hiked up to her waist and her panties down around her right ankle. It all started to sink in: this was a message, of anger and violence, the uncontrollable urge to do harm. I had to turn away and close my eyes, tried to wipe out the sight, envision nothing but a blank screen.

"Are you okay?" Hoskin asked.

I held a long-drawn breath, let it seep out slowly. "I'm good."

"Good." Hoskin pulled out his flashlight and pair of tweezers, and leaned over the body. "Then let's get started."

As Hoskin examined the body, Gilliard photographed. He reached down and gently rocked the body, checking for rigidity. She had long passed through the stiffness of rigor. He pressed a digital thermometer in the armpit. Thirty-three degrees. Hoskin estimated she had been dead for over a week. He studied the dried blood from her scalp.

"See the blood flow," he said. "It's running across her cheek. Her head is facing downhill. Wrong direction. May mean she was killed elsewhere and brought here."

Gilliard leaned in and snapped more pictures. He twisted the aperture dial on his wide-angled lens, focusing on the victim's face, which was contorted and bloated. Gilliard remained steady.

The air chilled, the rain ceased, the canopies of the tall trees shielded us from the harshest elements.

Hoskin knelt next to the body, searching for other signs of trauma. They would be pieces of the puzzle, storytellers, forensic evidence. His gaze locked on several wounds, but they appeared to be superficial.

Gilliard raised his camera. "They're deep but don't appear to be defensive wounds. I'm guessing from the brush."

Hoskin continued, noted more of the same on her legs and feet. He drew an assumption, his voice sounding heated. "He held her somewhere, without proper clothing, without shoes to keep her from escaping."

Small glass vials containing clear, distilled water were opened. Hoskin removed his surgical gloves and replaced them with new ones. He had the team turn the harsh lights away, leaving only a grayness to hang in the air. Slowly, he panned his flashlight at an angle across the body, scouring for hairs and fibers.

"Chad, bring me a small plastic . . . I've got some foreign strands."

Gillard had already retrieved a small plastic bag for Hoskin. It had been opened, label affixed to the side.

There was a dark-colored strand of fiber stuck to her abdomen. Dried blood. Hoskin worked at it, gently tugging at it, careful not to break or damage evidence. He studied it for a moment, then held it up for my assessment. What was not dirty or steeped in blood appeared to be pink in color. From what I could tell, it appeared to be man-made.

"From a blanket?" I asked.

Hoskin gave a nod. "Very possible."

A blanket she used to keep warm, I assumed, while being held captive. Each search and every suspect would now be scrutinized for that blanket. The fiber was placed in the bag and passed up a chain of agents, where it was sealed, described and dropped in a box for transport.

Then he looked at her hands, knowing their importance.

If she fought her assailant, there could be valuable evidence under her nails, in her cuts, on her palms. But nails tend to fall off and Hoskin was not going to let valuable evidence disappear. He carefully slipped plastic bags over each hand and banded them tightly. She would be taken directly to the morgue for an autopsy and Hoskin wanted to secure any possible suspect hair, skin cells, or blood. Finally, she was swabbed for sweat, blood or semen around her face, chest and pubic region, hoping to capture the DNA of her killer.

It took almost an hour to complete the first round of examination. Hoskin stood up and stretched, wincing from the pain in his lower back. He reached into a duffle bag and retrieved a large butterfly net. Even in the cold, the floodlights exposed fluttering insects, gnats and moths. Hoskin gently swiped at the air, corralling each species into jars containing ethanol. They struggled for a moment before falling still, floating in the clear fluid. For them, time stopped. Knowing their stage in development might give us a clue as to the exact time of death.

It was now time to see what was underneath her. Hoskin waved me over, had me positioned over her legs while he took her shoulders. On the count of three, we rolled her body to her side, exposing black soil. Beetles burrowed, trying to escape the brilliance of the spotlights. But as important as the insects were, that's not what we were looking for.

It was the note.

His search began around her upper torso, where the others had been found. A beam of light painted her upper body just past her breast.

"I got something," he said with an elevated tone.

I reached back in the toolbox, retrieved a pair of forceps and handed them to Hoskin. He slipped the tips of the tongs over the paper, carefully peeling the sliver off her skin. The note pulled away intact. Hoskin placed it on top of a paper bag next to the body so I could read it.

Catch Me.

I felt the blood rush to my head.

We bagged the note in a plastic sleeve before returning to our examination but I couldn't remember what else was done. My thoughts were consumed with the note.

After thirty minutes, Hoskin said he had gotten everything he could.

The search was completed and it was time to remove our victim from this spot of cold dirt. With the assistance of two other agents, she was lifted up and shuffled a few feet toward a black vinyl body bag.

There was hush.

We carefully slid her inside. Hoskin pulled on the zipper, her face still peering out from what remained opened. I saw the team and their endless stares, all attention on her. They held their position, watched her being transferred—out of respect. No words were spoken and none needed to be said. Hoskin gave the area one last look before pulling the zipper its last few inches. The bag was then placed in a second bag to ensure nothing was lost. Hoskin filled out a small plastic card, noting his formal bureau name, date, file number, ambient temperature and description of the contents: *UNSUB, Female.* He dropped the card into the bag, pulled the second zipper all the way up.

Even though the tag said UNSUB, we knew who she was.

CHAPTER 43

WE NEED A PLAN.
It was hard enough making our way into the crime scene, but getting Kate Jennings off this hill was going to be twice as difficult. The route out would have to be back up the hill, down the wet, slippery path to the front entry where the ERT box truck waited. Hoskin also told me because the trail leading to the site had not been completely searched, she could not be taken in that direction. Our only option: forge a new path. And that was going to take some work. Standing along the outer perimeter, I shouted back, "What do you need?"

"A chainsaw," Hoskin responded.

He traced an imaginary line in the air with his finger, then made a series of chopping motions with his hand. Heavy branches from the oak trees along the path needed to be cut. Two ERT agents darted up the hill and disappeared. Ten minutes later they returned with a large McCollough chainsaw.

"Clear me a path," Hoskin instructed, kicking a large pile of deadwood and debris.

Three agents retrieved hatchets from their gear bags and began shredding the manzanita brush, while a forth agent yanked the starter on the chainsaw. Puffs of smoke spewed before the chain took off in full rev. Settling the spinning, sharp teeth across the thick oak branches, wood particles spat, and soon the branches fell. Agents dragged the fallen waste to the side, and we had our path for Kate's body to travel.

"We're going to need a lot of muscle to get her over that ridge," I surmised, pointing up the moonless hill. No one complained but I saw apprehension. We were being asked to drag the body of a young girl like a sack of rocks over the top of a frozen hillside. Respect turned into a chore. I felt my chest tighten, my thoughts shifting between Kate Jennings and my daughter Justine, back and forth, until I couldn't see the difference. I knew it was Kate Jennings in that body bag but I couldn't help but feel it was a sign, a notion, guilt that it could have been my child who fell prey to the Bobby Rae Olsen's of the world. My hand steadied and my grip tightened. And I made a promise: *The killings stop here.*

The blades of grass were thin, straight, and slick. Geonetta's eyes betrayed her, fear of not being up for the task. I reached over, gently squeezed her shoulder.

You're going to do fine.

On my count, everyone bent at the knees, each person taking hold of a nylon strap along the sides. We heaved her off the blue tarp. The bag bulged and sagged in the center, demanding the laws of gravity applied here. The bag was too large for a young girl, making any movement clumsy.

We took a quick run at the hill, hoping the momentum would take us the distance. From the beginning, our footing was lousy. Where we didn't slide from the slick surface, the ground crumbled away. Halfway up, I stepped in a hole hidden by a patch of grass, falling to my knees, a hard jolt finding its way to the top of my head. The manzanita lay dark and hidden, exposing itself only to slice at our hands and legs in ambush. The wet, twisting, nylon handle ravaged everyone's fingers as the hill grew steeper. We struggled to stay upright. It would only take one of us to bring the precession to a halt, or worse, tumble back down the hill. I refused it to be me.

I'm not putting you down.

Ten grueling minutes past by the time we crested of the ridge and my arms felt rubbery, spent. Gently, we placed Kate's body down. Tall grass slapped across the bag from bursts of shivering cold winds, the damp air soaked deep into our clothes. I massaged my hands, trying to get the blood to re-circulate. We were all exhausted. I knelt down and placed a hand on top of Kate—feeling as though I owed her an apology for the roughness in getting her to this point. Geonetta saw my private confession. She knew what I meant, so she turned away.

We stood a moment longer, cold from the weather and sweaty from the climb. Tired as we were, everyone was anxious to get Kate off the hill, the hill she never volunteered to be on.

The rest of our trek went smoother, over a carved trail with gentle slopes. We got her to the bottom within fifteen minutes, the crew slowing down only twice to adjust their grips. Crossing the parking lot, no one paid attention to our presence. Workers continued on with their tasks not noticing the large, black bag being lugged through the middle of the commotion was the reason why they were here. The floodlights staged around several trucks and trailers grew brighter as we approached. The back of the ERT box truck was opened with two agents waiting for our arrival.

"Take her up," Hoskin instructed.

Bellows and I raised Kate's body, high enough for the two agents inside the truck to take hold, pull her forward, swallowing her up in the dark enclosure. She was slid to one side hidden, safe.

Hoskin heaved a deep breath and motioned a hand toward a stand of bright lights. "Let's get some coffee."

The team shuffled forward. I took two steps and stopped. My stomach went tense and my head buzzed. It didn't feel right, I thought, a sense of wrong to just walk away. I couldn't leave behind what I had just witnessed without some mixture of anger and sadness. Do something, whatever that may be. Pound my fists against a wall. Smash a glass window. Scream into the cold night. But to just walk away? I couldn't.

I turned back to the truck and stared silently into the dark enclosure before climbing in, next to her, resting my body against the wall.

"I'll stay," I said for no one to hear but Kate. It didn't really matter if anyone did. I sat, back braced against the inside wall of the truck, the knots in my body melting away. I closed my eyes and pulled my jacket tight to stay warm.

It was thirty minutes before I awoke, hearing footsteps approach the truck. Through tired eyes, I saw it was Geonetta.

"Thought you must have gotten lost," she said. "You all right?"

"I'm fine."

She stood for a beat then, hopped up into the box and sat next to me. She didn't say anything, just sat by my side, quietly.

"She shouldn't be alone," I confessed. "I'm just keeping her company."

Geonetta bowed her head, and took in a deep breath, "I understand." She gently leaned against me, pulled her legs to her chest and lay her head on my shoulder where nothing more was said. This time I didn't pull away.

The quiet gave way to the past painful visions of everything that had gone wrong. I felt it deep in my core, my body feeling a jolt to each vignette of Kate's broken body that came into my head. Here was a young girl, kidnapped and taken from her family over two weeks prior, helpless and alone, her only company being the monster that eventually ended her life. I couldn't help but think; everyone failed her. Her father, her friends, law enforcement. I failed her. I hadn't stopped the killer when he murdered his first victim and for that reason, Kate was taken, killed, and left in a cold dark patch of grass behind a hillside, alone for at least a week. I blame everyone, I blame the world. But mostly, I blame me.

I looked over at Geonetta, slumped against the wall, her eyes closed. Others walked by, saw us in the back, but went on their way.

HOSKIN CAME BACK AROUND, HANDED ME A CUP OF COFFEE. Before leaving, he said there was nothing more he needed to do, what was left could wait until the morning.

Now it was up to Kate to tell us what happened; the horrors of her death, told by the evidence gathered from her body. I was convinced her story would come screaming through her fragile frame as if spoken through a bullhorn. She had become a repository of microscopic details that would help me find her killer, maybe confirm it was Bobby Rae Olsen. I wanted her abductor to know, *Kate Jennings was not finished speaking and I was not done listening.*

Geonetta and I sat for another hour before the coroner arrived to take possession of her body. While we waited, I remembered leaning my head back against the inside wall and felt a shiver come over me—like the spirit of the dead passing through my body. Was it Kate wanting to tell me something? Or was it Em trying to give me comfort, tell me everything was going to be okay? Who knows. And that thing about manzanita? I swore I could smell it—a distinct aroma. One I would never forget.

CHAPTER 44

Friday February 28th – 7:25 a.m.

THE MORNING MEETING AT THE SHERIFF'S STATION WAS PACKED. There was a full staff briefing on last night's examination. It took nearly an hour. Phones rang and pagers chimed but they all went unanswered during the briefing. Everyone listened.

The search crews prepared their hunt for the Samuels while telephones rang nonstop between investigators and the bureau's forensic lab. News cameras crowded the parking lot, trying to steal vignettes of the Kate Jennings recovery.

"Can you get the P.I.O. out there to control those goddamn news crews?" Bellows had no patience for the media today.

A young deputy's eyes lit up as he dashed out to find the Police Information Officer.

"The pipe is being hand-delivered to our lab for analysis," I said. "Bobby Rae's DNA would lock in our case against him." Even with only a few hours of sleep, I was feeling energized. "I've asked Hoskin to get our evidence moved to the front of the line."

With everything back at the lab, it was a matter of time before I charged Bobby Rae, which would give me leverage in my search for the Samuels.

"Heather, I need you to meet with the Assistant United States Attorney in Fresno to brief him for Bobby Rae's pending bail hearing. Hopefully, the evidence discovered will be enough to convince a judge he's a danger to the community, at least until our lab returns with their full analysis."

"Until the lab comes back with something solid," Geonetta replied, "anything could happen."

"Do your best."

She threw me a half-hearted salute.

"I can't believe a federal judge would allow a piece of shit like Bobby Rae to make bail." Bellows howled, visibly frustrated.

"Have faith," I said. "With our source placing Bobby Rae at the barn and ERT finding the bloody pipe, I think we're on solid ground."

My words spoken with assurance, but secretly I was worried.

The large map of the park loomed in my view. More hatch marks were added all the time but too much land remained unchecked. I had to admit, my faith in finding the Samuels alive was slowly being stripped away.

CHAPTER 45

Friday February 28th - 11:40 a.m.

"**H**OW MUCH LONGER?"
        We were gathered in Bellows' office, listening to Hoskin's one-sided conversation with his counterpart at the lab.

"We're going to need answers, Paul, and fast. Those tourists have been missing for more than two weeks."

Hoskin again paused to listen. With resignation in his voice, he told Paul Petersen at the lab in Quantico, "I know . . . yes, yes . . . but I've got to go on the assumption that they are alive." More pauses, more listening, more frustration on Hoskin's part. Before ending the call, he asked Peterson to make this a priority. For the sake of the Samuels.

He hung up the phone. "I know Peterson won't let me down," he said. "Besides, he owes, me. But, it could take another week before getting the results back. Right now, he's short staffed due to reductions in his Funded Staffing Level." Hoskin tried to sound reassuring, "I know he'll come through."

But we didn't have the time. Bobby Rae's hearing was this week, and without additional evidence there was a good chance he'd be given bail.

"That won't happen," Hoskin said. "Besides, who's going to put up the money for that piece of shit?"

"His mom?" I said. "She believes in him. Probably would mortgage everything to get him out."

Geonetta was more upbeat. "If I have to, I'll compel Candy to testify, at least at the prelim. That should hold him long enough for the full forensic analysis."

I still came back to what was the real priority. "Bobby Rae is the only one that can get us to the Samuels."

Everyone agreed.

"I want to take another shot at Bobby Rae," I said. "I need his cooperation."

Bellows agreed. "Want me to get out the wooden shampoo?"

"I'm close."

Bellows punched the top of the desk with a meaty fist. The rumble sounded like a distant thunderstorm. "I'm in."

I had to take advantage of this opportunity even though the timing was still bad. I needed more time to pull together the evidence necessary to make him understand cooperation was his only option. Without it, it would be like dancing blind in a minefield: one misstep and the whole thing could blow up in your face. My only move: I had to make Bobby Rae believe I had it all.

And to do that I needed help. So, I made a call.

MY TELEPHONE RANG BACK.

Supervisory Special Agent Gerry O'Callaghan from the FBI's Behavioral Analysis Unit. At my request, he had just finished reviewing Bobby Rae's profile and felt confident he had a handle on the type of person he was, felt his suggestion would help get the cooperation I was seeking.

"Child molesters are intimidated by strong authoritative figures," O'Callaghan said. "Specifically, male figures like their father or a cop." He went on. "A child predator avoids challenging another male. Confrontation with an imposing male puts the molester at a disadvantage, makes them uncomfortable, nervous. A predator will bond closely with those they find their equal, exploit those they find their inferior. That's why the approach is the most important."

Having dealt with my share of predators, I agreed, but Bobby Rae was different. He had most of the traits but there were subtleties that made him oddly dissimilar. It was something I couldn't put a finger on. And that worried me.

"Be confident and credible," O'Callaghan said. "He needs to see facts, or what he perceives to be facts. No bullshit. That's not to say you can't bluff him. Your goal: keep him talking. No matter the disagreements or arguments, dialogue is your best weapon. Get him to talk long enough, there's a good chance he trips himself up."

I wanted to believe O'Callaghan. But what I learned about Bobby Rae gave me pause. He wasn't stupid. His past dealings with cops had made him suspicious and savvy.

"I know a lot of this sound like voodoo magic, Jack," O'Callaghan said. "It's all statistics with no guarantees."

O'Callaghan was a smart, experienced investigator. Came up the ranks as a street agent for almost fifteen years before transferring to the unit. Held a masters in psychology and oversaw the training program at Quantico for our state and local partners. He'd participated in hundreds of interviews with killers and molesters to boot. I'd come to trust the guy so I listened.

Presentation, he said, was key. First, the layout of the interview room. To convince Bobby Rae I had the goods on him, the evidence had to be displayed—everywhere. Pictures taken of the barn. Interior photos, the loft with large red arrows, the pillow where the bloody steel pipe was found. Display close-ups of the weapon with bold notations, fact or not, indicating a perfect match to Bobby Rae's fingerprints.

And files. Lots of files. Stacked on the interview table, serials and lab reports with Bobby Rae's name neatly amassed and spelled out. It didn't matter if the files were filled with blank paper. Size was important. Maps and charts were to cover the remaining empty space on the walls with more lines and more arrows indicating where the victims were found. He also suggested that agents and detectives should mill around the room, pretending to be working on analyzing data. Make it overwhelming. He even suggested we paint the room green. He said green is a comforting color, making the suspect more relaxed, cooperative. I laughed and told him I doubted I could find a painter that quick.

It was already 5:00 p.m. by the time the room was finished. It would only be a short shuffle across the parking lot, guarded by two deputies before Bobby Rae would be brought in for questioning.

I told Bellows, it was time.

I SAT ALONE, GOING OVER WHAT TO SAY. I felt nervous but kept my focus knowing this would probably be my last chance at getting him to cooperate. I had a handful of incriminating facts, but mostly I'd be dancing around pending analysis, skirting around what was really hearsay, even gossip. This was going to take finesse. The facts, I could easily state, but the bullshit part took a great deal of maneuvering. That didn't bother me. Honesty isn't the only pathway to the truth. Although living by a fairly honest creed, I found it easy to stray into the world of make-believe, knowing that in the end, it was about stopping a child killer. However I coax Bobby Rae to talk, the ultimate goal was to find the Samuels. I closed my notebook, pushed it forward and noted the hour.

This time, I was not walking out without something.

Let the games begin.

CHAPTER 46

Friday February 28th - 6:10 p.m.

THE SMALL METAL CHAIR SAT EMPTY across a long, thin table. I pulled another chair over, one that felt and looked more comfortable, directly in front of his, taking a place of dominance.

Geonetta leaned against the back wall, reading through files, getting prepared. She whispered questions to herself as if the interview had already started. Bellows sat just inside the shadows of the table lamp, rocking on the back two legs of his chair. I heard him punch a fist into the palm of his hand, a slow steady cadence. Then he laced his fingers together and cracked his knuckles. Even through his wordless silence, I knew what he was thinking.

Outside the County Jail

Bobby Rae Olsen

THE STEPS OUTSIDE THE JAIL WERE iced over. The hairs on Bobby Rae's arms spiked as the cold evening air hit his skin.

"This way, Olsen." One of two deputies stepped aside and pointed across the parking lot, instructing Bobby Rae to proceed toward the Sheriff's office.

He could see the media gathering just below the parking lot. Reserve deputies patrolled the yellow-taped barrier to stop reporters from sneaking a picture of the man purported to be a serial killer.

Bobby Rae squinted to escape the glare of a setting sun. Raising his chained and cuffed hands above his head, he blocked out the blinding rays as he shuffled across the icy black tar parking lot.

A tattered copy of *The Federal Rules of Criminal Procedures, 1997 Edition,* was tucked under his arm, pages tabbed with green cellophane post-its. Confident, filled with knowledge of the federal criminal legal process, Bobby Rae sported a grin, anxious to make this meet. He had a plan.

The Interview Room

THERE WERE TWO HARD RAPS AT the door. Through the small glass window, I could see Bobby Rae standing tall next to his two escorts, waiting to be let in. Another deputy walked up, stood to his right. The third one was formidable; 6'7", with a salt and pepper crew-cut and a Corporal stripe on his sleeve. An Amana side-by-side refrigerator had nothing on this guy. He pushed the door open, giving Bobby Rae a little nudge. I instructed the two escort deputies to stand guard outside the room. The Corporal pulled the restraints around Bobby Rae's waist, guided him into the center seat, then posted himself at the closed door.

The steel chain on his wrist spilled onto the conference table, tipping over the side, like an anchor dropped into the sea. I paid him no attention, held my focus on my papers, jotting notes. I felt his glare, heard his feet shuffle in place. I kept writing. From the corner of my eye, I could see Bobby Rae studying the pictures on the walls, the charts and the diagrams, scrutinizing each exhibit, seeing what we knew about his past. About him.

"Did you bring me in here to watch you write?" he asked.

I shrugged, pushed my legal pad forward, exposed for him to see the heading: *Robert Olsen—Capital Punishment, Recommended Sentencing.*

"You still representing yourself?"

A listless shrug.

"I'll take that as a yes."

Bobby Rae swiped his tongue across his teeth.

"I want to bring you up to speed, let you know where you stand."

He turned his head slightly, gave the walls a second look.

I pointed to my left. "I've got forensics, fingerprint examinations, DNA, blood." Then I placed a finger on an open file. "These reports confirm what we found belong to you." I slowly pushed another stack forward, just out of Bobby Rae's reach. "And these are witness statements.

Past accounts of your violent behavior." I leaned forward so he couldn't help but look me in the eyes. "Hell, the trunk in your Impala has enough evidence to convince a jury to convict you of just about anything."

He was unemotional, inexpressive.

"We found your barn."

Bobby Rae looked up, and I saw him stop breathing.

I opened a folder containing glossy colored photos. That caught his interest. "And a weapon . . . with your notes."

Still quiet.

"I'm asking you to tell me why," I added. "This is going to be your only chance." I laid the photos of each victim onto the table, one when alive and another when they were recovered. I hoped for a glimmer of empathy, compassion. "Look at them." I tapped a finger on the picture of Kate Jennings. In a calm whisper, "Look at her Bobby Rae. You hurt her. I have proof. Witnesses say you beat her pretty bad. Raped her. I've got the ER report after the incident. They took vaginal swabs. Now I have it. Want to guess what I found?" I leaned back, opened my arms wide. "And I have evidence of you being with the other girls." That was a lie, but I was on a roll and I felt like gambling.

Bobby Rae let his head rock back then forward, eyes to the table and shrugged. Slowly, his gaze tilted up. "Yeah, I knew them."

I went silent. *An admission?*

I waited for more.

"That doesn't prove I killed them."

He sat up and studied the evidence layered over the walls. Graphic, concise, specific to him and him alone. The display of evidence was compelling, damning, meant to frighten.

There was an empty laugh as he shook his head. "What does this all mean?"

I pulled my chair tight against the table. "It means I got you for murder. What I don't know is why you did it." I pointed at the file containing the victim's photos, getting his attention.

He looked at the files. I needed him to visualize the murders, see the severity of his situation.

"I want you to tell me why."

He folded his hands together like a man in prayer. "Why should I?"

That's good. Bobby Rae was talking. I just needed to keep him going, make a mistake, say something incriminating, something I could use as a bargaining chip in getting back the Samuels. I pressed my hands down, fingers toward him. "We're dealing with a murder charge so I'm trying to find reason to save you from cap punishment."

I stood and walked over to the wall. Strolling past each photo, I pointed at the pictorial of the gruesome murder scenes, explaining to him what we found at each location: the blunt force trauma to each victim's skull, the grease found embedded in the wounds. Pictures of grease containers found at the barn that matched what we found on our victims. There were several enlarged photographs of his fingerprints taken from the barn and on the personal property of our victims. This was only half-true. Fingerprints were lifted and submitted but the results were still pending.

Methodically, I continued, pointing at the pictures and diagrams, explaining how I found similar grease in his prized Impala—more enlarged pictures of the same hairs and fibers found in the barn and in his vehicle—about Kate Jennings' body recovery and the blowflies, time of death, a period when he was unable to provide an accounting of his whereabouts.

"And Bobby Rae," I said, pointing at a photo of a dusted fingerprint on steel. "I have the weapon you used to kill Kate Jennings." The 18 x 24 glossy spotlighted the bloody pipe. Red arrows pasted on the photo, a point of interest, suggesting the location of critical information. The pipe was real. The print wasn't yet conformed but he didn't know that.

"Even if I couldn't prove you killed all the victims—and I'm not saying I can't—*I can* with Kate. And that's all I need to put you on death row. You know what that means, right? Means you sleep forever."

"What does this all mean to me?"

"It means, you have a bargaining chip."

He locked eyes on mine, pupils dilated. "Go on," he said.

I had Bobby Rae's attention.

"Let me help you off this cliff." I walked around to his side of the table and sat on the corner, next to him. "I'm not going to bullshit you. With the evidence I have, a jury is going to want to see you pay for what you've done. Without you coming clean about what happened, they're seeing you as a monster. Give me something to show you're not."

I wanted the Samuels and he knew it. There was a long period of silence as his stare bounced between the pictures and the charts.

Geonetta walked up behind Bobby Rae, dragged a chair to his left and sat down. The stacks of reports she carried were placed on the table. A clear plastic sleeve displayed candid photos of his daughter Molly and his ex-wife Kelly.

His family.

"You need to protect them. If you don't talk, the media will make them part of this whole mess. They'll become part of this story."

He pressed both hands to his eyes and rubbed.

"You want to do them right." Geonetta pressed with the right touch.

His eyes raw and red, Bobby Rae looked back at the wall with considerable concentration.

"Your family deserves better," I said. I reached into my briefcase and extracted more pictures of our victims, when they were alive, smiling, innocent, happy—placed them on the table, kept my eyes on them. "They deserved better, too."

He touched the photos. One by one, sliding them to the side so he could see them all together. His teeth chattered.

A crack?

"These murders," I started, "they don't tell the whole story, do they? I believe there's a reason for everything. Whether or not I agree with the rationale is irrelevant. What is relevant is that it ends now. Your best option for mercy is to help save the Samuels."

An almost endless silence fell the room before he finally replied.

"I can't help you."

"That's a mistake," I replied, holding back my escalating fury. "The world is going to see you as a wife beater, child molester. Murderer. Convicting you isn't going to be a question. It's what will be your sentence."

Electrocution.

"Like I said, I can't help you."

I leaned close, my anger cresting a peak. "Tell me where they are."

"Don't threaten me, Chief."

"Last time: where are they?"

"You've got nothing on me," he said in hollow defiance. Words spat from his mouth. "Like I said, I can't help you."

Now in full rage. "I'm going to enjoy watching you fry."

I stood up. Geonetta followed my lead and pushed away from the table. I grabbed up the pictures, tried to keep it together, and forced myself to concentrate on what to do next. It would be a matter of days before the lab would come back with the evidence I needed to prove Bobby Rae was my killer, enough to convict and place him on death row. Then there would be at least fifteen years of appeals. By that time, I would be long retired. It would be far too long of a wait to help the Samuels. The search and rescue teams would be my last hope.

The short-haired Corporal lifted Bobby Rae out of his chair as though gravity was a theory. He didn't resist. Heading out the door, Bobby Rae grabbed at the frame, stopped his forward motion, and spoke one last time.

"What if I give you your tourists?"

"Wait!" I shouted. Everyone in the room froze.

"What did you say?"

Bobby Rae straightened his bent frame but remained facing away. His voice was tempered. "What will I get for helping you find your beloved missing family?"

Could it be, I thought, *I was going to get my answers?* I released a tense breath.

"That all depends," I said.

CHAPTER 47

Friday February 28th - 8:07 p.m.

THE WORDS CAME OUT SOUNDING LIKE A DEMAND.

"*What if*, Agent Paris?" he growled.

I looked over at the deputy and pointed at the empty chair. He whipped Bobby Rae around and shoved him back into the seat.

What changed his mind?

If Bobby Rae was agreeing to cooperate, the question was, what did he want in return? More importantly, what was I willing to give up?

He killed four, kidnapped two. Egregious was an understatement. To think the US Attorney or the DA would ever consider something less than capital punishment would be far-fetched. Appealing to his sense of civility was already tried. He had none. Only items of value: money, freedom, power. In this case, money was of no value. And for power, he was the sole keeper of the information I sought. Freedom was what he wanted. Something I couldn't give him.

I wanted to push him for answers but knew I had to remain steady, cautious. Anything else would signal weakness.

"You don't have much wiggle room," I said. "The murder of four teen-agers isn't something the prosecutors will negotiate. I need the Samuels alive so I got something to sell. They need to know you helped. That's what I can offer."

Bobby Rae combed his fingers through his hair, shackles rattled around his body like agitated rattlesnakes in a den. "If I said they were alive, would that be worth negotiating?"

"Where are they?"

"Not so fast, Chief." He leaned forward, focusing his attention on me. His energy returned, a rejuvenated vigor.

"First, get these shackles off me. They're cutting into my ankles and I'm starting to bleed." He tipped his head toward the Corporal. "I'm not going anywhere."

The Corporal looked at him, his right hand tightly wrapped around the top of the chair, twisting at the frame.

I nodded to the deputy, but instructed the handcuffs would remain.

"Here's my offer," he began. "I'll help you find the Samuels. In exchange, you take death row off the table."

"Not until I see them alive," I said.

"You're playing with their lives." He retreated back into his chair but his eyes were still on mine, black and endless. "Dead is dead, Chief. Whether I hang or not, you fuck up, they'll die because of you."

I pushed out of my chair, slid within inches of his face. I wanted him to feel my heat. "If they die one second after this conversation, you're going to wish I killed you."

Bobby Rae feigned a look of indifference, unfazed. He eased back. "Time's running out, Chief." He smiled.

"Take him back to the holding cell," Bellows barked. The Corporal reached down and grabbed Bobby Rae by the neck and lifted him out of the chair. He pushed the door open and dragged Bobby Rae down the hallway, his head out front and legs trying to play catch-up. The two deputies outside the door jumped to their feet and scrambled to help but the Corporal had the situation under control. I followed the commotion but stopped at the doorway, watched until I couldn't. By then, the others were around me, all eyes in the direction of the dark and empty hall.

I looked at the group. "He'd better be on the level."

BELLOWS WENT TO THE PHONE AND PLACED A CALL to Deputy District Attorney John Cohen. After thirty minutes of bantering, Cohen put the call on hold.

Elevator music.

Bellows had briefed Cohen on the interrogation and the reason for the call: forgo the death penalty in return for the Samuels. Negotiating a deal for Bobby Rae repulsed him, even for the safe return of our tourists. It sent the message that a monster like Bobby Rae had power over good, something Bellows despised. But this was a necessary evil. To justify his actions, he told himself he would find a way to screw over Bobby Rae, however long it took.

The drone of the music stopped and DDA Cohen was back. Bellows put him on speaker so we could hear.

"Hal, I spoke with the District Attorney. After briefing him on the situation, he is willing to forego the death penalty. He also said, unless the tourists are found alive, all bets are off. C.O.D., my friend. Cash on delivery. He's not happy about a killer setting the conditions."

"Frankly, I don't like it either, but this is where we are and I can't think of any other choice."

"Be careful," Cohen warned. "The way I see it, the bastard killed those girls and we can prove it whether he admits to it or not. I'd just as soon convict him of a capital punishment than play games over what he'll admit to. I think the issue with the DA is that Mr. Olsen will give you two more dead bodies and he'll argue we took the death penalty off the table, alive or dead, and that's just not going to happen. You make it clear to him that they come back alive or there's no deal."

There was a pause and a deep sigh from Cohen over the phone. "Hal, the DA doesn't like to be played with. If Olsen comes up short, don't expect him to ever consider another."

"I hear you, John." They exchanged a few pleasantries before Bellows hung up the phone.

I sat at the next desk, elbows on the armrests, hands tented. "US Attorney's Office also concurs."

Bellows picked up the telephone and requested the night clerk to tell the two deputies to escort Bobby Rae back to the interrogation room. We waited for his arrival.

"I want a front row seat," Bellows said as he stretched out his arms with his fingers weaved together facing forward, cracking his knuckles. He pointed at the cheap, hard, metal chair, currently vacant. "Give me the opportunity to watch him squirm."

BOBBY RAE LOOKED UP FROM HIS CHAIR AT BELLOWS.

"Evening, Hal," he said, gleefully, as if they were brothers.

Bellows' stare remained ice-cold.

"This is the deal," I stipulated in a cautious tone. "Prosecutors want the full story about what happened with the Samuels and their immediate return alive in exchange for no death penalty. Are we clear?"

"I got a last request."

I held back an exasperated breath. Another demand from a monster. "This one's important," he implored.

"Enough, Bobby Rae," I said. "Where are they?"

"That's what I am trying to do here, Chief. I'm saying you need to get out there before it's too late."

CHAPTER 48

Friday February 28th – 8:56 p.m.

W E LISTENED.
"They should be alive." His tone was flat with little urgency.

"Should?" Geonetta snapped.

"The more we talk, the less chance we're going have a deal." Bobby Rae tilted his head.

"We got a deal?"

I hesitated but had little choice.

"Now," Bobby Rae said, "I need a map."

Command Post

CLAMPED TO THE SIDES OF THE table, reading lamps illuminated a large map of the park. Bobby Rae leaned over it, gliding a finger through an area known for its abandoned mineshafts.

His finger stopped at a demarcation on a ridge, overlooking Mariposa County. He picked up a pen from the table and made an "x" on a patch of land that had not yet been searched. "You'll find them here. In an abandoned commercial mine two miles up this trail."

I noticed he didn't say *he* was the one holding them in the mine.

With his finger, Bobby Rae drew an imaginary line up the ridge to show them the direction to the holding sight. "Follow the road up to the top of the ridge. There's a road to your right with a locked gate and a sign that reads, *Keep Out—Private Property*. You'll need to cut the lock."

He straightened. "Stay on the dirt road for another mile to the entrance. There's a lot of mines up there. There will be several abandoned cars out front." He turned away from the map and leaned against the table, arms folded. "The mining company placed a locked cage inside for their equipment. That's where you'll find them. They've got food, water and blankets, but it won't last forever. It's going to take you about two hours to the entrance."

"Where are the keys to the locks?" I asked.

Bobby Rae stopped talking, curved an eyebrow and looked down.

He never intended on letting them go.

Bellows placed a hand on Bobby Rae's shoulder and squeezed. Bobby Rae's legs buckled as he fought back a wince. "God help you if they're not alive." Bellow looked over to the guards. "Keep him in the holding room down the hall." Then back at Bobby Rae. "I want you accessible if I find out you're feeding us a line of shit."

"Sounds good to me, Hal."

Bellows reached for Bobby Rae's throat. I saw it coming and stepped between them. As much as I'd love to see Bobby Rae take a beating, I needed his cooperation. Bellows pulled back.

"I'll be back for you," Bellows said.

Out Front of the Mariposa County Sheriff's Office

WE SHOVED OUR GEAR, INCLUDING AN EMERGENCY MEDICAL KIT and heavy blankets, into several large black tactical bags. Two paramedics from the local station were contacted and quickly made ready to travel with us. It was almost 11:00 p.m., too late to gather additional deputies at the station; rather they were called and told to be on stand by and ready to go. The search and rescue teams had been out all day and would be too exhausted to help. I had to work with what I had and get to the abandoned mine as quick as possible. The evidence and crime scene would be secured for Hoskin to manage in the morning.

I crossed the parking lot, threw my bags in the back of the FBI Suburban. "Hal, we'll take two SUVs followed by the medic truck." Bellows opened the back of his Tahoe and dug out his bolt cutters, then waved over a corporal to ordered him to join.

I jumped into the front Suburban. Geonetta slid onto the front passenger seat and shut the door.

"Do you believe him?" she asked, her voice filled with doubt.

"I don't trust anything he says," I confessed. "We'll know in two hours."

I called Hoskin, instructed him to wake his team and have them ready for a possible crime scene examination.

"I don't know if you'll be collecting evidence of a kidnapping or a homicide. There's no cell coverage out there. I'll have Bellows reach out through dispatch when we find our location."

The SUVs growled in a deep rumble awaiting our departure, the medic truck positioned close behind. Bellows pushed slowly forward and I followed him out of the parking lot toward the upper ridge in Mariposa County. The hills were littered with abandoned mines, each one identical to the other. One wrong turn could significantly delay our rescue, and the slightest deviation in Bobby Rae's instructions could be disastrous. I'm not a religious person but quietly I took in a deep breath and asked for help. At this point, I would take whatever I could get.

Mariposa County Sheriff's Department - Holding Cell

Bobby Rae Olsen

HE COULD HEAR AGENT PARIS LEAVING THE PARKING LOT.

Good Luck!

He pressed his face against the small window on the holding room door and smiled at the deputy standing guard. The deputy intentionally did not secure Bobby Rae's handcuff to the metal bar on the wall. He had asked Bellows for this favor when he was brought back to the holding cell. To his surprise, Bellows granted it. Bobby Rae never thought he would be so lucky. A golden opportunity that made things easier.

He scanned the hallway through the window, watching and studying every movement. His gaze followed each person that walked by. He counted until the next one passed, committed the time to memory. It didn't take long to confirm: other than the two guards and the receptionist, the building was empty.

CHAPTER 49

```
Friday February 28th - 10:35 p.m.
      East on Highway 108
```

THE MOONLESS NIGHT MADE IT DIFFICULT TO SPOT OUR LANDMARKS. We flew passed them in the evening darkness. The vehicle engine roared when pressed for more power only to be challenged by the rattle and squeak from the vehicle's rigid frame being torqued and twisted by the jagged, uneven path below our wheels.

I called to Bellows on the radio. "I've lost cell coverage. Maintain communication with dispatch through your two-way." Bellows double clicked his microphone, acknowledging my request.

"I'm still feeling uneasy about this." Geonetta asked.

"Same here," I had to admit.

She fumbled with her Surefire flashlight, shoved candy bars and bottled water into her fanny pack—nourishment for survivors. According to Bobby Rae's directions, we were still an hour away. I pressed on the accelerator, and the SUV began to dance a rough tango on the rocky surface.

```
Mariposa County Sheriff's Department - Holding Cell
```

Bobby Rae Olsen

HE SAT IN HIS HOLDING CELL, watching the two deputies converse outside the locked door. The hallway was empty and dimly lit. He could hear the echo of the receptionist's shoes clopping back and forth from the lobby to the Xerox machine in the conference room. Work got done at night when there was less commotion. He pressed his ears against the door, caught bits and pieces of the deputies talking on the other side.

One of the deputies yawned. "This is one fucking long night." He snorted long and deep, filling his lungs with air, hoping to shake off his drowsiness.

"If I drink one more cup of coffee to stay awake, I'm going to piss a river."

One of the deputies passed the window, placed a paper coffee cup on a small table near the bathroom door. There were muffled words, something about "being awhile," before disappearing from sight. The remaining deputy grinned, leaned against the wall with his arms crossed and closed his eyes.

It was time.

Bobby Rae tapped the window with a knuckle. "Deputy, a little help?"

The deputy rolled around and peered in. "What do you want, Olsen?"

He squinted and turned an ear toward the officer as if unable to hear. The deputy swore under his breath and unlocked the door. "Step away," he commanded. Bobby Rae complied.

"What's your problem?"

"Hey man, I gotta' piss—real bad."

The deputy peered back at the bathroom, stared at his partner's coffee cup still perched on the side table. "It's being used. You're going to have to wait a little longer."

"I'm going burst."

The deputy dipped his head and gave Bobby Rae a look of being inconvenienced before stepping out of his view. A second later, the door opened with the deputy dragging a set of ankle chains. He pointed at a chair. "Sit down."

Bobby Rae did what he was told.

The deputy bent down at Bobby Rae's feet, securing one of the large half-moon steel cuffs to his left ankle.

That was the moment he had been waiting for.

Reaching into his jumpsuit, Bobby Rae retrieved the ballpoint pen he stole from the map table; the one he'd taken when he told Agent Paris about mines and dead-end roads. A slight distraction of hope gave him the opportunity to slip it down his jumpsuit.

The deputy still crouched low, his focus on securing the other ankle bracelet had no inkling what was to come. With all his strength Bobby Rae raised his arm high before plunging the pen deep into the base of the deputy's skull. The plastic case flexed then broke from the force. The deputy's body jolted, jerked, then twitched. Bobby Rae wrapped his arms tight around the deputy's neck and squeezed, continuing to ram what remained of the pen even deeper. The deputy's body tensed and arched, his legs kicked at open air until slowly coming to a halt.

After a few seconds, he heard a slight gurgle, blood filling the officer's mouth. The convulsions slowed, then he fell still. Bright red spilled from his lips; a thick stream trickled across the stark white floor.

He shuffled the deputy onto his back, preventing the uniform from becoming soaked in blood. Without a clean uniform to change into, the killing would have been worthless.

Redressed, he slipped from the holding room and across the hallway. Knowing where the other officer was, Bobby Rae pushed open the bathroom door. He heard him in the far stall. The door swung shut as he drew the K-Bar steel blade he had taken from his previous victim.

This would only take a moment.

AT THE SINK, BOBBY RAE WASHED THE BLOOD FROM HIS HANDS, watching it swirl counter-clockwise, before picking up speed, disappearing down the drain. Tucking his hair under his newly acquired hat, he turned and quietly exited the bathroom, up the empty hall and out the front entrance. The receptionist was returning to her station. She looked up to the sound of the sliding door but Bobby Rae was too quick, already heading into the parking lot, out of sight and into the night.

CHAPTER 50

Friday February 28th – 11:22 p.m.

BELLOWS SLICED THROUGH THE FIRST SET OF LOCKS at the entrance to an old mining campsite. The gate grinded hard on the craggy surface and Bellows ended up having to boot it open. He stepped to the side and waved us in.

The unpaved road was pockmarked with deep crevices. Rocks and bushes besieged the way, making the travel impossible for anything but a four-wheel drive. It took another thirty minutes before I spotted a leveled clearing, covered in trash. Busted refrigerators and rusted washing machines that once kept this makeshift outpost operational were left abandoned. Portable out-houses tilted, doors wide open, having been forgotten, the stench still prevalent. It would have cost the company more to clear the debris than to pretend the rubbish didn't exist.

We drove past piles of empty propane cylinders before locating the opening. A pair of abandoned vehicles, Chevys, stripped to bare metal, blocked the entrance, just as Bobby Rae described. The cars had been gutted by scavengers, riddled with bullet-holes, used for target practicing.

I stopped in front of the entrance and stepped out, strained to see inside the dark, endless cavern. Bellows had parked next to me. He walked up, assessed the large black hole before pointing his flashlight forward. The immense depth, giving no clues to where it ended, quickly swallowed up the light. Geonetta retrieved two hundred and fifty feet of bright yellow nylon rope from the back of the SUV.

Slinging it over her shoulder, she knotted one end to her belt. "I'll have a deputy stay outside with a hand-held. He'll radio to help us find our way back."

I looked at the bulky rope. *Was 250 feet enough?*

The entry was tall and wide, more than enough to walk in without having to bend at the waist. The walls were sharp and jagged, cut by massive commercial drilling tools. The air was heavy, damp and musty. We were able to illuminate the interior to see smaller tunnels jutting out in different directions, all pushing deeper into the hill.

Bellows' voice echoed. "When these mines were active, shafts were drilled to locate large veins of gold or bauxite. Makes the opening look like an oversized ant farm."

"Bobby Rae's instruction pointed to the largest shaft." I pushed a finger to my right, toward a vein that disappeared into more pitch-black. "That's got to be it."

Geonetta took lead. Bellows and I followed close behind, my hand occasionally touching the yellow rope for assurance. The paramedics took up the slack, in case something bad happened. The walls were unstable; chunks of rock crumbled away as we passed, raining on our shoulders and necks.

The tunnel went on forever, swallowing up light from our flashlights, like a backyard telescope tracking a distant star. The farther we went, the narrower the tunnel became. Tighter, touching, scraping. The walls coned, and the narrowness forced us to hunch to avoid hitting our heads on the spikey ceiling.

Fifteen minutes in, Geonetta tugged at the rope. It stretched into a tight and straight line. There were only a few loops left on her shoulder meaning we had penetrated most of that two-fifty. At best, we had maybe twenty yards left and yet, we still hadn't found any signs of life.

Did I make a mistake, take a wrong turn? Is this the right tunnel?

Bellows moved passed me and disappeared. A second later, I saw his light dimly illuminate a ridge that dropped below his boots. He was gingerly standing at the crest of a ledge, overlooking a bottomless black pit. We quickly made our way to him and directed our lights into the drop. Shafts of light rays danced on every side and corners, surveying the surrounding walls in an attempt to comprehend the size. The walls were rougher, scalloped by heavy equipment, the dirt floor long settled into gray dust. Debris was left in place and trash not cleared. This was the end of the shaft. Where the miners gave up.

No one spoke but knew what each one of us were thinking. The cavern was cold but more obviously, undisturbed for at least a decade. I could still smell metal in the air. Other than the remains of discarded drilling equipment and bent scaffolding, there was no storage of food to keep someone alive, no lights to keep someone comforted, and no bars to keep someone captive. The Samuels were never here. Bobby Rae lied. He sent us on a two-hour goose chase. The question was why?

CHAPTER 51

Saturday March 1st – 12:28 a.m.

Chris Hoskin

H E SLOWED, ALLOWING THE PATROL CAR TO PASS.
The black and white stopped, then accelerated onto the darkened road toward the hills. Hoskin pulled the Suburban into the empty parking lot at the Sheriff's station. It was half past midnight and he wanted to get a jump on loading up his equipment for a possible crime scene. He stepped out of his SUV and dashed to the front door, trying not to catch a chill. The door flew open, slammed against the back wall with a heavy *clunk*! Carolyne gave Hoskin a stern look as he stomped his boot clean of snow on the linoleum floor. The slush quickly morphed into a small puddle in the warm lobby.

"Got called from Agent Paris telling me he may have found the Samuels?"

Carolyne shrugged. "They tell me very little." She pointed toward the holding cell. "Your prisoner is around back. You can ask the two deputies what's going on. I'd think they would know." Carolyne buzzed the door open and Hoskin quickly pushed his way in.

The hallway was quiet as he approached the holding room door. He anticipated hearing banter, officers joking, trying to stay awake. But instead, there was no conversation, no laughter. The hall was dark, lifeless. He rapped on the first door but no one answered. His eyes were drawn toward the floor where he caught sight of a pool of red slowly creeping around his boot, gooey and slippery. He straddled the pool, now spreading to the other side of the walkway linoleum.

Then he saw him.

"Shit!" He yanked hard on the door but found it locked. "Hey!" he yelled louder, pounding on the door, the sound reverberating off the walls. "Open the door!"

Carolyne peered around the corner, staring through frantic eyes.

"What's with all the shouting?"

"Get me a key to this door, now!"

Carolyne disappeared. The sound of her heels clapping across the floor in the adjacent room echoed down the hallway. There was a pause, the sound of a cabinet drawer opening and closing, and then Carolyne running back toward Hoskin. She passed a silver key to Hoskin, who jammed it in the lock and twisted. The mechanism clunked open. He drew his pistol, pushed it forward and around to the right, covering the blind corner. Slowly he peered in. A lifeless body lay crumpled on the floor. It wasn't Bobby Rae. Half-naked, a young male with a thin sharp object protruding from his neck. Thick, dark blood had coagulated and pooled along the edge of the floor. Holstering his weapon, Hoskin reached down, tried not to slip in the slurry and pressed two fingers on the deputy's carotid artery, hoping to find a pulse. Nothing.

He turned to see Carolyne, frozen at the door, her stare locked on the deputy. "Is he dead?"

Hoskin nodded.

"What do we do?" she stuttered.

Hoskin stood and guided Carolyne out the door. Suddenly, he remembered. You said two deputies? Where's the other?"

Mariposa County - Mining Camp

THE DIM LIGHT FROM THE MOON entered the opening of the mineshaft. A strong metallic odor from within the cave clung to my clothes as I stepped into the cold open air, making me feel gritty. The deputy holding the other end of the rope stood in front of the opening, watching each of us come to the surface.

"Did you find anything?"

Bellows answered by shaking his head, knowingly frustrated. His phone vibrated, then beeped repeatedly, as if a number of messages found their way in.

"What's happening?" I asked.

Bellows scrolled through his text messages.

He turned toward me but kept his eyes on his phone. "911 – CALL ASAP ON CH.10 ONLY."

That's the secure channel.

Bellows ran to his SUV, pulled open the car door and grabbed the radio mic. He switched to channel 10.

"Dispatch from 105, what's the emergency?"

He was surprised to hear Hoskin's voice coming over the airwaves. "Bobby Rae has escaped!"

Then came the news.

"He killed two deputies and has taken a patrol car. He's got a half hour head start on us."

Bellows' face turned a bright red, the veins in his neck bulging. "Put out an APB to all the surrounding departments." He didn't wait for a reply confirmation as the microphone fell from his hand. He stuck his head out the driver's window. "Move!"

Cursing, Bellows threw the transmission in reverse, tires slow to catch traction. We had a split second to avoid being run over. The deputy barely made it in the passenger side of Bellows' SUV before it lurched forward. His tires kicked up loose mud and dirt as the rear end slid wildly. I motioned to Geonetta to throw our gear into the back seat and we laid chase.

He duped me. And he killed. I may have lost the only leverage I had in finding the Samuels.

Things just went from bad to worse.

CHAPTER 52

Saturday March 1st – 2:01 a.m.

I PULLED TO THE EDGE OF THE road next to the Sheriff's station parking lot. Bellows nosed his vehicle up to mine. I could see him staring sharply through the front windshield, blank and distant, jaw clenched like a vice. His white knuckles had a stranglehold on the steering wheel. There was heat coming from his posture. Yellow evidence tape bordered the building; several deputies stood at guard, preventing the media from prying into their tragedy.

A deputy motioned me to pull forward. They had already allowed Bellows through. He had exited his vehicle and made his way to the front. In the cordoned-off area, a group of officers scoured for evidence. To my right, flashlights strafed the ground, following the direction they believed Bobby Rae made his escape. I walked inside.

Carolyne sat at the reception desk, hands around a cup of coffee, head slung low and face extremely pale. ERT had already arrived and started processing the scene. I caught up with Hoskin.

"I couldn't have been more than a few seconds behind him." Hoskin's voice was stricken with guilt. "He stole a patrol car."

Carolyne started to cry.

"Got an APB out and about a hundred officers searching for him."

I pointed down the hall and Hoskin confirmed that's where it all happened. I headed in the direction of all the activity, careful not to disturb anything along the path. A pool of blood solidified on the floor that had turned a dark purple. Smears from where the dead deputy had lain crisscrossed the floor, a pattern showing the struggle that had ensued. The bathroom door was propped open, crime scene tape secured diagonal across the frame.

Bellows walked up and removed his Stetson. "I've dispatched deputies to the families. He choked on his words. "I would go but I'm going to find him . . ." He paused.

Bellows didn't have to finish, I knew what he was going to say, saw it in his face. Bobby Rae should be afraid. I placed a hand on his shoulder trying to offer some amount of comfort. It was like touching stone.

My cell phone vibrated. It was Warren.

"I've got some bad news . . ." I started to say but before I could finish, Warren interrupted.

"He's here! Says he killed two deputies. He wants money and a ride out of town now. What the fuck?"

"Stall him. Don't let him get away."

There was silence on the other end of the phone. I could hear Warren running and his breathing labored.

"Are you fuckin' kidding? He killed two cops! I don't want him in my house." Another pause, more frustrated gasps coming over the phone. "Hold on. I'm running to the bathroom where he can't hear me." There was a snap from a door latch and the clunk of a locked being turned. "I can't have him here," he said. "Raley's spending the night. You can't arrest him here. It's too dangerous!"

"It's going to be okay," I lied. I needed Warren to calm down. "He trusts you. That's why he's there."

He said it again. "I can't have him here."

"Is there a place you can take him, somewhere away from Raley?"

I heard Warren stop pacing. The phone went silent for a long second. Then he spoke. "Maybe." His voice suddenly sounded sharp, focused. "There is a place, away from here. A trailer, parked near Foresta. I let a seasonal worker rent it during the summer. I'll tell him to lay low for the night. Give me an hour. I'll get him there."

I got the directions and told Warren to take a deep breath. I heard him inhale and hold it before letting it slowly seep out.

The last thing I said: "It's going to be okay. You just get him there and we'll take care of the rest."

THREE THIRTY IN THE MORNING AND THE WORLD WAS STILL ASLEEP.
Our car's headlights reflected off the snow, glistening along the

roadside but no moonlight penetrated the tall evergreens that encased the trailer park. I arrived at a clearing nearby and slowed the Suburban to a stop next to a patrol car and two Sheriff's SUVs. Bellows and Hoskin pulled up in separate vehicles. Sergeant Malloy from Tuolumne stood quietly as the crew gathered next to a flag pole.

Malloy looked at Bellows, knowing there weren't any words that would make things better, just a sharp tip of his hat. "I've notified our SWAT team," he said, looking down at his watch. "ETA, about thirty minutes. I've got two officers in a van on point. They got a good view of the residence and they'll call out any movement. I suggest the rest of us back away so that we don't spook him before the team arrives."

"Heather and I will set up at the end of the road," I said. "We'll block any cars coming or leaving while you prepare to make entry."

Malloy agreed.

We parked off on a connecting street hidden along a row of trees a few blocks down. The only sound other than the rustle from an intermittent breeze shaving through the trees was the *tick-tick-tick* of cooling metal coming from the car's engine.

"Do you still think they're alive?" Geonetta asked.

The Samuels.

"Maybe." I didn't want to say what I really thought. After this much time, it was doubtful anyone could survive this cold let alone a kidnapping.

I don't think she believed me. I didn't believe me.

Five minutes passed. We spotted three Tuolumne County Sheriff's SUVs speed toward the trailer park. Five more minutes and the radio chattered, coordinating their entry. I envisioned their response; simple. Entry: a series of flash bangs and breach the door. Penetrate: five cloaked in dark Nomex suits clearing anything in their path. Secure: three cover the outside windows in case Bobby Rae decided to shoot it out. Conquer: find their target and incapacitate. If the target responds with a threat, neutralize. In layman terms: kill.

My cellphone vibrated, broke the silence in the Suburban. It shimmied off the dash and fell to the floor. I reached under the seat, scooped it up and pressed talk. The call was extremely garbled. I stepped out of the car and walked toward an open area, hoping to find a connection. The voice on the other end became clear. I stopped moving.

"Did you hear me?" the voice screamed. It was Warren. More garbled words, then clear again.

". . . and he's in the trailer. He's spending the night until tomorrow morning. He's really spooked. Be careful. He's looking for cops and he's got a gun."

Before I could respond, the signal vanished. I tried several times to call him back but was unable to link to a tower. Back to the SUV, I grabbed the handheld radio and alerted Bellows and the SWAT team.

"Copy," Bellows replied. "Their point-man said they see movement inside. I'll inform SWAT their target is in pocket." Bellows stopped. "It ends tonight."

"We better get back to the trailer," I said. "SWAT is going in."

Geonetta nodded.

I cranked over the engine, threw it into gear and bolted up the road.

Clearing by the Trailer Park
SWAT Briefing

A PLAYGROUND WAS THE MEET SPOT. I killed my lights, exited the vehicle, and walked into a packed crowd of SWAT officers. Dressed in their black tactical uniform, they stood in a close huddle, intensely listening to the Team Leader's, or TL's, instructions.

Bellows whispered over his shoulder. "Shouldn't be more than ten minutes before they're ready to bang the trailer door. Nothing for nothing but I'm hoping he tries something stupid."

SWAT officer's hands high in the air, one by one, articulating their position and duty, confirming they knew their assignment as the TL called them out.

The TL nodded and looked toward Bellows and barked, "We're good to go."

The SWAT officers stepped onto a metal railing welded along the skirt of their Suburban. Silently, the SUV drifted out of sight and down the main road toward the unlit trailer. Geonetta and I climbed back into our car and followed from a safe distance.

It only took a few minutes for SWAT to cut along the curved road that led to the target location. As they rounded the corner, the Suburban lights went dark. In unison, they leapt off the railing and took their positions behind each other in a tight row. With the stiff chop, the TL whispered to his troops, "stack."

The TL saw us close behind, ordering us to park about fifteen yards back. Along with two deputies, Bellows stepped out of his vehicle and flanked the right side of the trailer, help cover the rear.

Making a fist and pumping his arm, the TL ordered his men forward, lining up against a row of trees near the edge of the driveway.

"Nuts to butts, boys," the TL ordered. He looked down the row of officers, all focused on the front door, weapons at the ready. The team held steady, prepared to move as a single machine. The TL gave the command: "Execute."

The team crept toward the darkened trailer door. Upon reaching the entrance, SWAT officer Number One advanced with the body shield as front man for the team. Number Two, with a ram slipped around the shield, prepared to breach the thin metal door. Number Three stood next to the breacher, bang grenades ready to toss in to stun their prey. With a point at the door, the breacher slammed the three-foot ram into the latch. The metal door crumbled inward. Two percussion grenades were tossed. Explosions cracked in a series of immense booms, rocking the trailer, the detonations deafening. Bursts of jagged light and smoke flashed from inside, windows shattered, glass fragments teething their frames. Only a microsecond had passed before the remaining team members stormed the entry, disappearing through the doorway and into a black hole. All I could do was watch and wait.

Outer perimeter of the Trailer Park

WE LISTENED TO THE RADIO TRAFFIC. Loud screams echoed from the SWAT team lead: "Sheriff's Department, show yourself!" The command boomed from the trailer as they cleared every inch inside the small aluminum box. Porch lights from surrounding trailers popped on, their occupants wondering what was going on. Deputies rushed to intercept curious onlookers as they slowly exited their front doors, walking toward the commotion. I waited to hear the fate of Bobby Rae, apprehended or dead.

Then came the word from the TL, voice crackled over the radio. "He's not in here. We don't have him!"

I took a moment, unsure of what I had just heard.

What the hell?

It didn't make sense. Warren confirmed Bobby Rae was in the trailer. In a sprint, I bailed from my vehicle and bolted forward, Geonetta a footstep behind. As I raced at full speed, out of the corner of my eye, I saw him. It was a movement in the woods at first, just within the trailer park perimeter. I stuck out my arm, slowed Geonetta, stopping her dead in her tracks. Her MP-5 submachine gun swung around, indiscriminately pointing into the black of the trees.

He's in there.

I strained to listen to the sound of crushing leaves, the rustling of snow-covered branches. A dark figure, blurry, staggered away. I pulled Geonetta by the arm, pointed in the direction of the shadow, for her to take notice. She thumbed the safety lever of her MP-5, scanned down range through her sights like a hunter tracking a wounded deer. We moved to an opening near the hillside, surrounded by evergreen trees, guns forward. The ground was void of light and thick in foliage, offering Bobby Rae places to hide and to ambush us if we weren't careful. I didn't care. There was little time for caution and I wasn't going to let him get away.

We continued sprinting toward the trees, moving faster, leaping over piles of brush and debris, chasing the sound of a running man. I put the distance no more than twenty-five yards or so. Intermittently our target would pass through the beams of our lights before disappearing from view. Hurdling a tight clump of pine branches, I spotted a figure cresting a slope and disappearing into a thick carpet of high Manzanita brush. My blood began to churn, knowing I was closing in on the man that had played me for a fool, hours earlier; more importantly he was a killer. Tonight, this game ends. Bobby Rae was coming with me in handcuffs or a body bag.

I cleared a field of tall grass, then came upon a ridge that dropped twenty feet down to a flowing river. Rushing water pounded against large boulders in the middle of the stream. I rounded the corner and saw a half-naked Bobby Rae balanced on a stack of rocks near the edge of the ridge, looking for a way out.

Cornered.

He was wearing only a pair of jeans and an old pair of boots. His face and chest were covered in cuts from jumping through a blown-out trailer window. In his right hand was a large blue steel revolver, presumably one he had taken from one of the deputies. My flashlight shone on Bobby Rae's white and bloodied chest. He lifted an arm in front of his face, shielding his eyes from the bright shaft of light.

"Drop the gun, Bobby Rae or I'll kill you where you stand!" I shouted my command while concentrating hard on placing my sights squarely on his sternum.

Geonetta approached from behind, the strap from her sub-machine gun clanging against the weapon's frame. The red dot of her Aim-Point laser painted a deadly mark on Bobby Rae's forehead.

"Don't give me a reason," she shouted.

I called out: "Your choice."

He was out of breath, fatigued. He looked too tired to run. Still holding onto the revolver, he contemplated his options. He heaved in deep, held it, and dipped his chin to his chest, eyes toward me. This time, his look was different. His mind was elsewhere. I could read it in his face. This was not going to go well. Not like the last time. And he knew, I knew.

He's going for it.

"Don't, Bobby Rae," I yelled. "You're going to lose!"

His expression grew defiant, breathing heavy, screaming in exasperation. "You kill me and all your answers are gone, forever!"

"I don't care. Right now, all I care about is having you drop that gun."

He choked out a pathetic laugh.

"Drop the gun!"

"Don't you want your tourists back . . . alive?"

"You killed two deputies. This game is over."

The three of us squared off in silence. Wind blew across the tall weeds and the rushing water continued to pound. Guns drawn and nobody relenting. If Bobby Rae flinched, Geonetta would cut him in two. If I flinched, Bobby Rae would think he had no other choice than to shoot it out. Either way, any movement would escalate this into a deadly firefight.

Finally, Bobby Rae spoke. "Do you know the difference between living and dying, Agent Paris?"

I wanted no more games, no more riddles, not tonight.

Bobby Rae pulled out a guttural laugh from deep within. "I don't either. I just know I got to make a change."

He raised his revolver and began squeezing the trigger. A chain of flashes erupted from the muzzle in quick successions as he stepped back toward the edge of the ridge.

Boom, boom, boom.

I dropped low in my stance, sights already square on his chest. I double-tapped the trigger. The rounds struck him center mass, splitting him open with the sound of two loud thuds. The blood pumping coarsely through his lungs from the chase quickly hemorrhaged from his body. Bursts of fire thundered from Geonetta's MP-5 as I felt the wind generated from the bullet's wake pass my right ear. Spiraling copper and lead ripped through Bobby Rae's body, like locust on a cornfield. His battered frame was thrown backward with unimaginable force.

The shooting stopped and quiet filled the void. I ran to the edge, found Bobby Rae's lifeless body crumpled on a pile of jagged rocks, bleeding from the gaping wounds to his body and face. His eyes were open, like he was staring up at the moonless night. Lifeless. There was no turning back on his final decision, choosing his fate, again under his own terms.

I stared at a dead Bobby Rae from above the ravine and started to wonder if I just ended my chances at finding my missing tourists. I turned to Geonetta, her weapon to her side, eyes open wide as if to say, *Now what?*

CHAPTER 53

Saturday March 1st – 6:08 a.m.

THE SUN SLOWLY MADE ITS WAY ABOVE THE RIDGE, casting brilliant rays of light through the clouds onto the wet ground where Bobby Rae fell dead. An early morning start gave ERT ample sunlight and maximum hours to perform their forensic examination. More yellow tape was drawn around the perimeter, this time to preserve the death of a serial killer. The coroner's ambulance had been parked up the road for the past two hours. The deputies, assigned the responsibility of removing Bobby Rae's body, leaned on the hood of their patrol car, smoking, neither one in a hurry or concerned about making any scheduled time. Geonetta and I rested against the side of the ERT Suburban, sipping hot black coffee from Styrofoam cups while watching the agents work. Bellows planted himself in an opening, eyes closed like a horse quietly asleep. The tension crept up my neck. With Bobby Rae dead, information leading to the Samuels was gone.

Bellows eventually opened his eyes, focused on a morning sun barely cresting over the next ridge. He decided to walk over, sensing my anxiety. "We'll find them."

What else could he say? Bobby Rae was a killer without a conscience. He gave me no other option other than the one that forced me to kill. To think he was going to help me find the Samuels was nothing more than fantasy.

The sun finally pushed over the ridge and flared. Bellows turned and shaded his eyes with a large hand.

"I better call Frank and get him up to speed before he hears it on the local news." I retrieved my cell phone, scrolled down to Porter's number. No signal.

I shoved the phone back into my pocket.

Bellows kept his eyes at the mountain range as the sun became brighter. "Get out of here and take care of business."

With this being a shooting ending in the death of a suspect, it was only a matter of time before I would be pulled from the field and placed on administrative leave. Just what I needed, taken off before finishing the job.

Strike one.

Policy is to surrender your weapon to your superior. It was now evidence in an agent-involved shooting investigation.

Strike two.

I thought about my options. Comply with bureau guidelines or ignore the rules and see it through. The Samuels were still missing. There were still too many unanswered questions. This was my territory, my land to protect.

The decision didn't take much thought.

There would be no strike three.

I called over Hoskin, explained my dilemma and what I planned to do.

"I'll take care of Frank," Hoskin said. He whistled and waved over one of his team members. A young agent jogged over, waited for instructions.

"Take them back to their hotel."

With little energy left, I gathered my gear, crawled into the back and closed my eyes, head against the window. The world started to swirl. A moment later, I felt a gentle hand on my shoulder. There was a beautiful and familiar scent. I felt her warmth. I knew who it was.

"Rest," Emily said.

"I failed, Em," I forced myself to confess. "I might have killed my one chance of saving the Samuels."

Emily's eyes saddened. "You didn't fail, Jack." She slid closer.

God, she felt good.

"Everyone has faith in you. That's because you don't give up. I know you won't." She lifted her head and placed a hand under my chin.

"What do I do next?"

"The answer is obvious," she said. "If he lied, someone else knows the truth."

Like I said, she was always the puzzle. But I knew what she meant. "I get it," I said.

Then she kissed me.

"AGENT PARIS? WAKE UP. WE'RE HERE." The agent who drove, gently touched my shoulder bringing me back from a dead sleep. Geonetta was already out of the Suburban and had retrieved her gear from the back. Still groggy, I scooped up my bags and followed her up the walkway to our hotel rooms. I fumbled for my key.

Geonetta was standing at her room door, already turning the handle. "Call me when you get some rest and we'll get something to eat."

I gave a half-hearted wave. "I'll call you in an hour." I yelled back, knowing it would be more.

CHAPTER 54

Saturday March 1st – 10:02 a.m.

I WOKE TO THE BLARE OF A Country and Western guitar riff coming from the hotel alarm clock.

Slim Whitman.

I checked the clock. I'd been asleep for two hours. I rolled to the edge of the bed when the telephone rang.

"Yeah? I'm awake," I answered, trying to hide the foggy haze still in my head.

"Sure you are," Geonetta boomed.

I rubbed my eyes and stretched out an aching back.

"Get cleaned up," she said. "Hoskin phoned. Got information from the lab, thought you might want to hear."

"Give me ten."

I hung up the phone, dragged myself into his bathroom, and turned on the shower. As the room started to cloud in hot steam, I felt the warmth wrap around me and it made me think of Em.

"COFFEE, BLACK PLEASE," I SPOKE FROM BEHIND A MENU.

Maureen, our waitress—at least that's what was printed on her name tag—scribbled on a small pad, paying little attention to my words, her head spun toward the door. She's been serving us these past few weeks, taking the same orders from the same menus. I looked up, saw Maureen glance back with a superficial smile. As often as we have frequented the diner, it was only right to be on a first name basis. Maureen shoved her pencil in her bee-hive styled hair and went back to the kitchen.

Hoskin sat reviewing a series of notes, an earlier conversation with the FBI lab examiner in Quantico. Geonetta crowded Hoskin, reading the reports over his shoulder.

"The pipe is good for the murders," Hoskin started out saying. That was great news. "The lab was able to confirm blood match with Jennings and Jenkins. There were a number of *partials* lifted from the pipe but nothing of value except one that had enough ridges to compare."

Hoskin pulled out a photo of the pipe, an arrow pointing at the lip. "He lifted a print of an index finger from *inside the pipe*. Pretty damn good, if you ask me."

"Is it Bobby Rae's?" I asked.

Hoskin dropped the photo to the table. "Didn't show a match."

"Then, who's?"

"They're still working on it. Also running it in the Cal DOJ database. They should have an answer soon."

Hoskin continued scanning his notes, told us about the hairs and fibers but nothing that would help create new leads. "Picked up more pink fibers from Kate's body." He pulled another photo. "Re-checking all our searches to see if we have them at any of our other sites."

"How about the accomplice theory?" I opened the question to everyone.

"With an unidentified print on the murder weapon, it's a viable possibility," Geonetta added. "Those fibers could be key."

"I'm going out to see Warren. See if he's heard anyone making a move to get out of town, now that Bobby Rae's dead.

"I'll go with you," Geonetta said.

Maureen brought our food. We ate, this time without the talk of larvae and maggots. After, we gathered up our files, notes, even the doodles on our paper napkins. Leave nothing behind for others to scrutinize. Everyone tossed money on the table before sliding out of the booth. I turned and tossed an extra five. For Maureen.

CHAPTER 55

Saturday March 1ˢᵗ - 6:01 p.m.

BEFORE HEADING OUT TO SEE WARREN, I had gone back to the Sheriff's station to finalize my report on the shooting. Porter called, said he was just checking up on me. He really called to order me home.

Leave.

I told him I couldn't.

Won't.

He didn't like my tone, but understood my frustration. After enough bantering, we came to a compromise. He'd give me another day to "collect my things." I acquiesced. If it took longer, I'd ignore our agreement.

Sue me.

My head hurt. Too little sleep, too much coffee. Pounding in my brain rattled like a hammer against an oil drum. I massaged my forehead, eyes closed, as the office printer whined, pushing out my supplemental report.

He escaped, he ran, he drew his weapons, we killed him.

I stood up from the squeaky metal chair to stretch my legs and decided to check in with the others in the conference room.

It was noisy. Volunteers, officers, dogs darting in and out, as gung-ho as the first day of the search.

The large map spread across the conference room table was becoming worn from people leaning up against the edges, dragging dirty shirt sleeves and sweaty arms across the paper. More red lines continued to advance on all fronts: Tuolumne, Mariposa, Calaveras, and Stanislaus.

I hovered over it and folded my arms across my chest, amazed at the dedication and drive from each and every person working this event. It felt good.

If they weren't giving up, how could I?

Find the Samuels.

With Bobby Rae dead, my next best source of intel was still Warren.

THE WINTER SUN DROPPED OVER THE MOUNTAINS. By early evening, it had become bitterly cold. I stood by the driver's door of my car, watching Geonetta pull on her winter jacket and toss her bag in the back.

"Ready?" I said.

She leaned across the roof of the car and nodded. "Yep."

I drove out of the parking lot, calling in our destination to the Mariposa dispatch operator. On the way, I thought about what to ask Warren and what he didn't know, how I could get him to find the answers. The priority was to locate every barn, building, or house Bobby Rae slept, ate, or crapped in. It had to be secluded, I thought. It wasn't an apartment; that would draw too much suspicion by the other tenants. Bobby Rae couldn't be smart enough to hide every detail about himself. He was a bragger and a drunk. Talking was something they can't help doing. Warren had to know.

We soon came to an intersection which took us off the main road and down a path that led to a remote home surrounded by tall trees, backed up to the forest. This was our first time coming to Warren's home. Small, neat but simple. Hidden within the trees, away from everyone. The house, the location, a statement of who Warren was.

The front porch light was on. I could see a glow coming from the main room in the house. The front door was ajar with only the screen door closed.

We approached. I searched for a doorbell but couldn't find one, so I knocked.

No answer.

"You in there?" I called out.

We waited for a moment before trying the doorknob. It was unlocked so we entered into the main room. Several lamps on both sides of the couch framed the evening news as it blared from the television. Geonetta checked the kitchen. From the shadows, Warren stepped from one of the bedrooms. He spotted me, got startled and fell against the hallway wall.

"Sorry," I apologized. "I tried calling."

Warren grabbed his chest and sucked in a deep breath. "What are you doing here?" He blew out a sigh as I followed him back into the living room. "Raley's here."

I looked back toward the bedrooms.

"I don't want her to know about you guys."

"Bobby Rae's dead," I said. Just like that.

"You don't have to worry about him anymore."

Warren remained quiet but I noticed the tension in his jawline.

"It's not over, yet. I still need your help." I added.

He walked to the couch, stood next to an open suitcase.

"What are you doing?"

"I'm packing." He stopped and looked at me. His eyes were heavy, shoulders slack. "This whole thing with Bobby Rae . . . I knew sooner or later, I'd have to leave.

He threw a handful of T-shirts into the suitcase.

"This has been too much for Helen and the kids. As soon as the world finds out about Bobby Rae, they'll hear about me . . . talking."

I knew what he meant. It was about Bobby Rae's associates, the theory of an accomplice. The threat to him and his family still very real.

"If it's okay with you," he said. "I'll leave tomorrow. For a little while. Going to find a new place for Helen and the kids to live. Start over."

Another handful of clothes into the suitcase.

"It's better this way," he said.

I couldn't disagree.

"Word's out and people are already talking about me snitching out Bobby Rae. I'm a leper." Warren turned away as if he couldn't look me in the face. "I'm glad he's dead. He was evil. He didn't deserve to live. And whatever happens now, he can't hurt me."

I could see his nerves were unraveling like a fraying rope.

Geonetta came out from the kitchen, cellphone in hand. "Text from Hoskin but I can't get a damn signal from inside the house."

"Can she use your house phone, Warren?"

Warren's attention was elsewhere, giving a response that was automatic. "Yeah, sure, whatever."

Geonetta looked at Warren, then at me. "I'll step outside and try grabbing a signal."

Warren paid little attention to the back-and-forth before waving a dismissive hand while he continued to gather clothes. Geonetta stepped out the front door.

I stopped Warren as he tried to pass, made him give me his attention. I needed help.

"Sit down," I said. "I need to ask you a couple of questions before you leave. It will only take a moment."

Warren remained edgy but gave in, sat down on the couch.

"Where's Raley? I inquired.

Warren pointed out the front door. "She's in the garage. I asked her to get me another suitcase."

"Warren, you know we're still looking for our missing tourists. I need you to think of any other places Bobby Rae may have mentioned, where he could have held them."

Warren looked down at the floor as he placed his hands over his mouth. "I don't know any other place. I swear."

Then the second question: "What about what we talked about? Someone that would have helped him."

"Your theory of another person?" A pause. "So, you really do believe he had help?"

Warren's face turned ashen.

"I'm not saying it's fact, I'm just asking."

His breath went short and quick. "This is not making me feel good."

I went back to the person he saw meeting Bobby Rae at the bar. "Are you sure you didn't get a look at him?"

He touched the side of his face, the bruises still there, turning a darker shade of purple. His lips started to move like he was about to confess something, then a hesitation. "No, I didn't see who he was."

I asked three or four more times, each a little differently than before, a friend, a cellmate. Same dead end. I had no choice but to give in. "Look, if you think of anything, call me, no matter where you're at. Understand?"

Warren nodded nervously, attention turned down the hallway. "I got to finish packing."

I put a hand on his shoulder. "You're going to be all right."

Warren faked a smile but I could see he wasn't convinced.

My cellphone vibrated with an incoming text message. Amazed it got through. It was from Bellows.

Call me at the office. I have info from the lab – Hal.

I looked at the bars for coverage. Same as Geonetta.

No Service.

Hit-and-miss out here. Who knows when Bellows sent the text? Could have been an hour ago.

I looked down toward the bedrooms and yelled, "Warren. I need to use your phone."

No response.

I walked into the living room, located a small desk pushed up against a corner wall and found the house phone. A brass lamp was crammed up against a computer that looked more useful as a boat anchor. The phone was old, boxy, the cord stretched and weak. The push buttons worn smooth, several of the numbers obliterated. A small glossy black cylindrical wooden pencil holder with oyster shell inlays of a Kimono-dressed woman carrying an umbrella was perched next to the telephone, the edges chipped, the oyster shell inlays gnawed at, like broken finger-nails. There were a handful of pencils, most of them blunt or unusable. A spiral school notebook, belonging to Raley, I imagined, was opened next to the telephone, the top page overflowing with scribbled words, doodles and drawings.

I picked up the receiver, heard a dial tone, and dialed Bellows.

"I'm here at Warren's. What do you have?"

"I just got off the phone with your lab," Bellows said. "They wanted to fax us a copy of their report. While I had them on the line, I got a quick update on what they found interesting."

"Tell me."

"For starters, they did a more extensive review of the indented writings."

The notes taken from our victims.

"They took a closer look hoping to identify the markings that were unrecognizable. What they discovered mostly came from the note found on Amanda Jenkins.

Dragoon Tattoo and Pretty Thing

There appears to be numbers but followed by an "@" sign. They think it's part of an e-mail address, possibly belonging to one of our victims. Shouldn't be too hard to find out if we check with the parents.

"But we collected all the computers from our victims. There's nothing connecting them to Bobby Rae."

"I don't think Bobby Rae communicated with our victims through emails."

"What are you saying?"

"Maybe our killer used a notebook belonging to someone who knows our victims.

Other teenagers?

I grabbed a pencil off Warren's desk. "Give me what you got and I'll ask Warren what he knows."

I pulled open the top drawer of the desk, looked for a clean sheet of paper, and found another notebook, weathered. I filtered through it.

Then I saw something.

There were pages of written notes, top to bottom. But the last couple of pages were different, containing shortened words and symbols, dates and numbers.

E-mail addresses.

Addresses, neatly documented in this cheap white twenty-weight notepaper, the same type of paper used for the notes left on our dead victims. I quickly worked my way down the pages. Coming to the bottom of the second page, I read out loud the familiar words: "*prettything17@ hotmail.com.*"

"Katie," a voice softly replied from behind me. I turned around. It was Raley standing at the door, grasping two large suitcases. She carefully placed them down, continuing a long stare.

"That's Kate's e-mail address. *Pretty Thing 17.*"

I asked, "How do you know that?"

"We all have them. They're free. You just sign up on-line."

It took me a moment to process what she said and what I found.

The paper.

Then I heard Bellows on the other end of the phone. We were still connected.

"Hal? You better get out here now."

"Before you go, I got one more piece of news. I ran all the known prints against the latent lifted from the pipe, mostly to eliminate our friendlies. I thought it was a mistake but now I'm not so sure. The print lifted *inside* the murder weapon . . ."

I knew. "Warren's."

There was a pause. "Get out of there, Jack."

"It might be too late."

CHAPTER 56

Saturday March 1st – 8:12 p.m.

I DREW MY WEAPON.

Raley took a step back and froze, her eyes clouded in confusion. In a whisper, I pointed toward the door. "Go to the garage and stay there."

Her body stiffened, pupils dilating double, fixated on my pistol. This time my words hardened into a command: "Go!"

There was a loud creek from the wooden floor down the hall. I turned and pointed my weapon in the direction of the sound, seeing nothing but darkness. Looking behind, I saw Raley still standing at front entrance. "Get out!" I finally yelled. Her body quaked at my demand. She stumbled back and out the door. Spinning around, I advanced, looking for Warren.

A door slammed from somewhere in the back.

I pushed forward in the dark, feeling my way along the wall. At the end of the hallway was a glass-panel door leading to the side of the house, grey shadows and twinkling starlight filtering through. There was no time to check for danger; I had to get outside before Warren could escape. I reached for the latch, twisted the handle and placed pressure. Then there was a gunshot.

I rolled away, flattened against the wall and squatted low. It was too risky to peek out, too dark to see through the glass pane. Warren could have a bead on my head and I wouldn't have known. Stepping outside was suicide, but remaining in place rendered me a stationary target.

Make a decision and fast!

I turned and bolted back to the front of the house. The entry door was left open, cold air rushing in.

Raley made it out.

Then it hit me: *Where the hell was Heather?*

I called out and waited, hoping to hear her voice, that she was okay. No response. I called out again. Still nothing. I knew, something bad had happened.

Heather Geonetta

SHE HELD HER CELLPHONE UP IN the air, hoping to catch a signal. Along the side of the house, evening gloom swallowed her up, sandwiched between her vehicle and the side porch. The call went nowhere.

Maybe I should use Warren's house phone.

She slid the phone into her pocket, turned and started for the front door when she ran legs-first into the trash cans around the back of the house.

Clang!

Trash tumbled. Glass bottles clanked against one another as they cartwheeled down the walkway. A lid rolled away landing in a ditch across the road. Geonetta stood up the first barrel then peered into the second.

That's when she saw it.

A trash bag. White, thin. Torn. What drew her attention was what was inside: a dirty and ragged, but clearly visible blanket. She lifted the plastic bag and held it close to her eyes as she stepped back, grabbing enough moonlight to discern its color.

Pink.

Eerily similar to the type and color found on their victim's body.

The pink fibers.

The discovery froze Geonetta.

Could the blanket match the fibers found on our murdered victim?

The blood drained from her face, the connection too evident.

Warren.

She had to warn Jack. Geonetta shoved the bag under her arm and made her way to the porch but hesitated when she saw the dark figure. She strained to identify the face.

Jack?

The shadowy figure raised an arm. Then there was a jagged flash, the sharp bang of a gun, and the feeling of fire raging through her entire body. Geonetta was thrown back, crashing hard onto the cold wet ground.

I SPOTTED MOVEMENT THROUGH THE SCREEN MESH. A form appeared under the harsh porch light, a body, shuffling feet finding its way up the steps.

It was Geonetta.

She was standing with her pistol in hand down by her side, face flush and gaunt, eyes glossy; her shoulders, dropped. Bright red soaked through a stark white blouse, under her winter coat.

Geonetta pushed on the half-open screen and stood at the doorway. In a daze, she shook her head in disbelief.

"Jack," she stammered. "He shot me . . . the son-of-a-bitch shot me." Beads of sweat formed across her face. She dropped to her knees, then fell forward. I bolted but couldn't catch her fall. Her left cheek slammed square onto the hardwood floor, her head rebounding like a basketball from the impact. Her pistol flew from her hand and rang a high-pitch clamor as it tumbled and bounced, coming to rest on the fireplace hearth. She fell still, her eyes dull before slowly coming to a close.

I reached down, searched for any sign of breathing. Her breaths were shallow and rapid, her pulse thready. Blood began to pool. She was going into shock. I rolled her onto her back, cleared her airway and hunted for the entry and exit wounds so I could put pressure, hold off the blood loss.

I tried to appear calm but the tone in my voice failed me. "Hang in there, Heather, I'm going to get you help. You're going to be all right, I promise."

I remembered Warren's suitcase, the stack of T-shirts. I reached over the couch, dug deep, and pulled out a handful of shirts and pressed them on her wounds. Her blood immediately soaked through. Geonetta was turning pale, her skin tacky, a sure sign her blood pressure was crashing. I took two pillows off the couch and slid them under her ankles to elevate her legs, getting blood to flow to her heart and brain in hopes of keeping her blood pressure up. Without adequate perfusion, it would only be a matter of seconds before her brain would be deprived of the needed oxygen.

Her blood continued to stream like spilt paint. My hands were covered, slick, as I worked frantically to stop the exodus. Geonetta's eyes opened for just a moment as she tried to speak. I leaned down close to hear her voice.

"My fault, gunslinger."

"Don't talk," I said, forcing a smile. "I'm going to call for back up and an ambulance." From the corner of my eye, I could see a shadowy figure slowly approach the walkway. I rolled away, drew my pistol and pointed it at the door, squaring my sights onto the center of mass. Seeing the front sight post, moved onto the trigger. Four pounds of pressure would send 230 grains of lead and copper hurling forward, spiraling at 1100 feet per second until striking its target. As the figure drew closer, I saw it wasn't Warren.

It was Raley.

She had returned, frightened, but too scared to run away. I holstered my weapon and reached out. "Get in here!"

She continued walking but slowed, unsure if she could trust me.

"Raley, she's a police officer and hurt! She needs your help!"

The plea finally got her attention, realizing we were not the enemy. She sprinted through the entry and knelt next to Geonetta.

"She's bleeding," Raley said, her eyes wide and her jaw falling open. I took her hands and placed them on top of the blood soaked shirts on Geonetta's abdomen and back.

"Keep pressure here. It will slow the bleeding. I'm going to call for an ambulance."

Raley nodded, intimating she understood but it was obvious; the situation was more than she could comprehend. She continued to fixate on the bloody shirts, unable to take her eyes off of the gruesome sight. I stood up, looked back toward the house phone. But before I could make a move, there was a sharp crack of gunfire. Someone screamed. I fell to the floor, felt a growing burn that turned into excruciating pain.

I had been shot.

CHAPTER 57

Saturday March 1ˢᵗ – 8:18 p.m.

I SCRAMBLED FOR COVER.

The pain radiated with each movement. More gunshots. I reached under my coat, felt a tear in my shirt and blood between my fingers. The round lacerated my skin, long and deep, but struck no bone, no vital organs, as far as I could tell. I flattened against the wall and tried fighting off the pain. Raley was lying on top of Geonetta, shaking. Two more rounds blasted through the front window, glass raining shards. I rolled onto my stomach, took aim at the silhouette outside and fired two rounds. The muzzle flash from my Glock lit up the room. I looked over the top of my sights, hoping to see Warren lying dead on the porch entrance. Nothing was there.

"Raley!" I scrambled to her side and grabbed her shoulder. "Go to the phone and call 911. Get help!" She hesitated a second, then took off.

I looked down, saw the left side of my shirt soaked crimson red. The pain started to move up my shoulders and was getting sharper. I went back to the wall, reached up and turned off the lights.

If I couldn't see Warren, I wasn't going to let him see me.

On the count of three, I dashed through the door, praying Warren was not lying in wait for a clean shot. I dove for the front end of my car, hoping to use the large metal frame for cover. Sliding onto the front panel, I collided against the metal, scanned for him with my gun, panning left to right, then back.

Tree branches rustled in the wind, a garbage can clambered in the distance. What I didn't hear was the sound of the cavalry. This was on me and me alone.

I made my way around the house, saw droplets of blood leading down a snowy path. He was hit. I sprinted until reaching a thicket of trees, stopping at the widest trunk for cover. That's when I saw the large structure.

The barn.

The entry door was opened, creaking from a stiff breeze, bouncing against the outside wall. I heard sounds of movement coming from inside.

I felt the pounding of my heart, so strong I feared it would give away my position. I pressed the magazine release on my pistol, dropped the half-spent mag and replaced it with a full one. Taking in a deep breath, I raced full-tilt through the front door, sliding to a stop behind an old rusty tractor. It took a few long seconds to get my orientation and for my eyes to adjust. From above, I heard objects fall, cabinet doors open and close.

Warren was searching for something.

Another fifteen seconds and my eyes cleared and everything fell into focus. There was a metal cage propped over a pile of filthy straw. A large padlock hung on the open cage door. Inside was a dirty porcelain bowl on a metal tray, abandoned. A wool blanket was tossed in the corner, wadded into a ball.

This is where he held them. This is where they were killed.

I moved toward the sound, toward a set of wooden stairs. I looked up, saw the steps disappear onto a landing. Slowly, I worked my way up, cautious not to strain the wood panels or creak the frame of the rickety workmanship. My eyes again focused on the front sights of my weapon, leading me forward. I followed the staircase. A sharp right bend led onto a small landing. Two more steps and a large loft with what looked like a small kitchen and a bed. There was a blurry figure moving in the dark.

Warren was frantically searching through wall-mounted cabinets with one hand while grasping a long barrel shotgun with the other. The moonlight streamed through a large window, silhouetting him moving between cabinets and drawers. Shadows spirited across the walls, plastic cups and empty fruit jars launched off dusty shelves with volatile sweeps of Warren's arm. Suddenly, he stopped, stared into a high shelf. Thrusting his arm into the upper cabinet, Warren retrieved a box of shotgun shells and spilled them onto the counter. They rolled haphazardly. He snagged what he could see, jamming them into the shotgun's loading tube. There was little time to think about my options. I drew a fast bead on Warren's chest as I crouched low on the landing, began to put pressure on the trigger, ready to take a life. Ready to bring this to an end.

From below, someone screamed. "Don't hurt him!"

Raley stood at the bottom, tears running down her face as she continued to plead. The distraction forced me to pause, enough time for Warren to point the shotgun in my direction and fire. The floorboard exploded, the planks and railing splintered into flying shrapnel. Fragments ripped at my face and shoulder. I threw up an arm for cover and dove to the floor, my body slammed hard onto the upper landing.

"Get out of here!" I yelled to Raley, with little time to look back. I squeezed off three rounds at Warren, my sights desperately trying to stay on target as he advanced. I fired again.

He grunted and dove to his right. A trail of blood followed him. I again looked over the top of my pistol and spotted him scrambling for cover, behind an old iron stove. I fired another round but missed, shattering the large glass window into splinters. I held my aim, waited for Warren to show himself.

Peek out for a second, that's all I need.

Silence fell across the room. A bottled rolled across the floor, fragments of glass tinkled as they fell from the shattered frame.

"Give up, Warren."

I saw him move behind the stove.

"Back-up is on its way." *I hoped.*

No response.

"Think hard. You're better off surrendering to me because those deputies are going look for any excuse to kill you."

Still no response. I didn't expect one.

Even I knew my words fell on deaf ears. Warren had already signed his death warrant. Sooner or later, every cop in the world would know what he had done. He would never be given the option to walk away from this. Even if taken alive, Warren was staring at death row. The thought of a lengthy trial, and fifteen years of appeals only infuriated me.

"Why'd you kill them, Warren?"

I heard him move, repositioning. "They deserved it!"

"I don't understand."

"They slept with Bobby Rae."

And he raped those that didn't submit.

"I tried to show them what they were doing was wrong but they just laughed at me. They wouldn't listen. I couldn't let them continue. And I couldn't let Bobby Rae get away with it."

"So, you killed them because they didn't listen to you?"

"I had no choice. They had to learn."

"It's over, Warren," I said. "No more killing."

Warren's voice cracked, words spoken through tears and desperation: "I would have . . . I would have let Bobby Rae go on with his addiction. He was *my friend*, you know? *My friend*! I would have never told you about what I heard that night at the bar." He hesitated. "But he had to touch her . . . my Raley."

I could hear his tears flood pass every word spoken.

"He took her to the barn! He had to pay. He raped her!" Warren choked on the pain. "I don't know what he did with your tourists but I know he hurt my girl."

"Bobby Rae didn't kill those girls," I said. "You did."

"I had to!" His tone turned manic.

"Why the notes?" I asked.

I heard whimpering that turned to tears. "To stop me," he confessed.

"Let me do that, Warren. End it now."

The floor creaked from the sound of quick steps. Warren was moving away from cover. I leaned into the opening to see if I could spot him. As I did, I was met with a volley of shotgun blasts. As fast as he could, Warren racked the action, ejecting the spent casings after each squeeze of the trigger, barrel leveled in my direction. Fragments of wood splintered as the rounds struck the floorboard. I had to stay low, wait for Warren to fire his last round.

Boom! Rack. Boom! Rack. Boom! Rack.

Then a pause.

He's reloading.

The dust and debris started to clear. I popped up and began firing. The blasts were deafening, the muzzle flashes blinding. I continued until the slide locked back, empty. I ejected the magazine, letting it fall to the floor, reloaded and panned for Warren. He was sprinting toward the back of the room, too fast for me to square my sights on him. In a split second, Warren lunged toward the broken window, took a step and jumped, two stories to the ground below. Glass crunched under my boots as I scrambled after him. I leaned over the edge and peered down just in time to see Warren hobbling into the dense forest.

How could he survive the fall?

I sprinted downstairs and slid out the front, bolted in the direction he had fled. I reached into my pocket and removed a compact flashlight, tucked it close to my body and checked to make sure it functioned, before sliding into a pile of wet pine needles under a tall evergreen.

Through short bursts of light, I painted the forest looking for any signs of Warren. It didn't take long to see him hobbling deeper into the woods. He was hurt, leaving behind a trial of blood in the snow. Weapon extended, I ran after him with my light guiding the path. The beam bounced the faster I ran. Glancing to the ground every few seconds, I followed Warren's footprints and blood through the trees until coming to a ridge that unexpectedly dropped off into total darkness. Before my senses told me to stop, it was too late. I cartwheeled head first, down a snow and ice-caked embankment. My head struck a large boulder, sending an immense shockwave through my body. I squeezed my right hand, felt my fingers still wrapped around the grip of my pistol but realized I had dropped my flashlight.

Not good. I can't shoot what I can't see.

Frantically, I swept at the slushy groundcover. Three feet in front, my hand filtered through frozen gravel and dirt, felt the hard case of my flashlight. I squeezed the base; a brilliant beam lit up my surroundings. Warren appeared in my view, on his hands and knees, sifting through the snow. He'd lost his gun.

"Hands up where I can see them—now!" I commanded.

He squinted into the bright beam that I held steady on his face. I had the advantage, direct aim at his center of mass.

"It's over," I said.

Warren sat up, puffing like a steamer. He looked despondent, face flush from the chase. "He raped Raley. Tell me you wouldn't you have done the same?"

I felt those words.

Bobby Rae raped those girls. He was a monster, one that could not be tamed or fixed. Could I turn a blind eye if our victim's parents took on their own brand of justice? What if it were Justine? Would others understand if I did the same?

But this wasn't just about Bobby Rae. This went beyond the monster. Taking revenge on Bobby Rae did not justify taking the lives of his victims.

Victims. Not conspirators.

"He's dead, Warren. Bring this to an end."

Although his voice was filled with surrender, there were remnants of a last challenge. "Not yet."

He focused on a spot a few feet in front, diving forward and out of sight. There was a muzzle flash, a bang, and I felt an immense concussion. Another flash, another bang. A bullet whisked past my right ear. I dove to the left, returned fire. His profile lit up from the muzzle flash and I saw my rounds hit, punching him back into a stumble. Blood exploded from Warren's throat, splitting open an artery. He fell as I scrambled to my feet, keeping the light and weapon beaded on his body. By the time I got to him, he was puffing in spurts, clouded breath rose from his face, partially from his shallow breathing and partially from the warmth of the blood pulsating out from his neck. I knelt over him. He was still alive and I could tell he was aware of my presence. His eyes glazed as he looked away. Between inhalations, he continued to justify his actions. "I had no choice. I had to stop him."

Kill the Monster.

"I know."

I pressed my hand on his neck, tried to stop the flow but his blood seeped around my fingers. It was hopeless and too late for help.

But before you die . . .

"Where are the Samuels?"

I grabbed him by the collar and pulled him close. His eyelids hooded over a dull stare, his mouth filled with blood. He didn't even try to answer.

I shook him, hard. "Where are they?"

His body went limp.

I didn't ask again.

A few more seconds ticked by and Warren's eyes closed. I heard his last gasp of air before he lay lifeless on a patch of frozen pine needles, deep behind the barn, where he once held and murdered four young girls to revenge the rape of his daughter by a person he once called his friend.

I left Warren in the snow and walked back to the house where I found Raley watching over Geonetta. My partner was unconscious but still breathing. I looked around, took in the quiet and assessed the mayhem, thought about how much the world had just changed for everyone.

IT WOULD BE ALMOST AN HOUR before Bellows and his deputies arrived with an ambulance. Raley insisted on staying with Geonetta, held onto her hand, refused to let it go. Warren remained in the woods for Hoskin and his ERT crew to examine and prepare for removal. I waited for an agent to take me back to Mariposa. Tomorrow, I would start again.

This case was not over.

CHAPTER 58

Sunday March 2nd – 1:35 a.m.

BEFORE CRAWLING INTO BED, I CRANKED UP THE VOLUME on the alarm clock to make sure I didn't oversleep. The medics on scene had cleaned and bandaged my wound but wanted me to go the ER. I refused but promised to have it looked at the next day. I took four Advils and did my best to ignore the pain. As hurt and tired as I was, I could only think about how far Warren's death set us back, unable to get him to help locate the Samuels, unable to save them. That's if he even could. Missing for over two weeks, I questioned if there was any further point in trying.

I can't give up.

Search and Rescue was still looking, call-in leads still being investigated. By early tomorrow morning, everyone would be back out searching. That's all that mattered.

I barely had the energy to strip off my boots before crawling under the clean bed sheets, too tired to undress. The pressed linens felt fresh on my face, a contrast to the earthy grit that clung to my clothes. I pulled the blanket up to my neck and closed my eyes. Fatigue voided all irritation.

They are alive.

It took seconds to slip into slumber. As my thoughts passed between the two worlds of lost and found, the faces of the Samuels appeared in my mind.

They are alive.

Sunrise – ERT Crew at the Crime Scene

IT STARTED TO SNOW.

Along the ridge near Warren's house, the ERT crew continued at their usual steady pace, unaffected by the weather. The bright sun punched through the morning hazy cold, highlighting the barn and exposing the evil that took place inside. Bolted in one corner was a makeshift box, wrapped in heavy gauged fence material, specially constructed to house Warren's victims. Dirty wool blankets scattered on wet straw; his prisoners had been shackled to galvanized steel poles cemented into place. How his ex-wife or kids never wandered over to this place was beyond me. There was a lock hanging on the barn door. I could only imagine it being the only thing keeping the world at bay.

The words *lost souls* and *repent* were hand-written throughout a Bible found at the scene. Hoskin examined the words scrawled between the margins of specific verses, presumably left by Warren for his victims to read . . . and learn. Fingerprints were lifted from the pages. The crew photographed every inch of the barn, standard procedure.

For the first time, Hoskin saw a disturbed look on ERT Special Agent Chad Gilliard's face. Stalwart and unflappable, he had conducted hundreds of evidence collections throughout his career, but this time he looked overwhelmed. Not long into the examination, Gilliard had to take a break. He gently placed his camera down on the fender of a brokedown tractor and quietly stepped away to have a cigarette. I was told he hadn't smoked in ten years.

The house was also searched, room by room, the computer disconnected and marked as evidence. Specialized examiners filtered into the living room and cautiously removed the electronic equipment, making sure that no data was lost or destroyed during the transition. And the bag with the pink blanket was tagged and marked for evidence. Raley had retrieved it from Geonetta's hand. It would be left to the lab to confirm an exact match.

The notebook containing the e-mail addresses and screen names was also photographed and bagged. Later, back at FBI Headquarters, each address would be recorded with the subscribers identified. Hoskin anticipated our victims would be part of this unfortunate list. The others would be contacted and interviewed. They would also be reminded of just how lucky they were to be alive.

CHAPTER 59

Sunday March 2nd – 6:59 a.m.

I CALLED HOSKIN TO LET HIM KNOW I was heading to see Warren's ex-wife. I wanted to tell her what had happened in person. Also, I hoped, she might be able to give me something that would help me continue my search for the Samuels. At this point, I'd take anything.

My cell vibrated as I drove through the hills toward Helen Kramer's house. I decided it was best not to answer. It could have been by boss, Frank Porter, reminding me I was supposed to be home, an agreement he knew I would break. He was right. There were still things I needed to do.

I slowly pulled into her driveway, parking inches behind her vehicle. The SUV was covered in dew, a clear sign she had not driven it since yesterday. Clouds started to fill the sky, the distant sound of thunder filling the horizon. I saw movement through the kitchen window.

I sat still a beat, listening to the engine cool, wondering what I would say, and how I would say it.

Your ex-husband was a serial murderer so I killed him.

I walked to the door and knocked, waiting uneasily. There was rustling in the background. Fifteen seconds or so passed before the door slowly creaked open. Warren's son, Josh, peered out, trying to figure out who I was. Then he remembered. "You're that FBI guy, aren't you?"

I smiled as best I could. "May I come in?"

He considered, then stepped away and disappeared down the cramped hallway. I crossed the entryway and closed the front door. The smell of coffee filled the air as I made my way to the living room. Helen

Kramer stepped out from her bedroom doorway. Still in her bathrobe, she stood slack shoulder, eyes red and swollen. She pulled her robe tight across her body.

How long had she been crying? How long had she known?

She crossed her arms and squeezed tightly.

"Mrs. Kramer, my name is Jack Paris. I'm with the FBI. I wanted to come and tell you, in person, what happened last night, before you hear it on TV."

Helen's gaze dropped toward the floor. Her hair spilt forward, dangling, failed to conceal the tears that fell to the carpet.

"You're a little late, Agent Paris. Two deputies were here earlier this morning. Where's Raley?"

"At the hospital, watching over my partner who was injured." I held up a hand. "Raley's okay. Deputies will be bringing her home, shortly."

Helen headed to the kitchen and slid into a chair, taking deep breaths. I could almost see the words spinning in her head, trying to formulate her thoughts. She stuttered, hesitated, started to speak, then stopped. A mind twisted without order. She was struggling to find the right words to express herself. I didn't want to complicate matters so, I sat down and waited.

"When Raley was born," she started, "Warren was totally dedicated to her. I saw in his face, nothing but unconditional love. There wasn't anything he wouldn't do for her. When she started to walk, he stood behind her. When she cried, he cried. Her pain was his pain. It was as if they were one in the same. Don't get me wrong, Agent Paris: he loved the other two just as much. But Raley was special. He wanted to make sure he kept her on course."

Tears fell.

"But that wasn't possible. I mean, she was a teenager. Of course she strayed. And Warren took it personally. Like if he could save her, the same future waited for Josh and Squeak."

She wiped her eyes, the tablecloth spotted with her fallen tears.

"It hurt Warren to see Raley rebelling. It was one of the reasons why we never got along. The fights about the kids were endless."

Helen looked away.

"Things changed after Bobby Rae came into our lives. Warren and I had already separated, but he still wanted to see the kids. At first, Bobby Rae didn't come over without Warren. That's when he saw Raley."

She swallowed hard.

"He started coming around unannounced, alone. I didn't like that. It made me real nervous, but Warren said it was all right.

"He would watch her. Everything she did. I told Warren it made me uncomfortable, him over here, spending all that time with our daughter, but Warren said I was just being paranoid. Then one night when I was out, Bobby Rae came looking for Warren. He knew Warren wasn't here. I wasn't home."

Helen stood up from the table and walked over to the kitchen window, stared out into the morning sun.

"He talked Raley into going out for a drive. By the time I got back, they were gone. He eventually brought her home, late. She went right to her room. He had that look on his face, something that told me something wasn't right. I froze. I didn't know what to do. He just stood there and smiled."

She leaned hard against the sink. I saw her hands quiver.

"The next day, I asked Raley if everything was all right and she just said 'yes.' I didn't believe her but what could I do?"

I placed my hands flat on the table. "Did you talk to Warren about this?"

Helen's voice cracked, overwhelmed by her admission. "He blamed himself for allowing that man in our home." She turned toward me, looked into my eyes. "That son-of-a-bitch raped my daughter."

I said nothing.

"He did all this to get back at Bobby Rae. He did it to fix his mistake of bringing that monster . . . that goddamn parasite . . . into our lives."

I went over to Helen. She was trembling, her anger seizing her emotions. I offered what comfort I could.

Helen tried to regain her composure. She wiped the tears from her eyes, pulled her robe tighter around her body. She looked over my shoulder, spied Amelia standing between the living room and the kitchen, staring with an inquisitive look. Helen walked over and caressed her tight. Amelia wrapped her arms around her mother's waist. Helen bent down and smiled.

"Squeak . . . Daddy won't be coming to see you anymore."

Amelia looked up at her mother. "Is it because he's in heaven?"

Helen didn't know what to say so she just hugged her tight.

"It's okay, Mommy. Daddy told me that someday he would go away but that he would return as an angel. He said all good people come back as angels."

She pulled away from her mother and held out a hand. One-by-one, her fingers unfolded. In her palm sat a small gold fairy with large butterfly-like wings. An earring. A beautiful design that resembled an angel.

"I knew he was right because I found this."

Helen took the earring from Amelia's hand and held it in front of her eyes, studying the brilliance.

"An angel in the snow," Amelia said.

"Squeak, sweetheart, where did you get this?"

Amelia bowed her head as if she was in trouble and looked at the ground.

"Oh, Squeak, it's okay," her mother said. "I was just wondering where you found something so lovely."

I recognized the piece.

The missing jewelry.

It was the earring belonging to Judy Samuels.

I slowly approached Amelia, making sure not to frighten her. "Amelia, can you tell me where you found this beautiful earring?"

The little girl hesitated a moment, unsure if she wanted to talk.

"It's okay, Squeak. Tell Mr. Paris where you found it."

She pointed toward the front door. "Out there. In my cave!"

"Take me there, Amelia." I offered my hand and she took it.

She grabbed her parka hanging on the jacket tree, and, with a slight tug, guided me out the front door, down a dirt path, and into the woods.

MELTED SNOW HAD TRANSFORMED INTO DIRT-EMBEDDED chucks of ice along the path that trailed into the forest. Amelia held tight onto my hand as she hurried, careful not to lose her footing on the slippery ice.

The path led us to a gap in the trees, tall, closely spaced, allowing only partial sunlight to filter through, casting soft rays on bright white. The walk became more difficult. The snow was deep and not easy to walk in.

We trudged along for another fifteen minutes, stopping by a sloped hillside. Below, the sound of rushing ice-water raged in a stream from melted snow. The rumbling sound of an eighteen-wheel logging truck reverberated, gears clutched into low gear as it descended the steep grade to the valley floor.

I stopped to catch my breath. Amelia broke free and ran toward a clump of trees surrounding a small open space at the bottom. The sun was brilliant, washing out my view. Squinting from the reflecting light, for a moment, I lost sight of Amelia running ahead. My heart raced.

"Wait!" I yelled. "Amelia, wait up!"

I took off and hurried after her. As I drew near, I caught sight of her kneeling in the snow, swiping a hand back and forth, searching. Fresh powder had fallen over the past several weeks. A blur of white floated gently in the sunlight, cloaking her in a frosty haze. A gentle breeze rustled through heavy branches. Accumulated snow fell in clumps from the limbs.

When I reached Amelia, she was squatting in front of what appeared to be a large mound. As I inched forward, I began noticing unnatural colors speckled in the snow: red, black, gray. Metal appeared, mangled and gouged, transforming the mound into a steel structure covered in snow. A car. I stepped back and spied the road above, the one used by the passing big-rig. Over my head, I saw a section of railing was missing, busted through. I envisioned the driver of this car, lost, unable to find the way back to the main highway. The car drifted off course, I surmised, tumbling from a dark moonless night, maybe blinded by the sun's bright rays.

The car was upside down, wedged between two massive trees. Over time, snow fell, covering up the fallen vehicle. The end resulting in Amelia's *cave*. Their belongings must have rained from the fall, giving Amelia an opportunity to hunt for her treasures. To her, it was an adventure. To the driver and any passenger, it was a tragedy.

I didn't need to walk any closer to see it was a red Pontiac Grand Prix, the type rented by Maria Samuels. It was her car that ran off the road, plunging to the ground below. No murder, no conspiracy. A mistake, a wrong turn, an accident. No premeditated act of violence. It happened because of circumstance, however unfair.

I saw no one in the compartment but there were gaping holes in the windshield that drew my attention. The occupants must have been ejected from the car. I scaled down the slope, leading to an icy stream. I scanned the undisturbed powder and searched for any sign of the Samuels.

Two immense pine trees bracketed a knoll of glistening powder. I approached, catching a glimpse of a small object protruding. It was a hand. Finely polished red nails. Speckles of dried blood caked the fingers, the skin white and papery. Carefully, I scraped away at the snow, revealing the face of Maria Samuels. Her hair was matted in frozen blood and ice, a sign of a head trauma after being thrown through the windshield, I assumed. Maria's eyes were still open, cloudy, distant, as if looking for someone, anyone, to come find her. Someone to take her home.

There was another mound, no more than fifteen yards to my right, closer to the water's edge. I made my way through the thick powder, dropped to my knees, and brushed away the top layer of snow.

Judy Samuels.

As devastating as this must have been, Maria and Judy likely died immediately from the impact they sustained. The end came quick.

"Are they angels?" spoke the soft voice of a child.

Amelia stood behind me, her head curiously tilted.

"Yeah, that's right, Amelia. They're angels now."

I didn't want her any closer so I walked over and took her by the hand. This time, it was my turn to lead the way.

We ambled back to the house, stopping every so often for her to wander off and find a unique rock or a perfectly shaped pinecone. A child on an adventure, unaware of the tragedies that had taken place over the past few weeks. I watched her play, thinking how fortunate it was for her not to have to deal with the real world.

It took two days to process the accident.

Just like any crime scene, the area was meticulously scrutinized for evidence to corroborate what happened—an accident. The traffic investigators later verified how the Samuels met their end, something I already knew. Coming over the hill, Maria lost control around a tight curve in the road and smashed through the safety rail. The car plunged down the embankment, snapping limbs and branches. Upon impact with the ground, the two were ejected through the windshield. They weren't wearing their seatbelts. The investigators speculated Judy may have been alive when she landed, attempted to crawl away before succumbing to her injuries. Maria died instantly.

Their bodies were taken to the morgue; a week later they were returned home to their family.

A week after that, I attended their funeral services. Maria and Judy were buried next to each other on a peaceful hillside, surrounded by deep blue skies and bright green rolling hills.

That evening, Emily came to me.

I was tired and had too much to drink. We talked about everything leading to this moment; she listened more than talked. When I was done, she smiled, told me she loved me and that I did everything I could to bring this to an end. I guess I did.

"The end isn't always what you expect or want," she reminded me.

"People die. You don't have control over that.
Keep the living living, and the memories of those that are not, alive.
I laughed, then I cried. Then I kissed her.
She was always the smart one.

CHAPTER 60

I SLOUCHED LOW IN THE CHAIR positioned outside Geonetta's hospital room. The hallway smelled of antiseptic cleaner. I always hated hospitals. They reminded me of isolation and despair, of life lost. My mother spent her last days in an ICU, connected to a machine, listening to doctors talking about her in the third person. It was then, she knew she was never leaving that place. Since that day, every time I stepped onto a hospital ward, I swear, I would see her in some empty hallway, disappearing through a faraway door.

When Emily learned of her cancer, she refused to be admitted, even with all the pain. She wanted to stay in her home till the end, wherever that end took her. There were times I wished I'd gone with her.

"You can see her now," a nurse said as she touched my hand.

I stood and pushed open the door to Geonetta's room. The sun filtered through a shear window curtain. Geonetta was propped up in bed, pillows stuffed behind her back. She was perusing reports. Piles of reports. Paper, notes and binders stacked on a steel rolling tray, plastic water cups precariously balanced at its edge. She hadn't touched her breakfast.

"What the hell are you doing?"

She looked up over a pair of reading glasses. "Hey, gunslinger," she said before returning to her reading.

"Have you forgotten you almost became a chalk outline?"

"I'm bored. I thought this was as good a time to read what happened."

She looked tired and pale but in whole, she was alive and I could see, getting better.

"Relax, Crime Fighter," I replied, relieving her of the reports. "You got time."

Geonetta pursed her lips and surrendered to my order.

I leaned on the edge of the bed and winced, a reminder, I too had been shot.

"Did you get hurt during the shooting?"

"No."

"How did you injure your side, then?"

"I cut myself shaving."

Geonetta rolled her eyes toward the ceiling.

There was a slight pause before she broke the silence. "What a tragedy."

I looked down at the floor.

She said, "Warren should have never befriended Bobby Rae.

I nodded. "I'm surprised he didn't kill Bobby Rae after he raped Raley."

"Isn't that why he led us to believe Bobby Rae kidnapped the Samuels?"

I swiped an apple off her food tray and took a bite. "He was the perfect stooge." Warren wanted to protect his family as well as get revenge on the man that raped his daughter. With the news of two missing tourists, who would have made a better suspect? I think he actually believed Bobby Rae was involved.

"What about the pipe, the notes?" Geonetta asked. "They were at the barn."

I could only speculate. "When he learned of the location, it was the perfect opportunity for Warren to plant the evidence that drew us away from him."

"You think Warren made the whole thing up about hearing Bobby Rae talking about the kidnapping at the Captain's Lounge?"

"To the contrary, I think that's where he got the idea."

Geonetta's lips tightened into a straight line. "I got to ask, why didn't Bobby Rae just deny the accusations when we arrested him?"

I could only assume. "Guys like Bobby Rae lie because they can't help themselves. And who knows what else he *was* guilty of. That man didn't like cops, didn't trust cops, and I'm sure he has more than enough skeletons to fill a few closets. It was about power, control. In his world, it was a game."

"Looks like he lost."

I agreed.

"And Warren . . ." Geonetta's words trailed off.

I just nodded. There were few words left that hadn't already been said. "Yeah, a real tragedy."

BEFORE SUNSET, I DECIDED TO HEAD NORTH, back to Sacramento. The highway was endless and quiet. The only sound taking me in and out of a daydream state was the hum from the car's tires as I pushed the speedometer above 90 mph along the desolate Central Valley corridor. The plain ahead was covered in dried grass, the color of wheat as far as I could see, disappearing over the unreachable horizon. Majestic size Oak trees, winter-stripped and bare, like soldiers standing post, in my rearview.

I couldn't stop thinking how different things had turned out. Had the Samuels never fallen to an accident while on vacation, maybe Warren would have never come forward with Bobby Rae being the red-herring. And Warren would have moved on and the murders of those unfortunate teenagers might have passed through time, unsolved.

As for Bobby Rae, he made the mistake of his life. His craving for young girls was bad enough, but molesting his best friend's daughter broke the bank. He took advantage of Warren's trust and that cost him his life. A friend is a friend until you do them wrong. Bobby Rae did Warren wrong.

EPILOGUE

Tuesday March 4th – 6:20 p.m.

I PULLED INTO MY DRIVEWAY AND PARKED. The street was empty.

Stepping from the car, I spent a minute looking at my home. I wasn't in any hurry. The roses out front, planted because Em loved color in spring. The water fountain, because she found the sound of falling water calming. There was a wreath hung on the front door because it was a sign of love and invite. It was Em that made the house a home.

Then I blinked and looked again.

This time the house was dark, windows void of life, empty. The roses were bare from winter's cold, and the fountain was silent. The wreath was withered and dead.

I opened the door and dragged my luggage into the hallway, then walked into the kitchen.

Liquor bottles stood tall on a silver tray next to the wine rack, awaiting my return. I took a short glass from the cupboard, dropped in an ice cube and poured a splash of twenty-year-old scotch, my reward for another case brought to an end. I took a sip. I retrieved my suitcase, dragged it up the stairs, leaving it in the middle of the floor, to be dealt with tomorrow. I didn't bother turning on the lights.

There was a sound coming from downstairs, tapping. I walked down to the den and saw the floor lamp was on. The desk was bathed in soft gold, the corners of the room falling just outside the light's reach. She was sitting on the couch, her MacBook perched on her lap, fingers strolling across the keyboard. *Tap, tap, tap, tap, tap.*

Emily.

As much as I wanted to reach out and hold her, I took the seat at the desk. It gave me a chance to see all of her.

She stopped typing, looked up and smiled.

It was like old times.

"Have you learned to accept everything good and bad?" she asked.

"I'm not sure, Em. Some things should never have happened."

"You don't get to choose."

She was right. I hated that. I smiled.

"When does tragedy end and the healing begin?" I asked.

Her eyes softened. "I know it's hard to accept. Misfortune finds everyone. Eventually the light gets through."

My lady of positivity.

"I don't know if I can do this without you."

Now an empathetic look. "You don't need me anymore."

The words stung. I took another sip and slid the glass onto the table. "The thing is, I don't want to."

"You'll do just fine. Besides, you have others that need you. And you need them."

Justine and Michael.

"No matter how dark it gets, I will always be there for you."

The alcohol was taking hold. I let my eyes close.

The telephone rang. I reached for the receiver. It was Michael.

"You're home," he said.

"Just got back."

"I hadn't heard from you so I thought I'd check in. Did I catch you at a bad time?"

I leaned back and look around. Em was gone. Usually, the moment left me empty but there was a warmth in hearing Michael's voice. "Just talking to your mom," I started to say.

"Huh?"

I took a moment to clear my head and get my bearings.

"I was just thinking about your mom."

"Me too," he replied.

For a long time, we talked. Just talked.

Keep the living, living and the memories of those that are not, alive.

I took a moment to let the statemtent soak in.

Words to live by.

GEORGE FONG spent twenty-seven years as a special agent with the FBI, investigating kidnappings, serial killings, white collar, gangs, bank robberies, drug trafficking, and other violent crimes. He was also a lead instructor at the FBI's International Law Enforcement Academy in Budapest, Hungary, presenting on organized crime, undercover techniques, informant development, and electronic surveillance.

In 2002, Fong was promoted to supervisory special agent, managing the Violent Crimes and Major Offenders squad in Sacramento, to include the undercover program and the Forensic Evidence Response team. In 2007, he was again promoted as the Unit Chief, overseeing the FBI's National Violent Gang Program at FBI Headquarters in Washington DC.

He became an assistant inspector during his last year in the bureau before retiring. Currently, he is ESPN's Director of Security and Safety.